A Recipe for Bees

Gail Anderson-Dargatz

HARMONY BOOKS

NEW YORK

Published by Harmony Books, 201 East 50th Street, New York,
New York 10022. Member of the Crown Publishing Group.

Random House, Inc. New York, Toronto, London, Sydney, Auckland
www.randomhouse.com

HARMONY BOOKS is a registered trademark and Harmony colophon
is a trademark of Random House, Inc.

Originally published in hardcover by Alfred A. Knopf Canada in 1998.

This is a work of fiction. Any resemblance to actual persons,
living or dead, is entirely coincidental.

Excerpt from *The Georgics* by Virgil, translated by L. P. Wilkinson
(Penguin Classics, 1982) copyright © L. P. Wilkinson, 1982.
Used by permission.

Printed in the United States of America

DESIGN BY CATHRYN S. AISON

Library of Congress Cataloging-in-Publication Data
Anderson-Dargatz, Gail, 1963–
A recipe for bees / Gail Anderson-Dargatz.
I. Title.
PR9199.3.A49R43   2000
813'.54—dc21   99-25269
CIP

ISBN 0-609-60451-1

10 9 8 7 6 5 4 3 2

FIRST UNITED STATES EDITION

-A Recipe for Bees-

-Also by This Author-

The Cure for Death by Lightning

-For Eric and Irene-

-Acknowledgments-

A great many people have participated with me in the writing of this novel, providing details and suggestions. In particular my thanks go to Alberta provincial apiculturist Kenn Tuckey, beekeeper Ted Kay, and my own beekeeper, Floyd Anderson-Dargatz, for their help with the beekeeping passages, and to the staff at the Kamloops Museum and the R. J. Haney Heritage Park in Salmon Arm for helping me place this novel in time. I am also indebted to Diane Martin and Louise Dennys for their loving approach to editing. Bible quotes in this novel were taken from the Jerusalem Bible; the Ryrie Study Bible; the Thompson Chain-Reference Bible; and the New Marked Reference Bible, edited by J. Gilchrist Lawson. Virgil's recipe for bees is taken from *The Georgics*, translated by L. P. Wilkinson and published by Penguin. Sections of this novel were first published in the story "Turtle Valley" in *Canadian Forum* magazine. Photos in this novel are from my parents' photo albums. My most heartfelt appreciation goes to Eric and Irene Anderson for the lives they've led and the stories they tell.

-A Recipe for Bees-

– one –

"Have I told you the drone's penis snaps off during intercourse with the queen bee?" asked Augusta.

"Yes," said Rose. "Many times."

Before Augusta dragged her luggage upstairs to the apartment, before she checked on the welfare of her elderly husband, Karl, even before she hugged and greeted her seven kittens, she had made her way, with the aid of a cane, across the uneven ground to inspect the hive of bees she kept in Rose's garden.

"They won't mate at all unless they're way up in the sky," said Augusta. "The drones won't take a second look at a queen coming out of a hive. But when she's thirty, a hundred, feet up in the air, *then* she gets their interest. They'll seek her out, flying this way and that to catch her scent until there's a V of drones—like the V of geese following a leader in the sky—chasing along behind her."

"You were going to tell me about Joe," said Rose.

"As soon as the drone mounts and thrusts, he's paralyzed, his genitals snap off, and he falls backward a hundred feet to his death."

"I don't want to hear about it."

In late summer, hives full of ripening honey emitted a particular scent, like the whiff of sweetness Augusta used to catch passing by the candy-apple kiosk at the fall fair, but without the tang of apples to it. She should have been smelling this now, but instead the hive gave off the vinegar-and-almond scent of angry bees. They buzzed loudly, boiling in the air in front of the hive like a pot of simmering toffee. There were far more guard bees than usual, standing at attention at the mouth of the hive.

"Something's been after the bees," said Augusta. She took a step forward to examine them, but several bees flew straight at her, warning her off. "I'll have to look at them later," she said. "When they've settled down."

She turned to the balcony of her apartment, directly above the garden. "Do you think Karl remembers today is our anniversary?"

"He hasn't said anything to me," said Rose. Later that evening, though, Augusta would learn that Rose had hidden Karl's flowers in her fridge. He had walked up and down the roadsides and into the vacant lots, searching for pearly everlastings, sweet tiny yellow flowers with white bracts that bloomed from midsummer right on into winter, and held their shape and color when dried. They were the flowers Karl had picked for Augusta's wedding bouquet forty-eight years before. He had brought the flowers to Rose's apartment in a vase and asked her to hide them in her fridge until later that day.

"You'd think he'd remember, wouldn't you?" said Augusta. "Especially after everything that's happened these past three weeks."

"You'd think."

"You can hear it, you know."

"What?"

"The snapping. If you're listening for it, you can hear a sharp crack when the drone's penis breaks off."

"Oh, God."

Rose followed Augusta as she headed through the sliding glass doors into Rose's apartment to retrieve her luggage. "Can you carry this one upstairs?" she asked Rose. "And this one? I can only manage the one bag with this cane of mine."

Rose took the bags, one in each hand. "But you were going to tell me the story, about seeing Joe again."

"Not now, Rose. I want to see if Joy's phoned with news about Gabe."

"But you promised."

"We'll have plenty of time later."

"You'd go and tell something like that to some strange woman on the train, but you won't tell your best friend."

"I like Esther. I think we'll be seeing a lot more of her. I promised to show her my hive."

"*You'll* be seeing a lot more of her. I don't care if I ever see her again."

"Well, since neither Esther nor I can drive, you'll have to drive me, so yes, you will be seeing her again."

"Oh, isn't that just great? Now I'm your personal chauffeur."

Augusta turned around at the doorway. "Rose, what's this all about?"

"Just tell the story. About Joe. I thought you never saw him again."

Augusta shook her head and started up the stairs to her apartment. "I'm sure I told you all that already. I can remember showing you the brooch he gave me. Ages and ages ago."

"Yes, the day we met. But you never told me the story. Are you really going to give that brooch to Joy?"

Augusta had met Rose five years before, on the ferry, just after she and Karl had sold the farm. Augusta and Karl were moving to the warmer climate of Vancouver Island. Rose turned the corner into the ferry bathroom and there was Augusta, sitting at the mirrored makeup counter they have on those boats, rummaging through her big purse. Augusta had looked up at Rose in the mirror, smiled, and said, "Do you have a comb? I can't seem to find mine."

Perhaps it was an inappropriate request to make of a stranger, she thought now, rather like asking to borrow someone's toothbrush. Rose said no. "They have them at the newsstand."

"Thanks. I'll get one from there. That's a lovely brooch you're wearing."

"It was my mother's," Rose replied, and Augusta promptly caught her in a web of conversation about the brooch a man named Joe had given her, a brooch Augusta pulled from her purse and showed Rose: a silver setting hemmed a real bee suspended in amber. When Augusta held it up, it cast a little pool of honey light on the floor. "It was the only lasting thing he ever gave me, in the way of presents," she said. "And that was decades after I'd stopped seeing him. I still dream about him, you know." Rose nodded and smiled and moved slowly backward, away, to a toilet stall. Augusta, seeing her discomfort, left before she came out again.

Yet Rose did turn up at the newsstand where Augusta was buying a bag of combs. Augusta was talking to the clerk because the bag of combs had been opened and who knew how many were missing? She was successful, too;

the clerk gave her the bag of combs for a dollar. Augusta grinned and winked at Rose when she saw that she'd been watching her dicker. Augusta enjoyed haggling. She often checked out the plants displayed at supermarket entrances, and if there was one going brown from too much water or sun, she took it to the produce clerk and (leaning a little more than usual over her cane, with a hint more creak in her voice) talked him into giving it to her. She always got her fern or African violet, and without fail she would bring it back to the car and say to Rose, "Look what I scored." Augusta nursed nearly every plant back to health; her apartment was filled with plants that the kittens regularly knocked from the plant stands, the shelves, the windowsills.

After Augusta had collected her change, she walked right up to Rose, holding out the bag of combs. "What color do you like?" she'd said, as if she and Rose were old friends. Rose selected a blue one, a comb she still carried tucked away in her purse, though she never used it. Augusta introduced herself.

Then Karl was there, opening a canvas bag for Augusta to put the extra combs in. He looked up at Rose, surprised, as if to say, *Who the hell are you?* And Rose stared back at him the same way. She later said that she had imagined Augusta a widow, like herself. Rose's husband had been dead ten years by then. Augusta introduced her to Karl, and when Rose shook Karl's hand, her hand slid right up his wrist, as there was no thumb to stop it. He grinned at the look on her face. He took a quiet, perverse delight in offering that thumbless hand to strangers last minute, so they didn't suspect. He had shot the thumb off while hunting when he was a kid, and there was nothing but scarred flesh from his forefinger to his wrist. When he flexed the muscles, even though he was in his eighties, he still felt the missing thumb bending. It itched but he couldn't scratch it. That itch would have driven most people to distraction, but not Karl. He appeared to bear all things, as he had his father's demands and Augusta's infidelities, with equilibrium. Augusta believed he was missing a certain quality of imagination. He accepted things as they came to him because he couldn't see the use in trying to change them. She had spent a lifetime battling this quality in him. Still, he was a dear man, and Augusta couldn't help loving him, even if he sometimes did put cheddar cheese into his tea instead of milk, even if he sucked his coffee loudly through a sugar cube held between his teeth.

That meeting was how Augusta and Karl came to live in Rose's apartment building. The three of them had got to talking on the ferry and Augusta said she and Karl had sold their farm in the Shuswap, in the interior of British Columbia, and were staying with their daughter, Joy, and son-in-law, Gabe, outside Victoria until they found a place of their own. Rose said that she managed an apartment building for seniors, in Courtenay, and that there was an apartment coming up for rent at the end of the month, as Mrs. Meecham was getting too old to live by herself and was moving into a home. One thing led to another and Karl and Augusta moved into the apartment. There was a three-hour drive or train ride between Karl and Augusta, and Joy and Gabe. That was a good distance between a mother and a daughter. Close enough, but not too close.

"Joe asked me to give the brooch to Joy," said Augusta.

"Joe? When?"

"At the auction." Rose sat Augusta's two bags on the landing of the second floor and crossed her arms. "I'm not going any farther until you tell me the story."

"Oh, Rose. I'm too tired for this right now. All this worry over Gabe—" She made her way to the apartment door, hooked the cane over her arm, and put the key to the lock. She sighed. "You bring the bags inside and I'll make a nice cup of tea, and if Karl's down at the seniors' center I'll tell you all about it, okay?"

But Karl was there in the apartment, as Augusta knew he would be, sitting at the kitchen table by the phone. The kitchen and living area were all one room and each wall was lined with shelves filled with teddy bears and dolls and ceramic figurines; not a collection, exactly, just a lifetime of purchases and gifts. It was a hot day; Karl had the fan in the living room going. He stood when the door opened. "Anything?" said Augusta.

"Nothing yet." He walked up to kiss her, but Augusta was already leaning down to scratch the spines of the many cats that slid and meowed around her unsteady legs. Karl hoisted the bag she had carried, took the two from Rose, and hauled them all into the bedroom. Augusta hugged the kitten she had named Blondie to her chest as she watched him walk away. Why did she do that? she wondered. Why hadn't she accepted his kiss? Now and then Augusta still caught Karl watching her, when she was busy putting together tea for the two of them, or washing the breakfast dishes while Karl and Rose took in a game of crib. He didn't smile or say anything, but she saw it in his face, how he loved her. Then he glanced away, at the crib board, or lifted his cup for a sip, and she really saw it—

burning in his face, reddening his ears—all the years of unsaid things.

Even so, Augusta took Karl somewhat for granted and even turned her eyes elsewhere. She had a crush on the old man with the garden beside the seniors' center, and she had never even met the man. She knew nothing about him, other than what he revealed of himself through his garden. When she walked by his house, she sometimes caught him hovering out of sight behind his dark window, watching; there was some movement there, the flick of a curtain, a shape in the black. Although he lived right next door, he didn't go to the seniors' center; he kept himself locked away.

She had once stopped at the old man's garden, leaned across the fence, and broken off a piece of bittersweet. It was a bush that produced bright purple flowers all summer long, and then brilliant red berries come fall. The twig tasted bitter, then sweet, as its name promised. Karl's father, Olaf, had once told Augusta that sheepherders hung bittersweet around the necks of sheep they thought had been rendered sick by the evil eye. She chewed the twig with a deliberate slowness, knowing the old man was watching, knowing she should really walk on. But instead she leaned on her cane and inspected his garden. He had filled the lawn with snowball bushes, a flowering plum and quince, a hazelnut tree too lanky to produce nuts, and trembling aspens with leaves that now scattered like spilled pennies. Here and there he grew beds of sunflowers mixed with banks of pink and white cosmos, and yellow marigolds and calendulas. Against the warmth of the house he grew tomatoes, love apples, Eve's temptation.

She wanted to know the old man. She wanted to share the time of day with someone capable of sweet talk and tenderness in a way that Karl wasn't. She wanted to hold hands and feel the thrill of a secret so dangerous she could tell no one, not even Rose.

Augusta sighed and put the cat on the floor. "Let's get some tea on," she said. But before she plugged in the kettle she picked up the receiver and listened for a dial tone.

"Funny that Joy hasn't phoned," said Rose.

"They did say the operation could take anywhere from five to eighteen hours."

"We could be waiting all day, then."

"You don't have to stay if you don't want to. I've asked a lot of you today. Missing the train and then having you drive all the way to Parksville to get me."

"And driving that woman back besides."

"Esther. Her name's Esther."

Esther had got on the train at Langford, just outside of Victoria. Augusta had been struck by a weeping spell on leaving the city, and was blowing her nose when a very fat Native Indian woman struggled up the last step onto the train with a huge basket. A mother and her young son of perhaps four followed the woman on board, and waited as she turned herself sideways and made her way slowly down the aisle. The boy asked his mother, in a voice so clear and loud that it made Augusta wince, "Why is that lady so fat?"

The Indian woman closed her eyes for the briefest of moments. She turned awkwardly in the aisle and bent down toward the boy, showing her ample backside to Augusta and the three young men sitting two seats down from her. The young man facing Augusta looked at the big woman and then sniggered with his two companions.

"It's okay to be big," said the woman. "Like it's okay to be small like you." Presumably she smiled and tweaked the boy's cheek, but all Augusta could see was the shake of the woman's massive shoulders. The boy's mother made some half-hearted apology, then pulled him off the train. Augusta watched her as she led the boy down the platform and onto the second car of the train. Augusta's car wasn't completely full, but someone sat in each set of seats except those across from Augusta. The Indian woman glanced from seat to seat and then smiled apologetically. "You mind?" she said. Augusta could hardly say no. That seat was the only one in which the woman was likely to fit. She moved her feet to one side as the woman sat down heavily facing Augusta; she took up the whole of the two seats. She slid the huge basket between their feet on the floor, then rummaged through her handbag, found a cloth hankie, and dabbed the sweat from her face. "Hot," she said.

Augusta smiled and stared out the window to avoid further conversation. When she glanced back, the Indian woman had leaned back into her seat and closed her eyes. The woman's basket was decorated with woven designs of what appeared to be stylized feathers in purple and green. It made Augusta think of a basket Karl had brought home for Joy so many years ago. He had bought it from an Indian woman who used the baskets she wove to pick berries on Olaf's ranch. Augusta couldn't recall the design on that basket, but it must have been very like the feathers on this woman's; it had been decorated in the same way, with colored fibers woven right into it, to form patterns. A bundle of Shasta daisies drooped over the side of it. The old man living by the seniors' center grew Shasta daisies, a huge patch of white that delighted the butterflies. But the flowers could be a nuisance. They took over a garden, just like mint; there was no getting rid of them. You could dig them out, but you'd always miss a root and they'd come right back next spring. They refused to die.

The fat woman's name was Esther Joseph, though Augusta didn't know that then. They didn't introduce themselves until they were stranded in Parksville. Esther was a good three hundred pounds, and tall, a giant of a woman. She wore glasses but no jewelry, and her stumpy ankles disappeared into white runners. She wore a dress with a floral print, and its short sleeves exposed a gardener's tan that ended at her elbows.

"I'll stick around," said Rose. "Maybe you can find some time to tell me about Joe."

Augusta lowered her voice as Karl came back into the kitchen. "For God's sake, Rose. Not while Karl's here."

"He wouldn't hear anyway," said Rose. "Eh, Karl?"

"What was that?" said Karl.

"See?"

"Rose!" said Augusta. "Have a cookie." She put the cookie in Rose's mouth.

Rose took a bite and spoke with her mouth full. "I suppose you've got bigger things to worry about."

"Yes."

"Have any inkling how Gabe's doing? I mean, any more premonitions?"

Augusta set teacups and saucers, milk and honey on the table. Karl and Rose took their tea black, and Augusta normally didn't put honey in her tea, but today she craved sweetness. "No, not really," she said. "Nothing since that day I found myself on the floor." Augusta had predicted Gabe's illness; that is to say, she'd had a vision of it. She was fussing around in the kitchen, making supper as Gabe and Joy were about to arrive for a visit when, no matter which way she turned, she saw a patch of white appear in front of her, the edges sloping off into the kitchen scene around her, and in this white was Gabe's face—or almost Gabe's face, because his features retained little expression and his skin held the milky pallor of the gravely ill. His eyes were closed and there was a honeybee on his lip. Then, as suddenly as it had appeared, the vision was gone, and she found herself on the floor beside the kitchen table. She sat there with her stiff legs stretched out in front of her. Karl was down at the seniors' center playing crib. If she had thumped loud enough on the floor Rose might have heard, as her apartment was below Augusta and Karl's. When Joy knocked on the door, Augusta had a hard time standing. She'd had to pull up her body using the edge of the table because her hip had locked on her. Then there was the rattle of keys outside the apartment, and the door opened and Joy pushed her way in, panicked, keys in hand. "Are you all right?"

"I'm fine," said Augusta.

"You look so pale."

"I fell."

"You fell? Are you all right?"

"Yes, yes. Fine. Nothing's broken. I'm fine. I didn't fall, exactly. I had trouble getting up."

"You're sure?"

"Yes. Just let me sit. There. Get me a cup of tea, will you, Joy? And a biscuit from the box on the counter? I need to gather myself. Gabe, sit by me. No, here, in Karl's chair."

As Joy was pouring tea, Augusta told Joy and Gabe about the vision. She said she thought it was a premonition of illness, but they both laughed it off. Rose took it seriously. She said, "We should write it down, don't you think? So there's proof when it happens?" She did just that. She had

Augusta describe the vision again, and wrote down every detail, then put it into an envelope that she sealed with an Easter Seal and mailed to herself, so the cancellation mark would date it.

Then Gabe had the seizure. Sunday afternoon, three weeks back, he began staring over his right shoulder, with an expression on his face that Joy described as frightened, as if he were watching his back, as if he were being chased by some demon. "What's wrong?" she'd asked him. "What are you looking at?"

"I don't know," he said, and then he wasn't able to say anything at all. Joy went into the next room to phone for an ambulance, and as she was on the phone she heard Gabe howl, an inhuman howl, and fall to the floor. She extricated herself from the emergency operator and ran back into the kitchen, where she found the table askew and Gabe thrashing around on the floor under it. "Just like a dumb hurt animal," Joy told Augusta over the phone. "He wasn't human. He wasn't Gabe."

Augusta's first love had howled like that before each of his fits. Tommy Thompson was an older boy who had shown no sign that he knew Augusta was alive. The other kids made fun of him. He was an epileptic, and as a young girl still in school she watched him slide into possession as surely as into the water of a river. He'd turn his head stiffly to look first to the far wall, then to the stove in the center of the room, and finally to the line of pegs where they hung their coats at the back. He couldn't stop himself from turning; nothing could make him look away. That was the warning.

The other kids would giggle out of nervousness, because they knew what was coming. They called him *sav-*

age on the school grounds during lunch break, and *wild man,
crazy man*. Tommy Thompson, sitting at his desk, would
open his mouth and out would come a noise that wasn't a
human scream or the cry of an animal, but something completely different, a noise that seemed to come not from him
but through him, the sound of a soul departing under
protest. Then he would fall heavily, with a thud like a sack
of potatoes dropped on a kitchen floor. His body would jerk
and thrash for what seemed like an eternity, while the
teacher, Mrs. Sawyer, acting with the knowledge of the day,
tried to force a spoon between his teeth to stop him from biting his own tongue. Mrs. Sawyer never succeeded, which
was lucky for her; she might have choked him or lost a finger to his mindless bite. Some time later Tommy would stop
convulsing and begin breathing heavily, nearly snorting,
until he slowly came back to himself.

After she got off the phone with Joy, Augusta immediately phoned Rose to tell her the awful news. "I'll be right
up," said Rose. She barged into Augusta and Karl's apartment, broke open the seal on the envelope in front of them,
then waved her handwritten description of Augusta's
vision above her head, crying, "See! See! There's proof!"

Karl, sitting at the kitchen table with his arm around
Augusta, stared at Rose, bewildered, as if to say, *What the
hell is she doing?* Even so, he didn't question her about her
behavior. So much went on around him that he didn't
understand, didn't hear.

Augusta hadn't told Karl about her vision. Augusta had
never had much luck discussing premonitions or ghosts
with him, though early in their courtship she had believed
he would have to be sympathetic, what with that phantom
thumb of his.

Now, today, Gabe was having brain surgery, of all things. It seemed to Augusta an impossibility, a cruel joke, something from a monster movie. He had been in that hospital for three weeks, undergoing test after test as the doctors figured out what was wrong. Augusta went down to Victoria to be with her daughter and Gabe right at the start, the day after Gabe fell ill. Rose volunteered to drive her, but Joy asked her mother not to bring Rose. "I don't want to have to deal with strangers while all this is going on."

"Rose is hardly a stranger," said Augusta.

"Come on, Mom." Augusta knew Joy didn't like Rose, or more to the point she didn't like the way Rose was always hanging around. One day after Rose had visited with the four of them, Joy said just that to Augusta.

"Rose? She has no family left, and no kids of her own. She's my friend."

"She's always here, even Christmas and Thanksgiving. She gives me the creeps."

"Joy!"

"She does. I don't think she likes men." Augusta repeated that last bit to Rose and they'd had a good laugh over it. After all, Rose had been married for thirty years.

So Augusta took the train down to be with Gabe and Joy. She went by herself. Karl didn't like traveling, but he would have gone and helped her with the frustrations of travel if it hadn't been for those cats. Seven of them. A young couple from church had taken in a stray cat and fattened her and then the cat had been killed on the road outside their house. It wasn't until a day later that they realized she'd dropped a batch of kittens in the attic. Augusta took the kittens on, even though Rose, as manager of the place, reminded her that she was not supposed to have pets in her apartment. "I'll find homes for them," she said. "But some-body's got to care for them now, or they'll die."

She fed them milk and canned catfood by spoon, twice a day, because if she put the bowl on the floor they walked through the food and tracked it across the carpet. When she was standing, they crawled up her pant leg, mewing and scrambling, knocking each other out of the way in a race to eat. The kittens pretty much set the schedule for the day, so when Joy phoned with the news about Gabe, Karl and Augusta decided that Karl would stay home. Someone had to take care of those kittens, and Rose wasn't going to do it.

Augusta spent her days sitting in a chair beside Gabe's bed with Joy, and every night she went home and cooked Joy and herself a late-night meal. She spent almost every minute at Joy's side, except the hour or so she slipped off to give Karl or Rose an update on the phone. One would have thought a daughter would appreciate all that help and want her mother around at a time like this, but not Joy. She had sent her mother packing today. That was why Rose had to drive all the way down to Parksville this morning, to pick up Augusta. Augusta had got off the train there to use the washroom—she couldn't maneuver in the one on the train—and the conductor must have thought that Parksville was her stop because the train had left for Courtenay with-out her. Why he didn't listen to Esther when she told him to wait, Augusta could only guess at. Just before Duncan, the conductor had opened the door to the train car and yelled, "Drunken Duncan!" The three young men seated ahead of Augusta had laughed. There was a large Indian population in Duncan. The town was built, in part, on reserve land. The train station at Duncan was like all the others, but several totem poles stood beside it. A sign proclaimed it *The City of Totems.*

There was only one passenger train service on Vancouver Island, up island in the morning, down island in the afternoon. Augusta no longer drove; Karl's eyesight had failed to the point that he wasn't allowed to. Rose was indeed their chauffeur, among other things.

"I don't understand Joy," said Rose, taking the cup of tea Augusta offered her. "Why would she send you home today of all days?"

"We had a bit of a fight yesterday."

"A fight?"

"A disagreement."

"Over what?"

"It doesn't matter." Although it did. She felt foolish now, and ashamed of herself. They had been downtown, as Joy wanted to spend some time away from the hospital, to try to calm down, and at Augusta's urging they had gone to Munro's bookstore. The bookstore was one huge room with a high vaulted ceiling and elaborate quilted hangings on the walls. It was a magnificent bookstore, a cathedral devoted to books, and readers worshiped here quietly, whispering their questions to the clerks, smelling and touching the books—revering them as if they were sacred objects. Joy must not have felt she belonged. For her, it must have been like entering the tabernacle of another's faith. She rarely read, and what she did read was Christian. Reading was a luxury, an entertainment, and there were always other, more pressing demands on her time, or at least she made it seem so. Gabe used to read, and Joy bought him books in her more generous moments, but it made her angry to see him sitting there reading when he could have been putting up those kitchen cupboards or finishing that wall in the living room or installing the mirrors on the doors of her walk-in closet. So she was waiting on Augusta, all but tapping her foot.

A book caught Augusta's eye, that was all, a romance called *Savage Persuasion*. It was a book Rose might have bought. On the cover there was a picture of a hunk holding a dark-haired woman, he dressed in a Native Indian's loincloth, she in a purple gown that was pulled off her shoulders. Augusta felt its binding and smelled it with the same satisfaction with which she touched all books. It was impulse. She felt a compulsion to take the thing, a tension that wouldn't let go of her. In the moment after she pocketed the book, she expected her heart to race, the sweat to bead on her upper lip, but there was none of that. She felt relief; a sensation of freedom came over her.

But then Joy was standing right there, like an angry mother watching a disobedient child. "What are you doing?" she shrieked. As if she didn't know, as if Augusta were a naughty child. She made Augusta put the book back, and then apologized to the clerks as she pulled her mother out of the bookstore by the arm. *Apologized*, as if she had the right. She drove Augusta all the way back to the house without saying a word, but once at home she had plenty to say. "What on earth got into you?"

"I don't really know. I—"

"I've never been so humiliated!"

"It's not so bad. It's kind of funny. Don't you think?"

"Funny?!"

"I just mean—it's not like I meant to! It just sort of got in my bag."

"How can you say that? Never mind! I don't want to hear about it. Oh, God! I don't want to have to deal with you tomorrow, not while the operation's going on."

Joy looked old at that moment; she had her sweater folded across her belly and her arms crossed so her shoulders were rounded. Augusta thought at the time that they could be a couple of sisters wrangling away over petty jealousies. Then she caught sight of herself in the mirrored cabinet that held the television set. The tart red of her lipstick couldn't conceal the fact that she was a much older woman, neither could the outrageous purple of her blouse, nor the brightly patterned scarf she'd used to pull the hair from her face. All the color in the world wouldn't rejuvenate the withered skin of her neck. She was the aging queen bee, wings tattered and legs crippled from years of life inside the hive; her usefulness was all but over. "I'll stay at the house, then," she said. "I'll wait here."

"I may come back to rest. The operation could be as long as eighteen hours."

"I'll be quiet. I won't bother you."

"Please. Take the train tomorrow. Go home. Be with Dad. It's your anniversary tomorrow."

"I don't want to go. Not now. I want to be here."

"I don't want you here."

Augusta began to cry. "What about me?" she said. "You're not thinking about me at all."

"I'm not thinking about you? For heaven's sake, he's *my* husband."

"Well, it's just not fair, sending me off like that."

"Oh, *please*."

"Well, it's not."

"I can't deal with you. I just can't deal with you right now."

Augusta had been petulant, childish during that argument, she knew that now, now that she was back at the apartment. If she had eased up maybe Joy would have calmed down and let her stay at the house, or in the hospital waiting room. But it seemed so unfair to be shipped off like that, like old useless baggage. "You can tell if a queen bee is getting old, you know," she said.

"Ah-huh," said Rose.

"Her movements are slower. She's got less get-up-and-go. She lays fewer eggs. When she's failing, her daughters simply replace her."

"Oh, yeah."

"They build a queen cell and put in a freshly laid egg. Then they'll feed that new larva enough royal jelly to make a new queen. The old queen lives out her days in a corner at the bottom of the hive."

"Feeling a little down, today?" asked Rose.

Augusta shrugged. "I can't be a ray of sunshine on a day like this."

"No, I don't suppose so."

Augusta breathed in the scent of honey as she sipped her tea, and immediately thought of Gabe. Once, after putting new beeswax foundation in the frames of Augusta's hive, Gabe had gone inside and made tea for Augusta, Karl, and Rose in Rose's kitchen, then brought it outside to where they were sitting in the garden. When he handed Augusta her tea, his fingertips had left the sweet maple-syrup scent of foundation on the cup. She had inhaled the scent with every sip. How could a woman not love a man who smelled that wonderful? Even when he hadn't been working with the bees, Gabe carried a sweetness around him. Sometimes he smelled like honey, caramel, or canned peaches—the sugary scent diabetics often gave off. When he sneezed it was much stronger; the heady smell was exactly like that of black poplar coming into leaf, a smell Augusta remembered from her childhood. Maybe his scent was a symptom of his illness, like the sweetness of roses that sometimes surrounded the dying.

Where was Gabe now? she wondered. Was he floating off someplace as the doctors did those terrible things to his body? Or was he there in that operating room, listening in? Was the operation over? Had he made it back to his body okay? Joy had promised to phone one way or the other, but it was almost two now and they hadn't heard a thing. She would have to sit here with Karl and Rose and wait. There would be no visits to the seniors' center today.

That was where Augusta, Karl, and Rose spent most of their days—eating lunch, playing cards, and generally painting the air blue with the complaints of the day: of welfare bums and Indians who were getting too big for their britches; of girls having babies on their own, shame on them; and of governments misusing their tax money. Augusta was growing tired of the pettiness of the place, the grumpiness. But at least at the center there were others who could understand the complications of aging; there were others for whom arthritis had rendered fastening a brassiere an impossibility, buttoning a blouse maddening, brushing hair painful, and doing up shoelaces a feat of Olympian proportions. A number of women had trouble bending far enough to cut their own toenails, and so headed for that handsome Dr. Miles for a regular ten-minute toenail snip. At the center incontinence was not the embarrassment it was elsewhere—there was a definite rustle at lunchtime as Depends-clad bottoms settled into chairs. And many of them suffered from aching knee and hip joints, so that getting up was the same pain-filled ritual dance: there was the groan or two, the private swearing, the testing of the sore leg, the hobble to the left and to the right to see which leg was going to hold the weight. And many of the seniors carried canes, some fiercely equipped with a spike strapped to the end, to better protect themselves from icy patches on the sidewalk and teenagers on skateboards.

Sometimes Augusta sat in a group of women at the seniors' center and looked around wondering why she was there. She didn't feel like one of them; she couldn't possibly look the way they did, all white hair and stooped posture. They seemed an embittered old bunch to her, blinded to new sensibilities, digging their heels in against the pull of change, howling for a world long gone. But the white hair and aching joints were hers as much as theirs, and women her age died in town every week. *Do the other women feel the way I do?* she wondered. *Do they look at me and say, I'm not like that, am I?*

- two -

Augusta dipped her spoon into the honey as one of the kittens climbed the leg of her pants and nestled in her lap. Rose peered down at the kitten and shook her head, her hair bouncing like meringue. She had the sun-weathered skin of a farmer and wore no makeup. She was dressed in a pink sweatshirt and jeans. Augusta inspected her honey-dipped spoon. "Did you know eating honey protects your stomach from aspirin?" she said. Rose sighed and caught Karl's eye.

"How was the train ride?" asked Karl.

"Very nice. Except I got off at Parksville and the train left without me."

"That Esther woman made her miss the train."

"She did not."

"Did so."

"She told you to get off at Parksville, didn't she?"

Augusta licked her spoon. "Honey won't give you gas the way sugar can."

"Didn't she?"

Augusta sighed and put down the spoon. "Just to use the washroom."

"It was her ploy to get a ride to the mall."

"So you're saying Esther delayed her trip by more than two hours to get a ride to the mall?"

"Yes."

Augusta shook her head and took another spoonful from the honeypot. It was from her mother, Helen, that Augusta had learned beekeeping, and she had learned it almost as soon as she could walk. As a child she had walked barefoot through the orchard, carefully, slowly, lest she step on a bee or stir them into stinging. The air in the orchard was thick with Helen's honeybees and the renegade wasps that ransacked the fruit, so walking with her mother through the clouds of bees to the peach trees was sometimes like parting a curtain. The bees would sweep away from their bodies and then collapse in behind them. Neither of them wore black into the orchard, even on church Sundays, because they feared bees might mistake their large black shape for a ransacking bear and swarm around them, stinging to protect their hives. After making their way through them Helen would pick Augusta a peach and she would eat it there, surrounded by bees, pestered by wasps. The juice that dribbled down her chin was warm, comforting, sticky, sweet; bees landed on her chin and lips before buzzing off.

Helen taught Augusta to pet the hives. She brushed her hand affectionately across the many bees climbing across the frames of honeycomb, and Augusta followed in kind. It felt like petting the belly of a loudly purring cat, except the wings beating against the palm of her hand tickled. But she just did this with the calm hives, and only on a day when the bees had a good supply of nectar and pollen, and the weather was fine. The mood of the hives varied from day to day, depending on the supply of nectar and whether or not they had been pestered by robber bees or pillaging skunks.

In her turn, Augusta had got Gabe started in his honey business, and that had been the beginning of their shared affection. She had given him most of her boxes and equipment when she and Karl sold the Shuswap farm and moved to Vancouver Island. He didn't make much money at it. It was Joy who brought in the steady income, working as a receptionist at a paving company. Before he became ill, Gabe had taken jobs doing whatever he could: house construction, cabinetmaking, farmwork. His bees were more like a calling than an occupation.

He was as obsessed with beekeeping as Augusta was. His bookshelves were filled with books about the art of beekeeping, the biology of bees, myths and legends associated with bees. He told Augusta that bees were the souls of the dead flying off to the afterlife, or just returning to start a new life. He said Jesus created bees: he washed his hands in the river Jordan and the sparkling drops that fell from his hands flew off as bees. The image captured her. As they flew up into the sun the fine hairs on their bodies caught the light and sparkled. They looked like flying jewels, or raindrops. As long as the sweet smell surrounded Gabe, Augusta would believe almost anything he said: that a tablespoon of honey sucked on before bed would induce sleep. That a swarm of bees could be settled simply by tanging pots of iron and brass together. That bees were the "birds of the muses" and could bestow the gift of song or eloquence on a baby simply by landing on that babe's lips. She wished it were that easy; she would find a bee and coax it with honey onto Gabe's lips and give him back his gift of speech.

Gabe looked much as Karl had done when he was a young man, though Karl was a smaller man, built like his father, Olaf. Even so, Karl had carried his body tall, as Gabe did now—at least, unless his father was around, in which case Karl's body shifted from self-possessed grace to bone-sad clumsiness. But his eyes never changed. Eyes so blue, well, she could have drowned in a blue like that. It was a blue made bluer still by the red that fired into his face at any embarrassment. When they were first courting, back then, it took only the suggestion of a hello, the suspicion of a caress, the possibility that Karl might have to speak her name, and his face was alight, as red as the cloth handker-chief he carried.

Karl was twelve years Augusta's senior. He was already beginning to bald when she first saw him, as she and her mother were walking down the road to see Mrs. Grafton, Martha Rivers' mother. Mrs. Grafton's husband, Harold, was a Rosicrucian and wouldn't allow his wife and children to eat meat. That was a problem for Mrs. Grafton, as she was anemic much of the time and too tired to chase around after all her children. Harold also believed that plants and ani-mals had spirits and so he wouldn't chop down a tree, but he would cut and stack the wood once the tree was fallen. Helen could never see the sense of it. "He'll spare the soul of a tree but not a head of lettuce," she said. Harold was away most weekdays, working at the sawmill, so that was when Helen slipped meals of meat up to Mrs. Grafton: lamb chops, roast lamb, roast beef and Yorkshire pudding. "We Anglo-Saxons need our meat," she told Mrs. Grafton.

On this day Helen carried a syrup can filled with beef stew. It was midsummer and the grass along the road was dry and dusty. A few wildflowers bloomed: shaggy daisies, blue bachelor's buttons, chicory, violet aster, vetch, and del-icate white pearly everlastings. Helen hadn't changed out of her housedress for this visit, which embarrassed Augusta so much that she couldn't bear to look at her. She herself had changed into her good blue pinafore, and stockings that itched. She was hot and couldn't understand why she had to accompany her mother on this visit. It would be the same as it always was. They'd knock on the door of the Grafton house and one of the children still at home would answer the door. (There were twelve children in the family, all of them white-blonds. Even then Augusta couldn't always tell them apart.) Helen would ask for Mrs. Grafton and the child would say, "Mama's hiding again."

From somewhere in back of the cluttered house Mrs. Grafton would call, "Is that Helen? Helen, I'm here. I'm not hiding. I'm just feeling poorly."

The child at the door might turn back to them then and, calm and quiet as a preacher's wife, say, "She's saying that 'cause she's embarrassed. She ain't sick. She locked herself in the bedroom and won't come out."

It was almost the same very time. Augusta would stare at the ceiling as her mother visited with the wild-eyed, pasty-faced Mrs. Grafton, and the children yelped and leapt around outside like savages. Martha Rivers was sure to be there. She was bossy, the oldest of the Grafton children and already thrice a mother herself. She spent as much time running her mother's home as she did running her own, and she wore responsibility like a cleric's robe.

Augusta's mind was taken up with dread of the coming afternoon as she watched her feet kick dust. Their collie, Sammie, was at her heels. Her mother hummed something—a hymn, likely—and crickets were singing in the grasses. Then Sammie yelped and darted off and her mother yelled at the dog and Augusta forgot all about her feet and the dust and the hot dry afternoon, because suddenly, there in front of her, was a blue like the blue she'd seen when she'd opened her eyes while swimming in the South Thompson and gazed up at the summer sky through water, layers of blue, a color that could fly her away if she let it.

That was the first time she saw Karl, the very first time, because there was a face around those two bits of take-your-breath-away blue; a red face, as Sammie was biting Karl's leg and was in no mind to let go.

"Git away!" Helen yelled. "Sammie, git!" But Sammie wasn't going to let go of the man's trouser leg and the bit of flesh he'd sunk his teeth into and, as Karl was making no real attempt to get the dog off him, Sammie had no reason to let go. Karl didn't let out one cussword, not one; he said nothing at all. But what he didn't say fired up his face and, with his carroty hair blowing all over, he looked the devil himself. Augusta stood back while her mother pulled the dog away by the scruff of the neck. "I'm sorry, Karl," she said. So this man was someone her mother knew. "Is your leg all right? Oh, I'm so sorry."

Karl smiled but didn't say anything, and the color didn't leave his face. He went on his way, limping, and Augusta, Helen, and Sammie went on theirs.

The next time Augusta saw Karl was when he was sagging beside his father, Olaf, in the truck, dressed in black, his head down, staring at his hands as they drove to the church on the day of his mother's funeral. It was painfully obvious that they'd had no woman's help in dressing. Olaf's socks were ridiculously mismatched—one blue, one green—and Karl had a red handkerchief poking out of his breast pocket. Red at a funeral! Those two men were the sorriest sight Augusta had seen in her short life, and though she was at a funeral she couldn't help the smile that crept onto her face. She was just fourteen and she could go right ahead and laugh at the grief of strangers. She hadn't known sorrow yet. She herself hadn't known Karl's mother, or the mangy old Swede Karl called Father. But her own father had worked with the Swede years before, and as Karl's mother had died from cold in a snowdrift out in the field not a quarter-mile from home—died in a manner that reminded everyone how close death's bite was—it turned out to be one of those funerals the whole town attended. Karl was twenty-six then, and she thought how funny he looked, how sad and how funny. She didn't see him again, even in town, until she was eighteen and her mother was three years dead and the studhorse man paid a visit.

Augusta stood up from the table and went over to the balcony to look down at her bees. They were still agitated, buzzing excitedly around the hive. Karl joined her, carrying his cup. "I take it you checked on the bees already," he said.

"Yeah. They're upset, like something's been after them."

"Boys," said Karl, "throwing rocks at the hive. I caught them at it this morning." He pointed at the parking lot behind the low white picket fence that surrounded Rose's garden. "They were over there, using the hive for target practice. I think they were trying to get the bees to swarm out. I was walking across the parking lot on my way home when I saw them. I chased them off."

"That explains it. I'll just leave the hive alone, then. Let the bees calm down. The less I fuss over them the better, after something like that." Augusta turned to Karl. "So where were you walking from? Seniors' center?"

Karl's ears blushed. "No. Just out walking."

Augusta looked him over briefly. He was up to something. Maybe he'd been out buying her an anniversary gift. She went back inside to join Rose at the table. Karl followed. "Did I tell you Saint Valentine is the patron saint of bee-keepers?" said Augusta.

"Is that so?" said Rose.

"He's also the patron saint of those with epilepsy, as well as lovers, of course."

"You're kidding me."

"No. It's true. Gabe showed me in one of his books."

"Then Saint Valentine is the one we should be praying to today. Gabe's a perfect candidate, a beekeeper who has fits."

Augusta laughed despite herself, then felt the lump of worry well up in her throat. Even without the vision, she would have known something was wrong with Gabe, long before he had that seizure. He had always been such a calm man; not even Joy's stormy moods would faze him. But now his own mood switched from honeyed light to thunderstorm in a heartbeat. He slept more than a grown man should and still walked around exhausted. He was fired from his construction job because he couldn't keep up. To Joy it seemed like pure laziness. She'd come home from the work that now paid their bills and have to clean house and make supper besides, because Gabe had nothing ready. He'd be sitting in his big green armchair, dozing. When it came time to harvest the honey from his own hives and bottle it for sale, he needed help from Joy, as he never had before.

It was Gabe who had collected the hive Augusta had now. When that swarm of honeybees landed on Rose's fence at the back of the garden, it seemed like Providence to

Augusta, because she had been telling Rose not two days before how much she missed having a hive of her own. The bees were clustered in a ball hanging from the fence. Rose told Augusta she thought there must be some round structure under them that they clung to, some construction of honeycomb they had created; she said it couldn't possibly be all bees. But it was all bees. Layer on layer of bees on bees, the outer ones jittering around and occasionally lifting off for short flights before returning to the globe. Under that first covering Augusta showed Rose the second layer of bees, sitting quietly, clinging to each other by the legs. They had created this marvelous fabrication with their own bodies.

Augusta phoned Gabe, and he came up the same day with his gear and a new box of frames and foundation. The only protective clothing he wore was a pair of yellow rubber gloves. He rarely got stung, though Joy was stung all the time when she helped him. Augusta herself could expect ten stings a day when harvesting. Honeybees tended to sting people in places where they sweated, like under the arms or waistband, where their animal scent was strongest. The bees were grumpy at the end of honey flow, as there was less nectar to collect and nothing to keep them occupied. They were protective of the ripening honey as it was all they had to see them through winter. The gloves she wore while working with them at such times were peppered with stingers. When she held the gloves up to the light, the stingers that stuck out of the leather looked like thistle spurs.

It wasn't that the bees ignored Gabe. They were interested in him, attracted to his sweet scent. They swarmed around him, lit on his arms and face, and got tangled in the fine hairs at the top of his head where his hairline was retreating. Like all good beekeepers he kept his movements slow and steady to avoid agitating them, but Augusta believed that they didn't see him as a threat because he smelled so wonderful. He smelled like the hive.

Gabe set the bee box under the swarm, then gave the fence one sharp tap. Rather than flying, startled, all over the place, the bees fell in a clump into the box with all its frames and the comb foundation on which they would store their honey. They sounded crunchy as they fell into the hive, like breakfast cereal poured into a bowl. With his gloved hand Gabe brushed the few that still clung to the fence into the box. Augusta ran her hand over the bees that crawled atop and between the foundation frames. They were warm, familiar.

Augusta hadn't realized how ill Gabe had become until that day Rose drove her back from the seniors' center because she was expecting Joy to arrive for a visit. Karl had stayed behind to finish off a card game. When they got home Joy was waiting in Augusta's apartment. "You're late," she said to Augusta. "Why are you always late? Doesn't my life matter? Don't you care that I've got things to do? It's like the whole world revolves around you. Other people have things they've got to do."

"I'm sorry," said Augusta. "I didn't know you were in a hurry today."

"That's not the point. You could be on time, for Christ's sake."

Augusta and Rose both gasped. There was righteous Joy taking the Lord's name in vain. Joy put her hand to her mouth, then she was crying.

"Rose, would you mind putting on the kettle?" asked Augusta. She took the Kleenex box over to Joy and sat on the couch next to her.

"I think he's nuts," said Joy. "He's like Jekyll and Hyde. One minute he's all sweet and nice and the next he's yelling at me."

"Gabe?"

"He never used to yell. We hardly ever got into fights, you know? Now he yells at me for no good reason. It's like he's some other guy."

"Maybe he's depressed," said Augusta.

"We don't go out any more or visit friends, because he can't carry on a conversation. I'm not even sure I love him anymore." Joy blew her nose into the tissue Augusta had given her. "Now God's talking to him." *God?* thought Augusta. While working on the hives or relaxing in the house, Gabe would get rushes of emotion, a sensation of expansion, as if he were ballooning outward, moving into everything that surrounded him. He said the feelings were pregnant with import and there were words attached to them, words he could never get out. He would rush to Joy and say, "I understand." He'd gesture excitedly with his hands, trying to get the words out. "Everything."

"You understand everything?"

"Yes. Sort of. Oh, shit. It's gone."

"You had an idea? Or what?"

"No, more than that. Like a light. Like—"

"God?"

"Yes, like that."

As Gabe described it to Joy later on, the feeling sounded like the times when she couldn't come up with the name of a person she'd known forever, a name that was on the tip of her tongue, the fumbling feeling of searching for a missing word. Only for Gabe the inability to find it went on for a long time and was accompanied by washes of transcendence, the effervescent emotions that might attend a visitation by an angel or, for others, a UFO sighting. "Sounds crazy, doesn't it?" he said to Joy.

"Yes. No."

Crazy, yes, Augusta thought. On the other hand, Joy went to see her pastor to find out why God wasn't talking to *her*. God was talking to Gabe, a nonbeliever—a man who'd *gone back to the world*, who'd *strayed from faith*, a *backslider*, a *black sheep*—and not to her. Gabe had been pulled into that born-again stuff after his parents died, but he didn't buy into it anymore, though Augusta was unsure of what he did believe. God talked to people in Joy's church. Any time someone got a good idea, or any idea for that matter, thought Augusta, they said, "The Lord spoke to me." A humble lot, she supposed, if they never believed they had an idea of their own. Augusta went to her own church most Sundays but didn't much care for Joy's; more to the point, the things her daughter believed made her laugh. In a fit of exasperation over her mother's beliefs Joy had once said, "How are you going to feel when I'm caught in the rapture and carried to heaven and you're left down here?"

Augusta laughed. "Well, I'd miss you. But I'd be quite all right here, with Karl and Rose and everyone at the seniors' center."

Maybe she shouldn't have laughed. It was all very serious to Joy, no joke at all. She really did imagine that the end times were so imminent that any minute now she'd be sucked up to heaven by a cosmic vacuum cleaner, leaving her poor unbelieving mother here on earth. How Joy had come to believe the things she did was beyond Augusta. She didn't get it from me, she thought. Augusta had her own brand of faith, one she had often described to Rose and

other ladies at the church as a gardener's faith, one that died
down in winter and grew in spring with the resurrection of
nature. Much of the time she didn't know what to believe,
but in spring and summer, when she worked in the abun-
dance of a garden—felt the mud between her toes, tasted
the ecstasy in a strawberry eaten fresh off the plant—she
had to believe God was a sensualist who enjoyed a good
tomato. Augusta couldn't help but feel that the God of Joy's
church was mighty thin.

"I wouldn't feel slighted," the preacher had advised Joy,
when she told him God talked to Gabe.

"But why Gabe?" said Joy. "He doesn't believe."

"Maybe He's calling Gabe home."

"But God has never talked to me. And I've never had
any miracles. I'm not asking for big ones, just little ones, like
Mrs. Tanner's when she found that five-dollar bill inside the
outhouse at the park when she was broke."

"But you have faith. What do you need with miracles
when you have faith? Gabe doesn't have faith and so God
is trying to get his attention, trying to tell him something.
But God may be too big for Gabe to handle. That's why he
can never remember what God has said to him."

"But what if it isn't God?"

"Well, that's just it. It may be the devil playing tricks
with his mind."

One would think a preacher would have an easier time
telling God from the devil, Augusta thought, as Joy told
her all this. As it turned out, Gabe was having little
seizures in his left temporal lobe, under his forehead. His
surgeon told him that seizures in this area of the brain
affected language, but also created the sensations Gabe
was talking about. A sense of awe, words that seemed to

carry a divine message, a feeling of profound meaning. Gabe's spirit of God was nothing but a cascade of electrical impulses flowing through part of his brain, a nest of excited bees in his basket hive. Despite her opinion of Joy's church, Augusta found herself disappointed by this. What a bitter pill to swallow, if the Spirit really was only a manifestation of the flesh.

But then, she wondered, what was she to make of her own occasional premonitions? They suggested so much, that eternity had surfaced into the temporal for a moment. Was *this* God talking? she wondered. Bees danced their elaborate dances to tell each other where the best nectar was. It was a language that had for so long gone unnoticed, and then been misunderstood by beekeepers, because bees danced in the dark of their hive and on the vertical floor of the honeycomb, hidden away. It was a language of touch and smell, not sound, as they gleaned information by touching the bodies of the dancing bees with their antennae. They deduced the type of flower the dancing bee had located by the scent of it still lingering on its body. Dancing bees offered other foragers tastes of the nectar they'd collected so they would know what they'd find. It was a language so unlike that of humans as to be nearly unrecognizable. Was the language of visions and dreams—the strange, nearly incomprehensible images and symbols—God's language? Why didn't He speak up, she wondered, and say things clearly in a language she could understand? God seemed to be as much a tease as that old man down the road from the apartment, hoarding his garden to himself, allowing her only the bittersweet twigs she could steal. Why didn't he come out and introduce himself, she wondered, instead of watching the world from behind the curtains of a darkened window?

The day after Gabe was hospitalized, Joy picked up Augusta at the train station and dropped her off at the hospital cafeteria so she could refresh herself before going to see him. Joy then went home to catch a nap. The cafeteria had floor-to-ceiling windows looking over landscaped grounds. Augusta found herself a table right by one of these glass walls and, as she drank her tea, a small black rabbit bounded across the lawn right up to the window. Domestic rabbits ran wild over the whole south island. She had seen them on the hospital grounds when visiting friends from the seniors' center; rabbits speckled or tan, off-white or black, grazing on the lawns or begging from visitors who fed them limp lettuce from plastic bags. This rabbit of Augusta's sniffed the glass at her shoes and sat up, clearly begging for food, apparently unaware of the glass that separated them. The rabbit was so trusting that Augusta could hardly believe it. The creature seemed like a gift, a divine comfort. For a moment the anxiety that had tightened her neck slipped away.

After her tea, Augusta found her way to the intensive care unit of the neurology ward. The sign on the door said, "Knock and wait for a nurse to assist you." Augusta knocked and waited a long time out in the hallway, unsure if she should knock again or not. The pain in her hip gnawed away at her. Some kind soul dressed in white had seen her breathless confusion over the buttons in the elevator, asked her where she was going, pressed the appropriate buttons, and told her which floor to get off at. Then there was another agonizing walk to the nursing station, and still another down a corridor to the door of the unit where her son-in-law lay. She was staring down that hallway at an elderly woman tied into a wheelchair when the nurse finally opened the door. "Gabe Suskind?" Augusta asked her.

"Are you family?"

"I'm his mother."

The nurse led her into the long narrow room and to a bed occupied by a man Augusta didn't at first recognize. "Gabe?"

"You can try talking to him if you like," said the nurse. "But please keep it down."

It was Gabe lying in the bed, but it also wasn't. His hair against the pillow was as carroty as ever, but his skin was nearly as white as the sheet he lay on, and none of his expressions was there, certainly not his smile. The nurses were keeping him sedated so he wouldn't move around, as he had for much of the day before. A bit of dribble slid down the side of his mouth. There was no bee on his lips. Nevertheless, here was the vision she had seen in her kitchen the day she had pulled herself up from the floor to open the door for Joy. She took a handkerchief from her purse and wiped the saliva from the corner of Gabe's mouth, then leaned into the bed rail. There was no place to sit. One bed was arm's length from the next, and in between were an assortment of IV stands and drip lines. Augusta shifted her weight carefully, to dampen the pain in her hip and to steady herself, so she wouldn't hobble and knock something over.

A nurse came and took Gabe's blood pressure and his pulse; lifted the blanket and checked the catheter and the filling bag of urine. She left Gabe's bedside without having once acknowledged Augusta's presence.

Augusta took Gabe's hand. She didn't know what else to do. It was limp and cool. The whole room was cool. She could see, now, why the nurses all wore sweaters. Fevers, she guessed; they kept the room cool to help combat fevers. She had done that herself for Joy, so many years ago: immersed her in lukewarm water to help bring down a fever. An old remedy, but it worked. When she took her daughter in to that handsome Dr. Collier, he had congratulated her. After he moved back east, to London, Ontario, Augusta had written to him twice, but he hadn't answered. Too busy, she supposed.

Augusta stroked Gabe's hand and glanced around the intensive care unit. At the far end was a room made of glass, with curtains only partly covering the glass walls. Everything within the room was white—white blankets on the bed, a white nightstand with a glass vase full of white Shasta daisies. There was a woman in the bed. Dead, thought Augusta, that woman's dead. She stared at the woman for a long time, hoping for some sign she was wrong, then watched as the nurse who had opened the door for her led a young woman and two men, who were clearly brothers, from the corridor into the glass room. The young woman cried out. The nurses stopped what they were doing for a moment and braced themselves against whatever they stood beside—the foot of a bed, the counter, the sink, the open fridge with all its bottles lined up inside. The nurse closed the curtain around the inside of the room and shut the door as she left it.

The moment passed for the nurses and they went on with their chores, but Augusta couldn't let it go. The grief of the family intensified the pain in her hip, gutted her stomach, dizzied her. Now that the curtains were drawn around the inside of the glass room, Augusta could see herself, Gabe—the whole room—reflected there. *For now we see*

through a glass, darkly, but then face-to-face. She began to
sweat and became short of breath. Her heart fluttered. The
nurse who had opened the door for her unceremoniously
slid a chair next to her and moved on before Augusta could
thank her.

Augusta dropped heavily into the chair and placed her
fingers over Gabe's limp hand. Her face was level with the
high bed he slept on. Her feet ached. She wanted more than
anything to slip her shoes off and let her swollen feet free,
but a nurse had just scolded a very young woman standing
by a patient in the next bed for walking around barefoot.
"You don't know what you'll pick up," she had said.

Smelling Gabe's sweet scent, Augusta closed her eyes
and saw him in her mind's eye in the orchard, midafter-
noon, hunched over a bee box. Bees in his hair. Bees on his
cheeks. Bees hovering around his head. He smelt of God's
own fruits and flowers and of honey itself. His was the
sweetness of angels. Being stung so often, Joy had become
an expert on the many cures for bee stings: a slightly moist-
ened sugar cube applied to the welt, or a paste of baking
soda, or slices of raw onion, or poultices of summer savory.
But the sugar-cube treatment took the pain away immediately. Augusta must have nodded off to sleep then, sitting
in the chair, still clasping Gabe's hand, because suddenly
Joy was beside her, removing Gabe's hand from her grasp
and holding it in her own.

One wouldn't think a mother-in-law would be so fond
of a son-in-law. But there it was. Gabe had lost his parents
when he was in his twenties, to a car crash. Maybe that was
why he was more of a son than son-in-law to Augusta. He
was the one who had visited her every day when she had
been hospitalized two years before, not Joy. Joy had only

managed the one visit. Augusta was in the hospital because her young doctor had pulled her off her old heart medication too quickly and she had collapsed in the kitchen. When it first started she thought she was having another vision so at first she didn't call out to Karl. The room became soft, bent all out of shape. Objects she knew were solid were dancing around like drunken sailors. The table leaned so much that she was sure it would give way if she so much as put a teacup there. The only two things she was somewhat sure of were the floor she was standing on and the blue phone on the counter that was miraculously holding its shape. Then the floor began to shift under her feet. She leaned against the counter and called out to Karl but the television was on high and he didn't hear. She grabbed the phone and used the redial button to call Rose. When Rose answered she heard the phone hit the floor.

The next thing Augusta knew, she was in a white room and everything was fuzzy and moving. Nothing made sense. She tried focusing for a while on the objects around the room: the square box on an arm above her, the skinny stand to one side that she knew she was attached to, by the tube running out of her. Most peculiar of all was the big red shape beside her, moving and changing; it wasn't one shape, it was many. Jiggling and flowing from one solid into another. She wished it would stay still and become just one thing so she could get a good look at it. She reached out to touch the red shapes, and as her arm took motion it too multiplied, flowed from one shape to another. It was ridiculous—laughable—and frightening at the same time, yet she was drawn to reach out. Because the red shape smelled of honey. The whole room smelled of honey and the red shape was the source. Even as she reached out, she giggled at the red thing's duplicity. She giggled right out loud. "Augusta," it said. "Mom."

That was her. She was Mom. Of course. All at once the higgledy-piggledy shapes joined into one. There was her arm, one arm, reaching out to touch the red. And the red was Gabe's shirt, and Gabe was in it, smelling of honeycomb and peaches. *Her* Gabe. He was holding a teddy bear. "Thought you could use a friend."

Augusta named that bear Gabe, and slept with him tucked in beside her every night of her hospital stay. Joy didn't think much of that; she read all kinds of unsettling sexual things into Augusta's behavior and gave her heck. "The bear was comforting, that's all," Augusta told her. "And Gabe is the most comfortable person I know to be around."

Gabe had given her the teacup she drank from now, as she sat with Karl and Rose at the table. He had surprised her with it, in fact. During their last visit, they had all gone into that antique store together. Lovely place. China teacups set out on mirrored glass shelves so the whole place shimmered in the pretty colors of the cups. There was one teacup and saucer there of a pattern Augusta had grown up with— the pattern of a set her mother had owned: a delicate yellow with roses painted around the rim. Augusta admired the teacup but finally put it back on its mirrored shelf. She couldn't afford it and Karl wouldn't give her the money to buy it. "What do you need that for?" he said. "You've got teacups all over the house." When they all returned to Augusta and Karl's apartment that afternoon, Gabe insisted on making the tea, and when he brought the tea to the table she saw why. How had he managed to buy the cup without her seeing? Because it was Gabe's idea, she saw that clearly, though Joy smiled as though she were in on the gift. Joy wouldn't have thought to buy her that cup any more than Karl would have. Karl wasn't much for buying gifts, even for birthdays or anniversaries.

"You planning anything special for today?" she asked him.

"Special? What like?"

"I don't know." She glanced over at Rose as she took a seat beside her. "Just thought you might have planned something."

"Thought we'd be waiting around for Joy's call. Didn't think we'd be going down to the seniors' center."

"No, of course not." She examined him as he scratched the scar where his thumb was missing. His ears were a little pink, but not the red they usually bloomed when he was lying or trying to hide something from her. With all that had been going on, she doubted she would have remembered that today was their anniversary herself, if Joy hadn't reminded her. "You remember when we met?" she asked Karl. "When you came to the farm with that horse dealer?"

"Ah-huh," said Karl. His ears blushed. He glanced at her and back at his cup, smiling.

The stud-horse man who had introduced Karl and Augusta was named George Hucker. He hooked up two studs, stallions, to a two-wheeled cart and rode them around from farm to farm to service mares for a fee. His occupation was called "traveling the stud" in those days, and it often involved more than mating horses.

When George Hucker arrived at the farm in the early evening, after supper, Augusta was planting potatoes and her father, Manny, was shoveling out the calf stalls. They were both sweating, neither looking their best, but they dropped what they were doing and greeted their guests. "What you doing here?" said Manny. "Both my mares are pregnant; you know that." He waved his hand at the mares grazing in the field behind the barn.

"Got a young man here looking for a horse. You remember Karl."

"Yeah, Karl. How's Olaf?"

"All right."

"Don't think you ever met my daughter, Augusta."

Karl smiled and nodded but didn't offer a handshake.

"So," said George. "Got anything for us?"

"What you in mind for?"

"Karl wants a good riding horse. Something sturdy and reliable and in good health. Nothing fancy. Karl here can't afford too much."

"Don't know if I can do anything for you, Karl," said Manny. "Wasn't planning on selling."

"Are you sure there, Manny?" said George. "Maybe Augusta has some thoughts on the matter?"

"You'd have to ask her yourself. She's got her own mind."

"I don't know," said Augusta.

"Why not try Grafton," said Manny.

"Heard all his mares was sold. Ones not sold are a little on the high-strung side."

"I wouldn't know about that."

George offered Manny and Karl a cigarette. Karl struck a match on the side of the wagon and lit Manny's and George's cigarettes before lighting his own. It was then that Augusta noticed he was missing the thumb on his right hand; he expertly held the match between his index and middle fingers. The stud-horse man, and Manny, silently smoked their cigarettes as Karl stole glances at Augusta.

It was only after they were married that Augusta understood that the stud man was also a trader of another kind, a matchmaker, and that she was the merchandise being appraised that day. She didn't clue in, even after weeks of Karl's visits. He started showing up at the farm, smelling of soap and carrying things. Sometimes he brought copies of *National Geographic;* once he brought flowers. Neither Manny nor Karl was much for talk so these were awkward visits. Augusta set out coffee, and cookies if she'd had time for baking that week, and sat at the kitchen table with the two of them. Her father smoked his pipe and leafed through the *National Geographic* if Karl had brought one. Karl ran a fingernail back and forth along the grain of the wood in the kitchen table.

It was during one of these visits that Karl told Augusta about how he had lost the thumb. He'd shot it off himself when he was sixteen, while hunting deer in John Walter's field, about a half-mile from home, with a Winchester rifle that belonged to Olaf. The gun went off when he tripped over a log in the long grass of the field. There was no pain at first. He didn't realize the damage he'd done until he saw the thumb dangling from his hand. Olaf took Karl down to Chase in his truck. With no freezing to stop the pain, the doctor trimmed off the hanging shreds of Karl's flesh and detached the thumb. Then he and Karl took a night train to the Kamloops hospital for surgery while Olaf headed back to the farm to take care of the animals. Olaf had little sympathy for Karl. He said it was his own careless fault he'd shot his thumb off and he wouldn't pay the hospital bill.

Karl took care of the bill himself by trapping foxes and sell-ing the furs.

Augusta had to drag that story from him, as he was as economical with language as he was with most everything else. There was little conversation among the three of them, just statements thrown out and never collected. "Good price on wool this spring," said Karl.

Manny turned the page of the *National Geographic.* "Some fool's trying sugar beets back of Kamloops," he said. "Too dry there."

Karl slurped his coffee.

At some point Augusta sighed with impatience, refilled the men's cups, and left the house under the pretense of hanging laundry or feeding pigs or bedding calves. The notion that Karl had come courting never occurred to her until that one day when he followed her out the door. "You don't have to go," he said.

Augusta took the last step off the porch and turned to face him. "I've got chores." She waved a hand back at the house, at her father still sitting there in the kitchen. "If I don't do them no one will."

This wasn't quite true. Manny was still a hard worker, though since Helen's death he worked sporadically, in fits of frenzy that drove him to near exhaustion. After these out-bursts he did nothing for a week or more but sleep, or sit in the house or on the stump out back of the barn. The pigs and calves and chickens would have starved if Augusta hadn't made feeding them her chore, along with all the housework and laundry and meal making. Manny had even stopped fishing, though occasionally, very occasion-ally, he went down to Deep Pool to swim. Augusta dreaded those times, fearing he would drown in the fast undertow of the river, and then how could she keep the farm running? Karl fumbled in his pocket for a time. Augusta thought he was about to give her something but he didn't. He took out his red handkerchief and blew his nose. "The flowers," he said.

She couldn't think what he meant; then she remembered. He'd brought a wilting handful of roadside daisies and bachelor's buttons. Back then she'd called them cornflowers; they were pretty as the day was long. Karl had laid the flowers on the table when he took the coffee from her, but she hadn't thought much more about them. "They make you sneeze?" she said, because she couldn't think what else to say.

Karl shook his head and wiped his nose. He put the handkerchief back in his pocket. "I bring them all for you," he said. "Why you think I've been coming here all this time?"

His face burned brightly now, but so, Augusta supposed, did hers. He reached out and cupped her cheek in his right hand. It was a strange sensation to feel his thumbless hand on her cheek, the bumpy scarred flesh against her skin. Where had he found the courage? He was shaking, but he didn't take his hand away. He was like the barn cats she tamed. Jittery and scruffy, the tops of their ears frozen off, they were chased by dogs and coyotes and still they pushed past the urge that told every fiber in their small bodies to run away, and tentatively came to her for a scratch and a meal of leftovers. How could she turn away from him? How could she say no to a man who needed so much? She looked at Karl, into his eyes, and got caught in that blue; she floated in it.

Karl brought her more flowers, and raspberries, blue-berries, huckleberries, and saskatoons that he'd bought from the Indian women, and took her on drives and to the dances. As a twenty-year-old he had walked the twelve-mile round trip from Olaf's cabin to the schoolhouse for several of these dances, but had never found the nerve to go inside. He had just hung around the schoolhouse door, watching. It wasn't that he couldn't dance; he took home to his bedroom what he saw on the lighted schoolhouse floors and danced with the broom to the music in his head until his father banged on the wall and shouted for him to cut out the thumping around.

Those first few weeks Karl was like a lamb following Augusta around as she did chores or worked in the kitchen, sometimes helping, sometimes sitting beside her, blowing on his harmonica as she sang along. He courted her the way the heroes in the westerns he read courted their women, with flowers, shy kisses, and little gifts of berries. It would have gone on forever like that if she hadn't gone ahead and done the asking. Whatever possessed her? Because something did possess her. She didn't think she wanted marriage, not yet, not to this man who was so much older and had a life so run by his father that he didn't collect a hired hand's wage for working on his father's sheep ranch. Nevertheless, there were the words, coming out of her mouth. "Is marriage what you're after?" she said. "I mean, do you want to marry me?"

They were sitting together in the dark green International truck that belonged to Karl's father, on top of Bald Mountain, looking over the farmland below. Karl was dressed as he always was, in wool pants and suspenders, a wide-brimmed hat. He wore armbands to keep the sleeves of his white shirt from getting in his way while he worked. A man didn't show his forearms by rolling up his sleeves in those days. He'd been playing "You Are My Sunshine" on his harmonica and Augusta had been half singing, half humming along. Then the words were there, out of her mouth and hanging in the air between them. Had she really said them? Karl quit playing and tapped the spit from the harmonica onto his pant leg. He cupped her cheek in his hand. For a moment she couldn't catch her breath; her heart skipped once and when he spoke the terror settled into her belly. "If you'll have me," he said. He was so earnest, so desperately earnest. He was thirty. She was eighteen. Her mother had been dead three years. She said yes.

-three-

When she told Manny she was marrying Karl he said nothing at first. He stood up from the kitchen table and refilled his cup. Finally he said, "You know about Karl's mother."

"I know she died. I remember the funeral."

"That ranch is a long way out from things. A lot farther from town than here."

"I know."

"A woman shouldn't be that far from things."

"You don't want me to marry Karl."

"I have no say in it."

"So you want me to marry?"

"I have no say. You do as you like." He wouldn't save her from herself. She had made her bed and she would lie in it.

Augusta now wore the diamond engagement ring and wedding band Karl had given her the year Joy left. She had gone without a ring for most of their early marriage after losing her first engagement ring to a sink of dishwater. That first ring wasn't worth much. Karl had no money of his own. "You know the ring is glass, don't you?" Martha Rivers said.

The day Karl gave her that first engagement ring, Augusta was so excited that she asked him to drop her off at Mrs. Grafton's house. Mrs. Grafton was the only woman Augusta could think to tell. But Martha Rivers was there, visiting her mother.

"I know the ring is glass," said Augusta. "It's all he could afford right now."

In fact she hadn't known. She had supposed Karl had begged money from his father to buy her a diamond. She had known it was modest, all right, but she'd been proud showing it off to Mrs. Grafton and even to Martha Rivers. But Martha Rivers could never keep her big mouth shut. "You'll be living with his father," she said. "His father won't give him nothing. You'll be in that house with that old man and his dog. It's no life for a woman. You know the history of that place, don't you?"

She knew some of it, or thought she did. Karl's father had bought the ranch from a man named Doc Perry—Doc was a common nickname for a bartender at the time, around the turn of the century. Doc Perry had kept prostitutes at the ranch for the use of his customers, and the place had got its own nickname: Whorehouse Ranch. After Olaf bought the farm and he and Karl's mother moved in, the place was more delicately referred to as the W. H. Ranch, but the name still stuck.

"Oh, that reminds me," said Martha Rivers, "I was going to tell you I heard Shirley Matthews was raped by one of her daddy's herders. That little short fellow. Percy Martin. After a binge in town, on a weekend off. Caught her behind the barn, right under her dad's nose. Drunk as a skunk. You'd wonder how he found the stuff to do it."

"Well, the girl must have done something to bring him on," said Mrs. Grafton.

"She's gone to the police. Her father took her."

"He'll only make things worse for his daughter."

"They're already calling her Dirty Shirley. Not myself, of course. I wouldn't call her that."

Mrs. Grafton laughed. "Dirty Shirley. Oh, that's terrible, now. Too good. Too good."

Augusta didn't laugh. She couldn't see the humor in any of that. There was an awkward pause where all three women stared at their hands, then Martha Rivers turned to her. "Well, Karl's father is no picnic. Do what you want, but don't say I didn't warn you."

Augusta had met her future father-in-law by the time Karl gave her the glass ring. Karl had taken her to the cabin the two men shared and introduced them formally. But they'd had little to say. She knew from Manny's talk that Karl's father's name was Olaf, Olaf Olsen. Olaf was what she called him in her own mind, but to his face she called him Mr. Olsen, and that was what she went on calling him, even in discussions with Karl. He was not a man who lent himself to informality, though he lived in bachelor squalor.

Olaf was short like Karl, and he was as fair, though what little hair he had then was white. He wore a mustache discolored yellow from pipe smoking. That first visit he was shaven, but carried around him the sour yeasty smell of a man who has been years without a woman.

The cabin's rooms were created by partitions, walls that didn't quite reach the ceiling. There were two floors, with two rooms on each floor. At ground level the front door led into the kitchen, where Olaf and Karl took their meals.

There was a second room off the kitchen that had once, presumably, been a sitting room but was now used for storage of farm equipment and horse blankets and the like. The two rooms upstairs were bedrooms for Olaf and Karl. The only picture hanging in the kitchen was a photograph of a young woman in Victorian dress.

The cabin smelled like an odd mix of sheep's wool, boiled meat, strong coffee, pipe smoke, and wet dog, and was dark and colorless except for the chair on which Olaf sat; it had long ago been painted a rusty red, like the red of a barn, and that color was now peeling to reveal the wood grain underneath. When Karl ushered Augusta into the cabin on her first visit, she went to sit in this chair but Karl took her arm and offered her another. Olaf came down from his bedroom and claimed that red chair, from which he dominated the room. In Olaf's presence, Karl suddenly became someone Augusta didn't know. His shoulders turned in, he rarely looked up, and when he spoke he took on a tone of apology, of absurd formality. "This is Augusta, Father," he said. "Whom I wish to marry."

The old man filled his pipe and lit it. Eventually he looked at Augusta, or rather he looked her over—as if she were a ewe he might purchase. Though his eyes were the same startling blue as Karl's, one of them was half blind, clouded over. Olaf watched Augusta until she grew embarrassed and looked down. Neither of them had offered her coffee or anything that might occupy her hands.

"I worked with your father," said Olaf.

"Yes, he's told me."

"He's a hard worker," he said. High praise, Augusta supposed. "That was years ago. Long before Mother's death."

"I was sorry she passed away," Augusta said. "I went to her funeral. Of course, I was very young."

Olaf watched his foot rubbing the floor. "Well, she's long gone now," he said. He laid his pipe on the table and took out a red handkerchief like Karl's. He blew his nose long and noisily. The floorboards overhead creaked from one end of the house to the other, as if someone were walking there.

"Is someone else here?" said Augusta.

"It's getting to be an old house," said Karl. "Creaks a lot."

Augusta glanced up at the portrait of the young woman. "That your mother?"

"Yes."

"She was pretty."

"That was taken when she was seventeen. Before she left the old country."

"What was her first name?"

"Blenda."

Augusta heard a scratching under the table. There was a dog there, to one side of Olaf's feet. The dog scrambled out of the darkness and wrapped itself around Olaf's leg, alternately whimpering and snarling at Augusta. The thing was pitch-black, a mongrel. "You got to excuse the Bitch," said Olaf. "She never smelt a woman."

Karl coughed and went red. *Bitch.* Augusta thought at the time the old Swede was simply being offensive, trying to shock her or test her mettle. But Bitch was the name Olaf had given the dog. Bitch. In all things he was to the point. Augusta's mother had never allowed the dogs in the house. They smelled and shed their hair and rolled in offal. They were necessary but dirty things that should be kept outside.

There would be changes when she took over the running of
this house, or so Augusta thought.

The wedding itself was a disappointment, as shoddy
and small as that engagement ring. Olaf no longer believed
in churchgoing, and Karl, apparently, didn't seem to care.

"Don't you believe in God, then?" Augusta asked him.

"It's hard to believe in what I can't see," said Karl. "And
I'm not going to waste my time worrying about it."

Even so, Augusta insisted on a real church wedding, in
her own church, with the Reverend to marry them. Her
dress was the one she had proposed to Karl in, a blue cot-
ton print shift that was the best she had; her bouquet was a
handful of pearly everlastings Karl had picked from the
roadside. It was hot. Sweat beaded the foreheads of the little gathering—it was only Olaf, Manny, the Reverend, and
a handful of churchwomen, including Martha Rivers,
whom she had not invited. She had no women friends save
Mrs. Grafton, and Mrs. Grafton, though she'd said she'd
come, hadn't. It was a dreary affair, over quickly. Karl had
to put that engagement ring on her finger all over again
because he couldn't afford a wedding band.

On the way down the aisle Manny leaned close and
hissed, so only she could hear, "You can still get out of it,
you know." It was exactly what she wanted at that point, to
run away, to hide. She could pull her arm away from her
father and hightail it out of the church and run off, but to
where? What would she do? What work would she find?
Her face was red—she could feel it. Her father's grip on her
elbow was tight. The room collapsed in on her, gathered her,
propelled her hotly to that little carrot-haired, red-faced
man, and the hand that waited.

Then there was nothing. Karl was gone. Her father was gone. Everything was gone. She's wasn't in the chapel anymore; she was—where? *My God,* she thought, *it's a kitchen!* She almost laughed. There she was walking down the aisle toward a kitchen sink. It wasn't the kitchen of the Whorehouse Ranch; it was the kitchen of her home farm, her mother's kitchen, Manny's kitchen. She looked down at her dress. It was no longer the pretty garment she had chosen for her wedding day; it was a ratty old housedress, and her hands were in a sink full of sudsy warm water. She was evidently searching for something in the water. Something had been lost. A ring. She had lost her engagement ring. Then there was another hand in the sink with hers, also searching. A man's hand. Whose hand? This hand found hers beneath the water and took hold. Then suddenly she was back in the chapel, holding the Reverend's hand. He had taken her hand and Karl's, and was joining them.

Augusta never told Karl about that vision. She couldn't bring herself to discuss any of her premonitions with him. He simply wouldn't have believed her. She'd tried telling him once, during their courtship. As they sat in the International on Bald Mountain looking over the farms and the South Thompson below, she asked him, "You ever had a dream that came true?"

"Dreaming don't get you nowhere."

"I mean, a dream you have in your sleep."

"I don't dream."

"You must dream. Everybody dreams."

"If I do I don't remember."

"Doesn't that bother you?"

"No."

"How about a feeling, then? You get a feeling something's going to happen and it does."

"You believe in that kind of thing and somebody's going to make a sucker out of you."

Augusta knew that a man who didn't dream and, what was more, didn't care, wasn't a man to trust with a thing like a premonition. Karl was so like her father in that regard. Manny wouldn't have known a miracle if Jesus Himself had walked across the waters of the South Thompson and slapped him with a trout. Although Helen had often talked in the morning about the day to come as if she already knew it. "A good day for sewing," she had once said, staring out the window at the road that led to town, and that was the day the sewing-machine salesman knocked on the door.

" 'One for sorrow, two for mirth,' " she had said, looking out over the birds on the fence near the marshland. " 'Three for a wedding and four for a birth.' Four magpies. Cows will be calving today." Sure enough, three of the five pregnant cows picked that day for calving.

They were little coincidences, easy to dismiss, and nothing was said of them. But there were other times, like the day when Manny cut himself so badly on the mower, when Augusta was convinced her mother had some sort of foreknowledge. What were they doing together? Washing dishes, likely lunch dishes, when Helen stood straight and gasped. "Your father's in trouble. Quick, get one of his leather belts. I'll saddle a horse. Meet me outside."

Helen and Augusta rode together on the same slingbacked mare to the field where Manny had been mowing hay. When they reached him he was sitting on the ground next to the mower, gripping his wrist. Blood was pouring from his hand onto the green, freshly cut grass. The sickle bar on the mower had become jammed and he had been attempting to free it when he sliced the flesh between his thumb and forefinger. But this accident had only just happened. It had taken Helen and Augusta ten minutes to reach him. Certainly he hadn't called to them. How did Helen know? That was, in fact, what Manny asked.

"It doesn't matter," said Helen. She wound the leather belt tight around his arm as a tourniquet.

"You've been fooling with it again, haven't you?" he said.

"I haven't been fooling with anything."

"But how did you know? It's the devil's work."

"It's God's work. I'm here helping you, aren't I? You'd be out here bleeding to death otherwise."

"I'm not bleeding to death."

"That's what you think."

Augusta didn't think it was the premonition business that Manny minded, exactly; it was that his wife had a skill he didn't have, a powerful one, too. Manny himself was forever finding omens of bleak events after the fact. His favorite was a hen's crowing. Although Helen's yard was full of crowing hens, he refused to believe a hen ever crowed. That would be unnatural. Crowing, like fighting, was the job of the rooster. So when some misfortune took him by surprise—a pig having its leg broken in the confusion of a truckload of pigs on the way to auction—he remembered that a hen had crowed unnaturally just that morning, and hadn't that been a sign of the coming day's bad luck? *Spooky.*

So it was from her mother's side that Augusta's ability was passed on. Even Joy showed some budding signs of having the gift. She had had her own premonition of Gabe's illness. She had dreamed that she and Gabe were walking down the main street in Chase but that they were from a different time, not the time of the street. Another Gabe walked down the sidewalk toward them. Joy was afraid because she knew that if the two Gabes met, her Gabe, the one walking with her, would disappear. And that was exactly what happened. As the two Gabes passed each other, Joy's Gabe started to fade, lose color, become transparent. She picked him up and put him in a shopping cart in an effort to save him but he continued to fade, just as the other Gabe, a stronger, surer Gabe, kept on walking away. Perhaps it wasn't a premonition, Augusta thought. Maybe the dream was only a reflection of what was happening in real life. Joy's Gabe *was* fading away. His words flew from his grasp like so many swallows. He'd be talking quite animatedly and then he would *fade*. His sentence would trail off and he'd stare into space. Once, when Augusta was asking him some question or other about the hives, he said, "Could you slow down? I can't *listen* so fast."

But then Gabe had never been much for small talk, even before he got sick. During that tense visit when Joy brought him home to the farm for the first time, he hardly said a word. Augusta filled the silence with chatter about bees. The kettle whistled.

"I'll get it," said Gabe. Augusta was a little uncomfortable having this strange man make tea in her house. On the other hand, it was nice being served for a change. He made the tea, found cups in Augusta's cupboard and milk in the fridge. He poured milk in all their cups, though Karl drank his black, often with a lump of cheddar at the bottom. There was a long silence during which even Augusta couldn't think of anything to say, and all four of them drank their tea. It was Karl who eased things a little. "I haven't had tea with milk since 1945," he said. "Not bad."

Joy and Gabe were married just two months later, not five months after they met at a Christian retreat. Although Augusta didn't condone their haste, she did understand it. Good fundamentalist Christian couples often got married soon after they met. *It is better to marry than to burn.* But then, Augusta and Karl had been married only four months after the stud-horse man's visit. They had spent their honeymoon night in the Kamloops Plaza Hotel. She had no memory of that night—it had long ago been heaped over by other memories, thick and pungent, of Joe in a similar room in the same hotel. And in any case, that honeymoon night hadn't been her first time with Karl. They had lain together, tormented by mosquitoes, on a bed of pine under heavy clouds that threatened rain. They hadn't undressed; they'd simply pulled down their underwear. After he was done, Karl kissed her soundly and said, "That was good." Augusta had felt no pleasure at all. It was over quickly and it had hurt. From the start, Karl's lovemaking was brief, to the point, practical, and in the dark. It all had such a disappointing sense of hurriedness about it. The voice of the old Swede haunted him even in matrimonial intimacy, Augusta was sure of it. She could almost hear his voice over Karl's shoulder: *Don't you have something better to do? Hurry up, hurry up. What's the holdup? Can't you do anything right?*

Augusta moved her things—a trunk of clothes, a chair, some bedding, and a few dishes—into the old Swede's cabin, onto the W. H. Ranch. She slept with Karl in Karl's childhood room, which had only one short, thin partition dividing it from Olaf's sleeping quarters—a partition that did nothing to stop Olaf's snores from waking Augusta at night.

Olaf doled out bits of money for Karl and Augusta's purchases at Colgrave and Conchie's general store in Chase, but he gave Karl no wages and Augusta no housekeeping allowance, so she was forced to ask for it, to come begging to him if they needed groceries. He griped bitterly if they went into town more than once a week, or if he saw what he thought was an unnecessary item—like Kotex—in her grocery bag. Augusta had to tear up one of the old flannel sheets she had brought with her and use those scraps for sanitary napkins.

Olaf whittled away at Augusta as he must have cut down his wife. It started right off, as soon as she took over the household chores. He took one sip of her coffee and made a face. "This ain't coffee," he said. "This is Englishman's coffee. Brown water." He dumped the pot outside and made his Swedish coffee, so thick and bitter that even he needed to keep a sugar cube in his mouth when he drank it. He complained about her dishwashing habits. "Why aren't there any cups clean? Why do you use so many cups in a day? Use the same one all day; rinse it out after you use it." He complained about her cooking. When she first cooked lamb chops he threw one to Bitch. She sniffed it. "Look," he said. "They're so dry even the dog won't eat it." When she left the old porridge pot soaking overnight in the washbasin, he gave her hell for that, too. "I couldn't make my porridge this morning 'cause I didn't have a pot. You want me to starve?"

Augusta didn't defend herself against his complaints—not at first, in any case. She learned to make thick coffee, and stayed downstairs after Karl and Olaf were in bed to clean the pots that needed soaking. She tried to please Olaf, but it was an impossible task.

On top of that Olaf was never without Bitch, and the dog barked and snarled and nipped at her skirts every time she came near the old man. "Does he have to keep that dog inside?" she asked Karl. They were taking their morning coffee together outside under the big maple, to eke out a bit of time alone. They hadn't been married a month. "She's the only pet I've ever known him to have," said Karl. "He brought her inside as a pup after my mother died." "She stinks. And she's always at me, barking and pulling on my skirt. I'm sweeping up hair every day. She's brought fleas into the house. Fleas!" "I don't know what to say." "You can ask him to keep the dog outside." "I couldn't do that." "Yes you could." "It's his house. I can't be telling him how to run it." "I'm running the house now, aren't I? I'm the one cleaning up after that mutt! I should have some say!" Karl examined his feet. "Well, I'm going to say something." Augusta marched into the house, into the kitchen, where Olaf sat drinking coffee and smoking his first pipe of the day. His wool pants were slung over the back of his chair where he habitually left them before retiring to bed. He was wearing the long underwear that he slept in and hadn't yet put his socks on. His toenails were overgrown and one big toe was red, infected from an ingrown toenail. The bitch was lying behind his chair, nose on paws. The dog and Olaf looked up in unison when Augusta marched into the room. "I'd like to talk to you about that dog," she said, blunt as a rock.

"What about the dog?"

"I want it kept outside. The house is no place for it."

"It's my house. My dog. I'll keep her inside if I want."

"But I'm the one cleaning up after her." Augusta took a step forward with her hands out, to further emphasize her position, and Bitch was suddenly there, between them, barking and nipping at her skirts. Olaf didn't call her off. He sucked his pipe. Augusta took a step back and the dog followed, barking, snarling, baring its teeth. Augusta turned and fled, and the dog chased her as far as the front door. Karl was still under the maple, cradling his empty cup. "Did you see that?" she yelled at him. "You see what kind of welcome I've got here?"

Karl mumbled some endearment in apology and reached out a hand to cup her cheek, but she shook her head away. His bashfulness, so sweet in the beginning, was now the mark of a weakling. Well, she supposed at the time, she should count her blessings. At least Karl wasn't demanding and jealous, as her father had been with her mother. Manny had always tried to keep tabs on Helen's whereabouts, what she was doing, fretting over any man who might tip his hat to her on the street, especially a stranger.

"Who's he, then?" he'd say.

"Mr. Wallace," said Helen. "He and his wife bought the Michaels' house. I sold his wife eggs last week."

"Looks like a dandy."

"He's a lawyer. A very nice man."

"I don't like the looks of him. You stay away from him, hear?"

"I can't sell my eggs and honey if I've got to stay away from everyone."

"You watch out for him. You don't know what men like him are capable of."

"You don't even know him."

"I know his type."

The infrequent dances were the worst for Manny as they attracted bachelors from miles around: herders and cow-boys, lonely and bushed and sick for female company. There was always a shortage of women dance partners, and it was a niggardly husband who hogged his wife all for himself. So Manny was forced to stand back against the wall, with his arms crossed, watching his wife dance with other men.

The dances went on in the schoolhouse, with the desks pushed back into the corner, on Saturday nights—but only until midnight, as right on into the fifties there was no dancing on the Sabbath. The RCMP drove there from Chase just before twelve to make sure of it. No alcohol was allowed inside a public building so there was no booze in the schoolhouse. There were few drinking places in the area at the time—Yep Num, who owned the café and roominghouse in Chase, rented a room to men so they could sit and drink— but there were plenty of bootleggers. In Chase an English butcher named Miller made beer and sold it along with his meat, and there were stills hidden all over the mountainsides, especially across the lake in Celista. Home brew was passed from man to man around the back of the schoolhouse, where the horses were tied and where fights were taken. There was almost always a fight at these things, though no man ever seemed to get seriously hurt. The Christmas dance was the worst for it. If there was a fencing dispute, or a suspicion over a missing cow, or an unpaid debt, the bitter feelings floated to the surface on booze, or were carried to the front on petty jealousies over who danced more than his share with the schoolteacher.

When a fight erupted it went outside and took all the men with it. It was so like a cockfight, with a circle of men egging the fighters on. The women and children were left in the schoolroom by themselves to wait for the men to come to their senses. No nice woman dared go outside, not at any point, not until it was time to go home and she and her children left accompanied by her husband. No woman except one of the Grafton girls, who was given to sitting in cars with men and their beer. When the fight was done the men swaggered back in, laughing, to seek out partners for the next dance.

Manny got into a few of those fights himself as he challenged any man who had more than one dance with his wife. The son of one of those men got a group of boys together the following Monday and threw rocks at Augusta. She was perhaps eleven at the time. They followed her home after school for that whole week, hurling rocks at her, almost always missing, but terrorizing her out of her skull. One of them was a snotty-nosed Grafton boy, she remembered that.

What moved boys to throw rocks, she wondered now, as she drank her tea. Just today, boys had thrown rocks at the train. The train was passing a playing field behind a school, and along the fence that separated the tracks from the schoolyard boys were lined up, facing the train. Augusta couldn't see the expressions on their faces, but she could see their hands raised and she lifted hers to wave back before realizing that they weren't waving at the passing train. They were throwing rocks at it. One rock banged against the side of the train, and Augusta flinched back from the window. Boys had done that in her day as well, thrown rocks at trains, at the windows of abandoned homesteaders' shacks, and at neighbors' dogs, not to shoo them away but for the fun of it, to see the dog run. She supposed that was partly why those boys had thrown stones at her so many years ago. She had run home and, crying, breathless, finally told her mother about the boys' harassment. The next day Manny walked with Augusta to school and, out on the school grounds, cuffed the ears of all three boys and told them to leave Augusta alone. Of course Manny's visit only made things worse. The boys did stop throwing rocks at her, but took up words instead; every afternoon they ran after her, calling her all manner of obscenities. She wouldn't tell Helen or Manny again. Instead she learned to avoid the boys on the schoolyard, to scuttle home right after school before they took a notion to go after her. She was always on guard, watching for them, and if the boys came her way she fled, often to the girls' five-seater outhouse behind the school. She avoided the eyes of boys, held herself close and contained, and learned to be invisible.

In the forties a man like Manny was called a leghorn rooster, after the small scrappy birds that strutted around the yard as if they owned it and dared anyone to say they didn't. He might have even liked the nickname, as he was always going on about the "pecking order." He saw the true natural order of things there in the chicken coop: man at the head, protective and paternal, and under him a hierarchy of women who in turn ruled over the children. He ignored the fact that given free run of the fields, the hens mated with nearly every rooster, not just the nastiest one, and that there were plenty of bossy hens who beat up on deferential roosters. Helen had one of those roosters in the scratch run at the time, a bird Manny had named Sorry, as he thought any rooster who let hens boss him around was a sorry rooster indeed.

He'd sometimes rant on about this sort of thing at the dinner table, stabbing his fork into a bit of chicken breast and swinging it in the air to make his point. "Those chickens out there, that's your model for womanhood. They're hardworking, thrifty, good mothers, they submit to the will of the rooster. On the other hand the rooster's always scouting for danger, always scratching up feed for his hens and calling them over to eat it. There's the ideal family."

"So you want thirty wives, then?" said Helen.

"That's not what I mean." He tucked the chicken into his mouth and talked with his mouth full. "On the other hand that would be all right, wouldn't it?"

"You wouldn't last a day."

"There you go, talking back at me."

"Ah, go on with you."

"No, really. What are they going to think of me in town if you're never listening to a word I say, always giving me lip? They'll think this is a woman-run house. They'll laugh at me."

"They already do."

Manny's face flushed. "I should be treated with respect in my home. You shouldn't talk to me like that. Go cut me some more bread."

The phone rang, startling all three of them. Karl was the one sitting closest to the phone, but he made no attempt to answer it. He was uncomfortable with phones; he would never answer it if Augusta was there with him, and if a call had to be made it was Augusta who did the dialing. She pulled the phone off the kitchen counter and placed it on the table beside her so she could check the call display to make sure it was Joy phoning. She didn't feel like fielding well-meant questions from the women at the church or seniors' center about the outcome of Gabe's surgery.

"Damn it," she said. "It's Ernest again." Ernest Grey had been phoning for months. Augusta didn't know him, or anything about him other than what she could guess from his phone calls. He still had an old rotary-dial phone; she could hear the click and spin on her answering machine as he tried redialing in his confusion, after reaching the answering machine. When she first heard that rotary dial she wondered briefly if there hadn't been some accident in time, if someone from the past was dialing into her present to leave a message on her machine. But that was just a flight of fancy. If Ernest were from the past, why would his name appear on her call display?

Ernest was ancient; his voice was cracked and faded, and his mind was slipping on him. He was trying to phone someone else when he phoned Augusta, someone named Linda. A daughter, perhaps? Augusta guessed he was living alone, and not in some home, because no one seemed to be there to stop or help him. Occasionally she answered the phone and explained once again that he had the wrong number. More often than not he would call only once, and that was the end of it for a while. But sometimes he'd try over and over, all through the day, until Augusta unplugged the phone. She hoped this wasn't going to be one of those days. She didn't like talking to him. He was befuddled and half deaf and she had to go over and over it, explaining the situation until he understood. She hated talking to him because the thought of being caught in her own dreams like that—living like a sleepwalker—scared her to death. She had watched Edna from the seniors' center, who was ninety-two and had a daughter who was a senior herself, decline into twilight over the last two years. No one wanted her sitting at their card table. She talked and talked, repeating herself over and over, because she forgot what she had just said. She used to know the games, but now she needed someone to coach her every step of the way. One day Faye Risby yelled at her, "If you don't know the game, get out!"

Edna said, "You can't tell me I'm dumb. I've got a right to be here." Maybe so, but when there was a meeting now everyone tended to sit hurriedly, in long rows of seats that excluded Edna, so she was forced to sit in the front row alone.

Gabe was walking around the hospital in that kind of confused state for days after the seizure, making it clear he wanted to go home, though it was equally clear he had no idea where he was. He was only dimly aware of the nurses, the hospital bed, and the other patients in the intensive care ward. They all blended and disappeared into the fictions his mind created. That past week he had told Augusta and Joy that the first couple of days in hospital he thought he was sleeping on top of the washer and dryer at home, with his feet through the wall. If Joy went off to get a bite, and wasn't there to stop him, he would pull out the catheter tube and try to use the washroom, though he wasn't sure where it was and would go wandering out into the hallway with his gown open at the back. At one point he put the long blue plastic bedside urinal on his foot, thinking it was a shoe (Augusta knew another man, Ralph Fielding from the seniors' center, who did the same thing after a stroke. It made her wonder what was going on inside men's heads that made them equate their penises with their feet).

Before the seizure Gabe had walked in his sleep now and again, a symptom of his illness. Joy once woke to find him poised and ready to urinate in the closet of their bedroom. She woke him in time, thankfully. Other times she'd wake in the night and find him sleeping in odd places, curled in a corner of the kitchen, or spread out on the floor of Joy's sewing room. He never remembered how he'd got there.

Augusta was a sleepwalker. A couple of months before, she had leapt out of bed in the night convinced the apartment was on fire. She ran into the kitchen, where she could see and smell the smoke and hear the fire alarm blaring in the hall. Then all she could think of was getting back to Karl to wake him, as he wouldn't be able to hear the alarm. She was desperate to reach him but somehow the space of living room between the kitchen and the bedroom door stretched out of proportion, seemed so much longer than it was in reality. It took forever to reach the bedroom, and when she finally did and cried out, "Wake up! There's a fire!" the shrieking of the fire alarm stopped. There was no smoke. No fire. Even so, she made Karl help her check every electrical connection. She phoned Rose and made her go hunting around the apartment building for smoke. There was no fire. Yet she couldn't shake the feeling that she had been warned, of what she wasn't sure.

Augusta had begun walking in her sleep in her teens. She'd clamber out her bedroom window, then run around the house. Climbing in was a good deal harder than jumping out, so at the point of return, when she had to figure her way back through the window, she'd begin to wake up, conscious of what she'd done but not why. She would sense the chill of the early morning, the dewy or sharply frosted grass under her feet, but only just barely, as in sleep one was aware of the surrounding darkness and that darkness became incorporated into the dream. Anxiety was the trigger for her sleepwalking. That dream she had about the fire followed the vision she had of Gabe with the bee on his lip.

And the sleepwalking she did as a teen started after the vision she had of her mother's death.

Just that day on the train, she had dreamed she had woken from sleep to find a hole had opened up in the train floor between her seat and Esther's. There was no flash of passing ground as she would have expected. Instead, extending from the floor, there was a rectangular pit of sorts, though there was no dirt. The walls were white and smooth, and lit up from within, in the way snow seemed to glow from within on the night of a full moon. Esther was still sitting with her, smiling, swaying with the train. Her basket had disappeared, presumably into the hole, but the Shasta daisies were on her lap. She handed them to Augusta and invited her to throw the flowers into the hole. When she did, the pit was suddenly full of flowers. Augusta stood to jump into those flowers, but Esther said, "Wait a while." And so they sat together, swaying with the train, talking of inconsequential things, with the pit of flowers absurdly open between their feet.

When Augusta awoke, into the real world this time, Esther was looking at her, smiling. "Did I snore?" said Augusta.

"No, you were laughing."

That dream had the quality of a premonition, a dream foretelling her own death, though she didn't want to believe that. Wasn't she just preoccupied with Gabe's illness? she wondered. With the possibility of his death, her worrying mind was manufacturing nightmares. Yet it hadn't felt like a nightmare; Esther said she had laughed.

Augusta set the phone back on the kitchen counter, then glanced at Rose as she sipped her tea. She wouldn't tell Rose about the dream she'd had on the train, though she'd told her almost all her other premonitions. It would scare Rose to death. She believed in Augusta's visions, considered them a gift, and was hungry for stories about them. And Augusta had no shortage of strange tales to tell her. She'd had more than her share of premonitions and ghosts. Even Olaf's cabin had been haunted, or Augusta felt it had. It was a wretched house to live in, dark and full of squeaks and shifting timber. There was so little privacy. When she knew the men were out feeding the sheep, she bathed hurriedly near the kitchen stove, pouring warm water from the stove reservoir over herself with a saucepan as she stood in the square galvanized steel tub she washed laundry in, fearful that any minute she'd be caught naked in the kitchen. She never felt alone there, even when Olaf and Karl were in the mountains with the sheep for the summer and she was by herself for weeks on end. The first winter of her marriage she had a dream about the place. She was standing in the room she shared with Karl, only in her dream there were two beds in the room, a twin set, covered over with gray army blankets. She stood between them, looking down at a corpse that lay in one of the beds. The corpse was Karl's mother, Blenda, as she looked in the portrait that hung over the table. Someone stood behind Augusta. She turned to see who it was and saw her own self standing there. "That woman died in this house," she said to herself. "We have to be careful not to step in her shoes."

When she turned back to the bed, the corpse was gone and a mannequin was in its place, covered up to the chin with blankets. She turned around to say something to herself but her companion was also gone. When she looked back at the dead woman's bed a third time it was herself lying there.

"Your mother didn't die in the house, did she?" she asked Karl in the morning as they sat at the breakfast table. Olaf had been gone when Augusta awoke, out checking for newborn lambs.

"No, she died outside, of cold."

"I thought you might have found her before she died and brought her inside."

"No, she was dead out in the field. Why're you asking?"

"No reason."

Ranch life was different from the mixed farming she'd grown up with. Karl and Olaf crossed Rambouillet ewes with black-faced Suffolk rams to get a heavier lamb, but the Suffolk were a knotheaded bunch, prone to wandering off by themselves rather than flocking, always finding ways to break through a fence, and their offspring acted more like goats than sheep. They kept a few goats as well, milk goats to feed orphaned lambs if there were no ewes to take them, and to provide fresh milk to the herders when they were on the mountain ranges.

Olaf often hired Indian hands over whites, as he could pay them less and get more work out of them. Manny had done the same, though not with the same tightfistedness. He'd hired Indians and strays in the Depression, when no one else would, and during the war, when there was no one else to hire. He'd hired others, too. One summer when Augusta was still a girl, he'd hired a white man with a Japanese bride. The man's girl-bride scrubbed dishes silently beside Augusta, as she spoke no English. When they left at the end of the summer, the girl handed Augusta her blue silk parasol, printed with birds and bamboo. Manny had been generous with the Indians and strays; when they left, they left with their bellies full. Occasionally, when times were better for them, these men returned to say thanks with cigarettes for Manny, candy for Augusta, and tapioca pudding for Helen. When she was nine or ten Augusta rode the saddles the hired men left on the wooden benches inside the implement shed, breathing in the smell of leather.

Manny traded horses with the Indians from the Neskainlith band, horses that were broken only because they were underfed and tired. When he fed these horses, their strength and fight returned. While Augusta tamed the horses with apples, Manny mastered them. In the catch pen he jabbed at them with pitchforks, hit them around the head with the bullwhip, and forced them into the squeeze. The horses jerked their heads against the wood of the chute with eyes wild and rolled back, and when the bullwhip cracked, the skin on their necks rose up. Augusta flinched with them.

These horses were runaways, predisposed to taking off out of control, dragging the buggy or farm equipment behind them. They ran with harrows in spring, hayrack in summer, disc in fall, feeding sleigh in winter. Once a gray dappled mare ran wild, pulling Manny and Helen in the buggy down Shuswap Hill, spooked by the dust that chased her. She thundered over the ridge and down the gravel road that was the highway with her mane flapping in knotted clumps. Manny pulled back too fast. One rein whipped from his hand and kicked and jumped against the mare's front hoof. Helen dug her fingers into the planking of the seat; her hair and cloak were loose and flapping behind her. Manny clung to the back of the seat, his feet against the baseboard, the whole of his weight pulling on the one rein until it snapped. The buggy swayed close to the bank. Saplings whipped Helen's arms. She cried *God help me* over the thundering hoofs and flying rocks. At Peterson

Road, facing a fence, beads of sweat over her neck, the mare tired to a stop.

Back at home Manny removed the buggy wheel by tapping it off with a hammer and greased the axle with butter. A wheel rim was lost and the seat was knocked loose. Later Helen sat Manny down near the stove and rubbed butter into his hands. It was the year during the Depression that they couldn't give butter away. But when the war was on, Helen measured butter in her Blue Willow teacups for cooking. She weighed it on the kitchen scales and wrapped it in scrubbed flour sacks to sell in Chase. She traded butter, eggs, bread, and honey for ration coupons with Dr. Litwin's wife and the butcher's young bride.

Augusta was thirteen when Manny came home from town saying he'd hired Harry Jacob, an Indian man living on the reserve. "I told Harry and his woman they could set up a tent by the creek for the summer," he said to Helen. It was Harry and his woman, never Harry and his wife. The title "wife" was reserved for white women. The couple set up a huge canvas tent, the kind ranch cooks housed their stoves in, a tent with a hole at the top for a stovepipe. Harry's woman had no stove, but built a campfire under that hole, so the tent was always filled with smoke. Harry, his woman, and their children smelled of smoke; to Augusta their skin appeared stained with it. The couple had a six-year-old boy whose name Augusta no longer remembered, and a girl two years younger than Augusta named Alice. Alice went barefoot and wore the same dress every day, a flowered yellow shift. She spoke little English. Harry's woman spoke none. She had a ragged, indifferent air about her, as if she knew nothing she said or did would make a difference. The boy was sick. He spent his days inside that smoke-filled tent watched over by his mother. To Augusta's delight, Alice came out to play hide-and-seek, kick the can. They chased each other clear around the farm. It was the closest thing she'd had to a sister, to a friend.

Manny didn't like Augusta playing with her. After chores, while Augusta and her father were sharing the water in the washbasin, cleaning up for supper, Manny said, "Why do I have to keep telling you to leave that girl alone?"

"I wasn't doing nothing," said Augusta.

"I saw you run through their tent with that girl chasing after you."

"We were playing tag."

"They don't keep themselves clean. That youngest kid's sick. He'll never make old bones."

"I don't play with him. He just lays around anyhow."

"The boy could use some peace, I should think. He won't get any rest with you howling through the tent. You leave them be. You hear?"

"There's nobody else to play with."

"Augusta, listen to your father," said Helen. She set two plates firmly on the table and swung around to pick the whistling kettle off the stove.

"Why can't I play with Alice, then? She's not sick."

Manny pulled the towel off the nail in the wall and dried his hands. "She's a *Siwash*." Her face must have told him she didn't understand. "It means Indian," he said.

Next day when she caught up with Alice, Augusta tried it out. She had only meant to tease Alice. "Hey, Siwash!" she called. Alice turned and stared at her. "Siwash! Siwash!" Augusta sang out. Alice turned heel and ran, through the pasture, into the bush. Augusta ran after her. "Alice!" she called out. "Hey, Alice. What's wrong?" But Alice was a deer in the bush, practiced at hiding. Augusta shuffled back home with a knot growing in her stomach. She walked through the open door into the house holding her belly. Helen was at the kitchen table, gripping Manny's plaid jacket by the collar, rummaging in the pocket. She pulled out a handful of change and inspected it. "What're you doing in the house this time of day?" she said.

"I don't feel so good."

Helen turned; her face paled. She placed a cold hand on Augusta's cheek, on her forehead. "You been staying away from those kids like your father said, haven't you?"

"Yes, ma'am."

"You been coughing?"

"No, ma'am."

"That boy's very sick. You understand you could get sick too, don't you? If you play with him or his sister?"

Augusta nodded.

"It's just your tummy?"

"Yes. Can I go?"

"Lie down in your room. I'll bring you some ginger in sugar water. See if that doesn't fix you. I don't want you going outside again today. All right?"

The powdered ginger and sugar drink didn't fix the ache in Augusta's belly, as she knew it wouldn't. She had hurt Alice and nothing could be done. What could be done? She scanned her room. She had few possessions. Toys were scarce in those days. She had several dolls that her mother had fashioned from socks and scraps, but just one store-bought doll, a pretty thing with a ceramic head covered in blond curls; it had eyes that closed and a box inside that said "Mama" when she laid it flat. She had seen this doll in Eaton's catalog, dreamed of it, pleaded for it, prayed for it, and on Christmas morning when she was eight she had found it under the Christmas tree. Now it sat staring into the nights, on her nightstand. She had named it Carla, the most exotic name she could think of.

She slipped the doll out to the tent when Manny was doing barn chores and her mother was in the chicken coop collecting eggs. Her gift didn't produce the reconciliation she'd hoped for, nor did Alice make the show of gratitude Augusta had expected. Alice took the doll from her and walked away, down to the creek, making it clear by the set of her shoulders that she didn't want to be followed. Less than a week later, Alice's little brother was dead. Harry's woman took Alice back to the reserve, and once the field work was finished Harry followed.

Augusta had seen a young girl who'd made her think of Alice during her ride home earlier that day. The train was following the ocean at that point. Spooked by its passing, a heron lifted from the shore and flew for a time parallel with the rails. Augusta watched, prickling, as the great clumsy bird became graceful in flight. Gray and white, so like a flying dinosaur, surely it must have lifted from the waters of a whole other time. The heron veered and headed over the train; it cast a shadow over the train window as it disappeared overhead.

When Augusta faced front again she saw an Indian girl standing ahead near the track. As the train came on her, Augusta felt the girl was staring at her. She stared right back. She felt a little silly, but she couldn't make herself look away. The girl could have been Alice, she looked so like her. Why the girl was staring at Augusta she could only guess at. Perhaps the girl thought she recognized Augusta. But she didn't smile. She was a pretty girl, not yet a teen, standing limply and without proper posture, in a flowered shift. She had a limp bouquet of white and ragged Shasta daisies. She held these flowers up to the window as the train passed, offering them to Augusta, but unlike almost everyone else Augusta had seen beside the track that day, she didn't wave.

Still holding her hand to the glass in the beginning of a wave, Augusta went on staring out the window although the girl was long gone. Had she even been there? The memory of her felt like one of her crazy incomprehensible dreams. Maybe, lulled by the sway of the train, she had dropped off for a moment, and this dream girl, an echo of Alice, had escaped, skipped out of her head to go picking daisies. But that was foolishness, silly thoughts.

"You see some deer?" said Esther.

"Hmm? No, no. There was a girl by the tracks."

"A girl? I didn't see anyone."

"She had a bunch of daisies, like yours."

Esther shrugged and chuckled and pulled her glasses forward and let them drop down her face so they rested oddly on her chin. She rubbed her eyes and sat back, but didn't pull the glasses back on. They bumped there on her chin, still hooked loosely over her ears, with the movement of the train. She closed her eyes and a little while later she began snoring. Augusta watched her for a time, thinking the glasses would fall from her chin and land in her lap, waking her, but they didn't.

The night Alice's brother died, Helen grabbed Augusta by the shoulders and shook her. "See what could have happened if you didn't listen to your father? See?" She hugged Augusta. "You could be dead!"

Augusta pulled away from her mother and ran to her room. She sat on her bed and stared at the space where Carla had kept watch over her. She was sorry the boy was dead, sorry for Alice and her silent, unsmiling mother. But all Augusta could think of was how she hadn't listened to Manny. She had played with Alice, she'd gone into the tent with that sick boy, and in play had touched their smoky skin. Had she brought the boy's sickness into the house on her hands?

In the kitchen her mother was taking the blame for the boy's death. "We should have taken him to the doctor," she said.

"And who would have paid?"

"The doctor would have taken a calf in trade."

"Then we'd be out the calf."

"You put more value on a calf than on that boy's life?"

"He was his parents' responsibility, not ours."

"It was our Christian duty to help."

"Well, it's too late now, isn't it?"

"You could hire him back. Give him a raise."

"And risk bringing sickness onto the farm?"

"You'll hire off the reserve in any case. There's few enough hands left, with the war on. Ask him to leave his woman and the girl at home. He can see them weekends. He works well, doesn't he?"

That first summer after Karl and Augusta were married, Olaf hired a slight one-legged Indian man named Pete to do the packing for the summer—to take a packhorse down from the mountain where they pastured the sheep, into town to get supplies to bring back. As a kid he'd jumped off a barn loft onto a rusty nail, and the leg had developed gangrene and he'd lost it, but it didn't slow him.

When Karl brought Pete to the house to introduce him, Augusta didn't want to shake his hand. The Indians had sicknesses, didn't they? She wiped her hands on her apron when he offered his hand, refusing him, and mumbled that she'd been baking bread, that her hands weren't clean. But he could see as soon as Karl invited him in for coffee that she hadn't been making bread; she'd been cleaning up the breakfast dishes. "I don't want you bringing the hired hands to the house," she told Karl, after Pete had left.

"That's not sociable," said Karl. "They've got to come by sometimes. And there'll be times you're expected to make meals, you understand. For threshing crews. For the shearing crews when they come round."

"We'll feed them outside. I'll take the meals to them. There's not room in here, in any case."

Karl shrugged and nodded but didn't listen to her. He brought hired hands home and made them coffee himself, despite her objections. The Indians. The scruffy, high-smelling white boys who made sheep's eyes at her behind Karl's back. The shearers who traveled from sheep ranch to sheep ranch, from the state of Washington to southern British Columbia and on up to northern B.C., following spring. The Indians were generally quiet and avoided looking her in the eye. They tagged along behind Karl and Olaf like dogs as they went from one job to another on the ranch. Even Karl, who invited these men into his house, wouldn't have expected them to walk by his side.

Years before, while they sat fishing across from reserve lands, Manny had told Augusta stories about Indians, stories about the drunks—like Tommy Joe and Jack Moses, who'd gotten themselves pie-eyed and into a fight in 1919. Tommy Joe took after Jack Moses with a shotgun and ran him down to the river, where Jack threw himself into the water, hoping to escape by swimming the South Thompson. When he came up for air, Tommy Joe shot him in the head, killing him. Tommy Joe got just three years in jail for his crime. They were both Indians, after all. If Jack Moses had been white it would have been a different story.

The Indians had different manners, different expectations about how things were done. When Augusta was a child, Indian women came round to the farm selling huckleberries and blueberries from large baskets decorated with designs that looked like trees or deer faces or feathers. The berries were warm and juicy from the horse ride down the trails on hot summer afternoons; they stained Augusta's hands purple and tasted of heaven. Sometimes the Indians opened the gates and walked right through the farm, with their horses and dogs, on their way up the mountain to pick those berries, following old Indian trails. They seemed to have no regard for private property. Manny let them get away with it for the most part. The one time he did get all fired up and stood at the gate in the way of a group traipsing through the back pasture, it came to nothing. The Indians stopped a moment and stared at him, then formed two streams of bodies that went around him, engulfing him briefly before passing on.

The young minister at Augusta's church in Courtenay gave sermons, now and again, on the damage his white grandfathers had inflicted on the Natives, how they forced

Indian children into residential schools, splitting families and forcing whole generations into dependency, and how the church now had to support the Natives' fight for the land stolen from their forefathers. "What are they ballyhooing about?" Rose said after one of these sermons. They were all having tea and sandwiches, as they usually did after church, in Augusta and Karl's apartment. "They don't have to pay taxes, they get welfare. They've got a house on the reserve if they want it. More than I ever got. I had to work for what I got. And look at me. No house to show for all that work."

"We did take their land," said Augusta.

"I didn't take anything from them. Do we have to go on paying for the mistakes people made a hundred years ago? They should be thankful the government treated them as well as they did."

Augusta had half agreed with her at the time, though now, as she made tuna sandwiches for lunch beside Rose, she thought how that kind of thinking made her no better than a hive of senseless bees, acting on instinct, buzzing angrily about, protecting their honey even as they robbed other hives. A hive was so like a nation in miniature, complete with customs officials and border guards. Augusta could pick a guard bee out by its authoritative stance. It sat back on its haunches, on its four back legs, and raised its front legs and antennae to scrutinize every bee passing through the tiny entrance to the hive. The guard bees could tell their nestmates from bees of another hive by scent and by behavior. Each hive had its own customs; different races of bees had different dialects to their dance language. Often bees from other colonies were simply stonewalled, prevented from entering a hive by guard bees blocking the entrance with their bodies. If a wasp tried to get in, the guard bees *shimmered*, vibrated back and forth very quickly, to intimidate the foreigner. If the invader was an ant, they fanned their wings and showed their behinds to it, kicking at it. If the threat came from a mouse or skunk, or even a human, the bees flew angrily at the creature, or lighted on it to pull at its hair; then they tried biting—anything to avoid stinging, because stinging meant the guard bees' death.

During the poor times, when honey flow was slow, more guards were posted at the entrance to the hive to prevent robbing by bees of adjacent hives. When there was a lot of nectar coming into the hive, there were fewer guards and they acted out their duties with less conviction. There was more threat from raiding toward the end of summer, when the voluptuous scent of ripening honey surrounded the hive. The robber bee hovered in front of the hive, zigzagging back and forth, casing the joint, and then landed at the entrance before running quickly to try to get inside. Then the guard bee attacked, running up to grapple the legs of the robber, and the two bees tumbled around, each trying to sting the other. The guard bees were willing to sacrifice their lives to protect the honey in the hive then, because another, larger colony of bees was capable of taking all the honey they'd worked so hard to collect, and without that honey the hive would die come winter.

Even so, guard bees did let foreign workers in, especially novice foragers and deferential bees who had become lost or had drifted to this new hive on strong winds. But the new workers were only accepted after a diligent and lengthy inspection. Guard bees combed the body of the outsider with their front feet and antennae, assessing the stranger's willingness to submit. The guard bees weren't above accepting bribes. Newcomers hauling loads of pollen and nectar were readily admitted. If Augusta wanted to unite two colonies, all she had to do was lay a single sheet of newspaper on top of one colony, then set the box of the second colony on top of it. As there were no floors to these bee boxes, all that separated the two hives was that sheet of newspaper. By the time members of both communities ate through the paper, they had become accustomed to each other's scent and they wouldn't fight.

"Esther invited us over for lunch next week," said Augusta.

"She invited you."

"She invited us both." Augusta cut the sandwiches and set them on a plate on the table. "Karl," she called out. "Did I tell you I saw a lot of sheep on the train ride today?"

Karl had moved into the living room to watch television. "What was that?" he asked.

"Sheep. Everyone along this one stretch of track seemed to have sheep. On little five-acre plots." Late in their marriage, the land around Augusta and Karl's farm was slowly dissected by buyers she and Karl had called "acreage people" with enough contempt to make her now feel foolish. They were acreage people because they came from the city and played at farming, babied their livestock like pets, and let their pastures go wild. Worse, they kept too much to themselves. Augusta would have called them acreage people in play, rather than contempt, if they had let themselves be known to her, if they had waved or smiled when they passed her on the road. But no, they kept to themselves as they would have in the city, not knowing that the culture of the country was different, not knowing they had affronted her without even talking to her, *by* not talking to her. Now, when Augusta walked down the streets in Courtenay, she acted like those acreage people; she rarely waved or stopped to chat. There were too many people living too close by.

"Not enough room for sheep to move around," said Karl, turning from the television. "Makes no sense having sheep on this island. With all the rain, they'd have no end of foot rot."

"And there were goats along the highway on the drive home," said Rose.

"There were a couple of men with dogs herding goats," said Augusta, "just like you did with the sheep. Although there were only about thirty goats. You hardly see a thing like that anymore."

Karl and the hired men, aided by border collies, had once walked a thousand or more sheep down the highway on their trek to the mountain pastures. It seemed inconceivable to Augusta now, but then, in the fifties, the highways were still relatively quiet. One of the hired men walked ahead of the sheep, carrying a red flag to warn oncoming cars, and if a car did approach, Karl, walking the sheep from behind, would send a dog up the flock. Guided by his whistles and hand signals, the dog would force the flock to one side, to let the car by. Many people simply parked their cars and watched the flock pass. It was a living river of bodies: an amazing sight, a thousand animals controlled by a handful of men and dogs.

Karl and his father hired herders for the summer, and they all slept in tents in bachelor's bliss on the mountainside, watching sheep, watching for bears, trading stories with the lookout men who watched for forest fires from their lonely cabins. It was Karl who cooked for them, for the most part; he sometimes traded jobs with Pete and brought the horse down for supplies, as it gave him the chance to see Augusta. Later in the summer, lambs fat on alpine grasses were cut from the flock using a corral-and-chute system set up on the mountain, and they'd be driven, on foot, down to the nearest rail stockyards. From Queest Mountain, the lambs went to Malakwa to load; from Hunters Range they went to Salmon Arm. Once loaded onto stock cars, they were shipped to the Vancouver yards and from there to slaughterhouses.

Most of the time Augusta stayed behind, alone, on the Whorehouse Ranch. The summers were her quiet time, without Olaf or his wretched dog. She sat and drank coffee whenever she wanted, which was almost every morning. But she worked too: feeding and milking the cow, and feeding the pigs if they had them. The rest of her day was spent in her garden: tilling, planting, weeding, harvesting, and canning. They would depend on that produce through winter. But tending these crops was no chore for Augusta; here in the garden, her senses tingled. She went barefoot, ate sweet strawberries warm off the plant, and dug her fingers into soil, into living earth. If she didn't own the house she kept, at least she could call this bit of land her own. She had bought it with sweat, invested in it with care. Her soul bloomed here with the flowers, and the smell of tomato plants and lavender quieted her. Here she was at rest.

The only flowers in the garden on her arrival were ratty weeds blooming insolently in the vegetable plot over the heads of carrots, potato plants, and cabbage so infested with cabbage moth that it looked as though some angry soul had peppered it with buckshot. She dug into the dry sandy soil around the house and made rectangular beds with two-by-fours, and brought in wheelbarrow after wheelbarrow of sheep manure to fill them. Planting a flower garden on her arrival at the end of August was a risky thing to do, because it was only with luck that the weather held long enough for her to get a few velvety snapdragons, a scattering of stubborn petunias, and a patch of hardy Shasta daisies that sprang up triumphantly, rooting themselves there to bloom for years after.

Olaf couldn't see the sense in it. "Flowers aren't good for anything," he said. He was wrong. The garden filled her, extended her, made her more than she was without it. There was so little in that bachelor's cabin that she could call her own. The garden was her place, and she filled it with prettiness: lilac bushes cultured from saplings given to her by Mrs. Grafton, tulip, daffodil, and iris bulbs that she'd brought from home, and in the shade around back of the house, bleeding hearts split from her mother's plant.

On occasion Karl came down from the mountain with the packhorses to get salt for the sheep or supplies, or to oversee the haying done by hired hands or, later, to harvest the silage corn, turnips, and beets. On their first anniversary he surprised Augusta by coming down for no particular reason. He took her into town for pie and coffee at Yep Num's café, and to a movie called *The Egg and I*. It was the first of the Ma and Pa Kettle films, in which a young city couple try their hand at egg farming and befriend old Ma and Pa Kettle, poor country folk with too many kids. As they were driving back home in the International, Augusta said, "Why don't we keep some chickens? I could sell eggs."

"We used to. Bitch kept getting them."

"My father never would have kept a dog around that killed chickens."

"Dad won't get rid of Bitch. She's his pet."

"We're going to do without eggs and a little income because of that dog?"

"We can buy them."

"Your father foots the bill for eggs when he could have his own, because of that stupid dog?"

That was it—their one date for the summer.

Sometime in September, depending on the weather, the parade of sheep would march back down the highway to the Whorehouse Ranch, where they were pastured for the winter. Karl hauled feed out to them each day on sleighs: corn silage; swede turnips; and hay of mixed alfalfa, wild grasses, and alsike clover. During lambing, dried sugar-beet pulp was added to the ewes' feed.

Come lambing season, the cycle of work began all over again. They trimmed the sheep's hoofs and clipped the wool around the udders and flanks to make nursing easier, and the lambing pens were prepared. Once the ewes began lambing, Augusta and Karl and Olaf took shifts during the night, checking for births or complications. There were ewes that died giving birth, lambs lost. Sometimes a ewe that had lost a lamb would not accept another ewe's orphan. Karl would then put a sheepdog in with both the ewe and the foster lamb, and within a day or two the ewe would grow protective of the lamb and accept it, because of the dog's presence. At other times, when there were twins, Karl would leave one lamb with its mother; the other he would clothe in the skin of a lamb that had died, and place it in a pen with the dead lamb's mother. The ewe would smell her offspring on this changeling and nurse it. Once the ewe had accepted it as her own, Karl would remove the dead lamb's hide.

Sometimes, though, the orphaned lambs simply had to be bottle-fed, if there was no ewe to take them. That first lambing season on the Whorehouse Ranch, Augusta bottle-fed a sweet black lamb she named Molly. She brought it into the house and, sitting by the kitchen stove, held it like a baby and nursed it from a bottle until it grew too big to hold. Even after it was weaned and began spending its time tagging along with the flock, it always ran to Augusta and nuzzled her hand. Several days after Karl and Olaf shipped off a load of lambs, Augusta noticed that Molly was gone. When she asked where the lamb was, Karl was evasive. "She's around her somewhere," he said; then later, after a week had gone by, "Coyote must have got her."

"You shipped her off, didn't you?" said Augusta.

Karl's face grew red. "That's what we do here," he said.

"But you didn't tell me."

"I didn't want you making a scene."

"She was my pet."

"You can't make pets of them. We'd never sell any if we made pets of them."

"But just this one. Why couldn't you let me have this one?"

Thinking about that lamb now, Augusta believed it wasn't a pet she had wanted as much as a child. She felt herself drawn to the tiny dresses, miniature shoes, and sweet little blouses in the baby goods section of the general store. She once picked up a lovely white christening gown and felt the soft ruffles and silky ribbons between her fingers. But then Martha Rivers was right there, pregnant as an elephant. It would have been, what, her fifth? She had six altogether. At least she had been less productive than her mother.

Martha Rivers smiled at Augusta. "Too bad you won't have need of those."

Augusta smiled back. "How's that?"

"Well, Karl can't have children, can he?"

"Why would you think that?"

"Everyone knows. He had mumps when he was— twenty, I think it was. Or was he younger? We all know what *that* does to a man."

"I don't think it's your place to talk about things like that."

"We're friends, aren't we? I've known you since you were born. And in any case, I only tell things like they are."

In home in bed that night Augusta asked Karl, "Is it true you can't have children? Did you have mumps when you were a man?"

"Who told you that?"

"Martha Rivers."

"Gossiping woman."

"Is it true?"

"I don't know. I did have the mumps. I don't know what it did to me."

"We could try, couldn't we?" She ran her hand down his thigh. He was wearing his longjohns as the weather had turned cold.

"He'll hear us," said Karl.

"So what if he does?"

"Stop it!"

"Are we to go the whole of our married lives afraid to lie together as man and wife?"

"We'll find another time."

"What other time?"

"When he's out."

"And when is that?"

"When he's out with the sheep. We'll find some time alone together."

"In the day?"

"Yes."

"You're always out with him. If he's doing chores, you're doing chores."

"Enough. I'm tired."

Augusta thought now that she could hardly blame Karl, with his father always at him, always complaining. It didn't much matter what Karl or Augusta did—it wasn't good enough for Olaf. One night she served scalloped potatoes. Olaf picked up his plate and peered at it. "What's this?" he said.

"Scalloped potatoes," said Augusta.

"What's this they're floating in?"

"They're baked in cream."

"You don't cook potatoes in milk. You boil them. In water."

"Why don't you try them?"

"I'm not going to eat that slop. Looks like curdled milk. Turns my stomach."

Augusta threw down her fork and pushed herself away from the table and ran upstairs. But nothing went said in any part of that house without the rest of the house hearing it.

"What's the matter with her?" said Olaf.

"You don't have to complain so much about her cooking."

"If she'd learn to cook I wouldn't have to."

"The potatoes are good. If you'd only try them, for Christ's sake."

"Don't you talk like that to me."

Augusta sat on the bed but didn't bother lighting a lantern. Light slid up from downstairs through cracks in the floorboards. There was one knothole in the floor, and if she peered through it she could see both of them at the table, if she shifted from side to side. First Karl, then Olaf. They didn't say anything more. Olaf pushed the scalloped potatoes around on his plate. He took a forkful, sniffed it, licked it, put it in his mouth. Augusta watched him chewing. He took another forkful, and another. It was cold in the bedroom. Augusta lay back on the bed and pulled a corner of the gray camp blanket over her legs. The light from the floorboards hit the ceiling in slices so the wood there looked like the slats on a lambing pen or a crib. Then there was a figure behind the slats, a shadow moving across the ceiling. Augusta sat up. There was something in the room with her, something blocking the light from below. "Bitch?" she whispered. But the shadow on the ceiling wasn't the shadow of a dog. It was a human shadow. "Who's there?" she said. She didn't breathe. The floor creaked a little, as if under some weight. It was Blenda, Karl's mother, she was sure of it, though why she couldn't say. Augusta grappled with the matches at the bedside table and lit the lantern. The shadows vanished. She was alone.

She sat there for a while, staring into the dark corners of the room. It would be winter soon and the snowy roads would make the drive to town difficult. She thought of Blenda trapped in there all those winters. She must have needed to get out of that house, away from these men who could sit together in the kitchen for hours and not say a word, even if it meant walking between the sleeping bodies of the sheep in the cold fields. Was that what had killed her? The badgering and the silence? On a night when any sane woman would stay inside by the fire, had it driven her out into the snow?

-four-

A good deal of Augusta's train ride that morning had followed the ocean, the Strait of Georgia between Vancouver Island and the mainland. At one point she saw a pier jutting out into a bay. On the end of the pier a young woman and an old man were fishing together. The woman couldn't have been more than twenty, and the man was at least seventy. Augusta wondered, were they father and daughter? Father and granddaughter? Not lovers, surely. If they weren't related by blood, what interest would that young woman find in that old codger? Perhaps they were only strangers who had met on the pier and decided to sit together for a bit of fishing. Who knew what brought folks together? It was only important that they did come together, somehow, despite the odds.

She smiled to herself as she sat down to lunch with Karl and Rose. The gossips of Chase would have speculated in that way about Augusta and the Reverend when Augusta was, what? Twenty-three? When they fished the South Thompson. She had gone to church only infrequently following her marriage, as Olaf griped over her town trips, and she really didn't know the Reverend well, not in a personal way, when she went to his office. Where had she found the courage?

"I'm sorry to bring you this," she said. "But I've no one else to talk to about it. We've been so isolated on the ranch that I haven't made any friends, but now that I'm here I feel so ashamed. I mean, I found some magazines, belonging to my husband, in his old suitcase under the bed; *those* kind of magazines. Do you know what I mean? And I felt dirtied by them. What I mean to say is, they shocked me. Should I have told Karl I found them? But he would get angry. Or he wouldn't say anything at all. Most times he doesn't say anything."

The Reverend listened but didn't respond at first, and so out of nervousness Augusta babbled on until she drove herself to tears. The Reverend handed her a handkerchief. "How's your father?" he said.

"My father? All right, I guess. I hardly see him. I ask him to come for dinner, you know, but he never comes. I don't get over to the farm anymore."

"Manny stopped going to church years ago. I think he stopped right after your mother's death, didn't he? I sometimes see him in town. He looks so sad. I feel sorry for him, you know. He has no one."

"He doesn't want anybody. He never wants to see me. I could die for all he cares."

"Oh, I don't think so—"

"I know I don't get to church much. Olaf won't let me drive the truck."

"I see. I see." The Reverend offered her a second handkerchief. "You fish, don't you?"

"Fish?" said Augusta, wiping her nose.

"Fish."

"Well, yes. I used to fish with my father all the time, when I was a child. I don't think he ever goes fishing anymore. Karl doesn't fish. I miss it, actually."

"Me too. My wife doesn't fish. She says it's boring. And I don't like fishing with men. They get competitive. They compare their fish, for length." The Reverend smiled, a little slyly, so Augusta found herself laughing despite herself at his small, indecent joke. "Of course, I rarely catch anything," he said.

"I liked the sitting. It was an excuse to sit and be peaceful. With Karl and Olaf—well, I feel like I always have to be doing something. Housework or chores or helping Karl. He never says anything, but he looks at me, you know? Judging, if he catches me sitting."

"It's the same in my line of work. The congregation doesn't like to see me idle. That's why I never go to the café; I get these looks telling me I should be someplace else, helping someone. I suppose it's understandable, as they do pay my way. Nevertheless, even God's servants need repose." He reached over and patted Augusta's hand. "As does a housewife." He stood and took his coat from the rack by the door. "Shall we go, then?" he said.

"Where?"

"Fishing."

Augusta laughed, but she went with him, wearing her one good dress, her wedding dress, and a sweater she took from the truck seat before joining him in his Austin. They went fishing at Deep Pool, a fishing hole Manny had taken her to when she was a child. Deep Pool was on the town side of the South Thompson River, a short drive from Chase. From Deep Pool it seemed as if Chase had once been a much larger town and had been split in two by the changing course of water, because there were communities facing each other on opposing banks of the river. Whites lived on one side, in or near Chase, and Indians lived on the other, in the reserve village. For much of her childhood, there was literally no bridge between them. The bridge over the South Thompson wouldn't be constructed until 1938, only a few years before Helen died. Before that, Indians coming over to town canoed, or swam their saddle horses across. Sometimes on moonless nights the Indians went out in their canoes holding flaming pitch torches made from ponderosa pine, what they called salmon wood because they used the torch flame to attract the salmon to the surface of the black water. They then stabbed the fish with homemade three-pronged spears. They were glittering fireflies on the water; they were ghost lights rising from Deep Pool.

Every Saturday Manny had driven Augusta down to Deep Pool so that they could sit out on the dock and fish. It was an excuse to do nothing, because Helen could hardly complain about a missed half-day of fieldwork if they brought home a dozen trout to slice open and fry in fresh butter for supper, especially since Manny volunteered to cook them himself. The river was wide, and its slow-moving waters were deceptive. At Deep Pool, Augusta could walk for yards hip-high through water that reflected the changing sky and showed little of its underside. Then suddenly there was nothing underfoot—sand and gravel gave way to empty space. She sank like a stone, gasping water, down into the bottomless pool, where something slid past her legs before she swam back to the surface.

That first day she went fishing with the Reverend, they saw Manny walking the riverbank some distance away. He waved, but he didn't come over to greet them.

"We should make a habit of this," said the Reverend.

"I don't think I could. Olaf doesn't like me using the truck to come to town. And I know he wouldn't like me fishing with you."

"But you'd like to, wouldn't you?"

"Sure."

"If you change your mind, I'll be at my office. Saturday mornings are best for me."

The Reverend never addressed the problem that she had brought him, about finding Karl's dirty magazines. All he ever said about it, he said in the car as they drove to the river on that very first fishing trip. "God wouldn't give us those feelings if they weren't to be enjoyed," he said, out of the silence they had been driving in. It took Augusta a moment to understand what he was talking about. "But like eating," he continued, "one doesn't want to overdo it."

But the Reverend had missed the point entirely. Or perhaps she hadn't explained herself. It wasn't excess Karl was guilty of. In their few years of marriage she had come to consider him a man of many fears and few desires, and had resigned herself to a life of longing, and shamefully pleasuring herself. But when she found those magazines, it infuriated her. While she went without, he indulged himself! He had found the time, albeit in the outhouse, but he had found the time for *that*, when he could find no time for her. It was a meanness of spirit that extended into all areas of their lives together. Of course, what chance did he have of being anything different, with a father like his?

"I heard you went fishing with that Reverend," said Olaf. They were sitting at the dinner table.

"You heard right."

"You let her go fishing with another man?"

"He isn't another man, Father," said Karl. "He's Augusta's minister. We should feel honored he's chosen her for companionship."

"He has his own wife for companionship."

"She doesn't like fishing," said Augusta.

"He should be fishing with some other man. That ain't right, fishing with another man's wife. There'll be talk. Don't your wife care about how it affects us?"

"And just how does it affect you?" said Augusta.

"Haven't you heard the saying: *Watch out when the preacher comes calling on your wife alone?*"

"You dirty old—"

"Augusta," said Karl. There was warning in his voice. He was learning, from Olaf.

But then so was she. "The Reverend invited me to go again Saturday, and you know what? I think I will. I'm taking the truck. And I'm going fishing. If you want anything picked up then, add it to my list."

Augusta was surprised to find herself standing up to Olaf, and to Karl. But the Reverend's attention made everything all right, made it okay. He was an important man, a man of status. If he chose to fish with her, how could she say no?

His name was Gavin Lakeman, but he was always the Reverend to Augusta. Never Gavin, never Reverend Lakeman. He was tall, a good six feet, and barrel-chested. Although he kept himself clean-shaven he was never without that five o'clock shadow, and his arms were covered in a pelt of black hair. He had a temper that he had to fight, especially as he had high blood pressure.

These Saturday morning fishing trips became regular outings, during which the Reverend refreshed the meager fly-casting skills Augusta had learned from Manny, though at first she caught only bony whitefish. The Reverend, on the other hand, could land a fly in the exact spot a trout had broken the water's surface, and he seldom went home without a string of a dozen fish. He wasn't one to yank a fish out of the water and hurl it to shore, as Manny had when Augusta had fished with him so many years before. The Reverend cast out in the middle or far side of Deep Pool, and when he felt a bite he'd coax the fish in to shore for perhaps ten or fifteen minutes, talking to it all the while. "Come along, my beauty. There you are. There you are." Then, "You really are a beauty, aren't you?" as he admired the fish flopping in the sand at his feet. Then he killed the fish by grasping its tail and whacking its head against a rock, and that sudden whack, after all those persuasive murmurs, came as a shock to Augusta as well as to the fish.

There were often others fishing on the sandbars or from the rocky beach farther downriver, or swimming in the pools upstream. Sometimes Indian kids slid down the bank and swam along the opposite shore. Once Manny even floated by, fully clothed except for his shoes, on his back with his hands behind his head, serenely drifting on the water. Augusta called to him, but he didn't seem to hear. He went on floating downstream. The Reverend pointed at him with his chin and said, "If I could choose a way to die, it would be to slip under this water in midstream and let it carry me into eternity."

He often talked about death and souls and such; even the sex of angels (girls, the Reverend thought, certainly all females), and did fish have souls? (The Reverend didn't want to think so but felt they certainly must.) As for the appearance—or sex—of God, the Reverend didn't believe man had been created in His image. Rather he believed God took the forms of all His creations. At any given moment He could be a fish. A tree. A rock. The earth itself. Or He might be a stranger one came across, a fellow passenger on a bus or train. Woman or man. Whatever took His fancy. God spent eternity amusing Himself by seeing what it was like to be each of His creations, every single one of them. When He grew bored, He simply created something new. It was an idea that made Augusta suddenly careful of ants underfoot, and apologetic to the turnips she ate. "He could be any-where, anything, walking among us," said the Reverend. "Maybe He's you."

"Maybe He's you," said Augusta.

"Oh, no. Not me!"

"I notice you don't talk about these ideas in your ser-mons," said Augusta.

"Madam, if I talked like this from the pulpit I would be out of a job and we would not be fishing right now."

Augusta shrugged. "Might give you more time for fishing."

"Hmm. I'll consider it."

But he was only joking. When she was able to slip away from the farm to attend church, his sermons were always the solid, stoic affairs that were expected of him. At church they kept a polite distance from each other; he treated her like any other member of the church, shaking her hand at the back of the church once the sermon was over. His wife, Lilian, always dressed so beautifully in blue, stood beside him, also shaking hands. Most times Augusta tried not to catch Lilian's eye as she shook hands. But once she looked straight into Lilian's face. Lilian smiled and winked at her. It was the knowing wink women friends pass between each other in the kitchen as their menfolk blather nonsense in the living room. A conspirator's wink.

As the months of Saturday fishing trips went on, it grew harder for Augusta to think of that respected and dignified preacher and this fisherman as one and the same man. It dawned on her that the Reverend she'd known all the years of her childhood was a role played, a fiction. And here, holding a fishing rod, sitting on the banks of the South Thompson, was the actor, the man behind the fiction. His wife had also been playing a part, the tidy, perfectly organized leader of the Sunday school and women's church league who never lost her smile. Now Augusta discovered that under that smile something was boiling away. "She steals, you know," said the Reverend.

"Steals? Lilian?"

"Nothing she needs, mind you. Things that make no sense. A scarf. A bar of soap. Once a can of salmon. Always from a store; never from a member of the church, thank God. It's been going on for years. I've tried stopping it. I've made her take the things back to Colgrave and Conchie's and explain and beg them not to tell anyone. But it goes on. Now I have Ed Conchie watch her when she comes in, and add what she takes to our bill. The church elders all know about it. I've explained. They keep an eye on her. I suppose most people know about it by now. Though no one's ever said anything to me, or to her."

"I didn't know."

"It's my fault, I think. She wasn't cut out to be a pastor's wife. She had to learn how to look nice all the time, even at home, because someone's always dropping in. And she's expected to organize meetings and Sunday school, all of that. She didn't know how, at first. And I was hard on her. I yelled until she cowered. All that fear and tension had to come out somewhere, didn't it? So she takes things, useless things. I've never hit her, but I might as well have. Ranting on like that. And what have I to show for it? High blood pressure and a wife who steals. Well, she doesn't do it so much anymore. I guess I'm getting easier to live with. Getting older has a way of mellowing you. In any case I learned some things. Maybe it was God's will that I messed up so badly with my own wife. It makes me watch for other women in the same boat."

"That why you go fishing with me?"

The Reverend grinned at her. "You're doing me the favor. Not the other way around. Although I admit that when you came in that day I did feel guilty. I didn't do very well with you and your father, after your mother's death. I had your father in, you know. I had him come to my office and we talked. Or rather, I talked. He's a hard man to get a word from. I tried to get him active in the church again, and tried to offer some help for you. There were women in the church who would have come out, to help with housework or meals, to visit with you. But he wouldn't have any of that. He didn't want to see anyone. I guess I can understand, what with the talk going around that the baby wasn't his. Still, I should have pushed things, for your sake."

Augusta felt the anger flare up. "The baby was his."

It was a lie. Manny had hired Harry Jacob for another summer after his son's death, though Harry's woman and Alice never came back with him. Harry Jacob was a hard worker, practiced at working alone, unsupervised. Manny could leave him, even during haying, and catch a Saturday morning of fishing if he wished. But Manny wouldn't have him in the house, not with sickness raging through the reserve. So Helen took meals out to Harry's tent in the evening; she carried beef stew to him in syrup cans, and slabs of buttered bread, buttered sides together, wrapped in clean cloth. She rubbed apples to a shining red with her apron before taking them to him. Mornings and afternoons when Manny was in town or fishing, and Harry Jacob worked in the field alone, she brought him sweet coffee, and delicate cookies made from precious sugar, nuts, and beaten egg whites called Penna Dutch kisses.

Through the kitchen window Augusta would see Harry Jacob and her mother chatting in the alfalfa. Harry had a way about him, a slickness that reminded Augusta of Clark Gable, though he wasn't as handsome as all that, not dressed in field denims, not all greasy haired and sweating from a day's work. Yet even unwashed and dressed so poorly, he leaned against the tractor as if he owned it and all he saw around him; cocky and relaxed, he pointed at the hills or at the house with his coffee cup, talking and laughing, no doubt at his own jokes. Helen fidgeted with her apron, or hugged her belly, shy as a schoolgirl, and laughed at almost everything he said. He was younger than Helen by a good ten years and yet he made her behave like that, like a silly, flirting teenager. It made Augusta angry to see them together. She wanted her mother to go back to acting her age. She should quit all that silly giggling and get back to work. Here was Augusta, just fourteen and stuck with the summer's canning, a job she hated; here she was sweating over the stove in the heat of July when she could be down at the river swimming or fishing with her father.

"I saw you talking to Harry again," said Manny one evening.

Helen wiped her mouth with her napkin. "He helped me move the bee boxes after I took him lunch."

"You spend too much time talking to him."

"I'm being friendly. You don't want me to be friendly to our help?"

"You're being too friendly."

"Oh, Lord."

"Don't give me that look."

"What interest would I have in an Indian?"

"None, if you know what's good for you."

"Enough of this. Harry will work harder if he's fed and treated well. And that's what I'm doing. In any case, don't you think we owe him something? His son died on our land and we did nothing to help him."

Manny, red-faced, pushed his chair from the table and crossed his arms. But he said nothing more about it, and he didn't make a fuss when it was Harry Helen asked to work with her in the honey house for the final harvest, and not Manny. Extracting and bottling honey wasn't a job Manny liked. It was hot, sticky work and he was always stung badly. And besides that he'd take any excuse to go down to Deep Pool for a little fishing. Augusta was ready to help but Helen got her busy in the kitchen, canning plums. So it was just Harry and Helen out in the orchard, gathering the frames. Helen opened the hive, lifted off the inner cover, and slid out the frames filled with honeycomb, one by one, all the while squeezing puffs of smoke into the hive with a smoker, to calm the bees. She tapped the frame against a rock near the entrance of the hive, to rid it of as many bees as she could, then brushed the remaining bees from the comb with a handful of long grass. She then carried each frame, cleaned of bees, some distance away to put it into a covered super, or bee box. When she had a box full of honeycomb she had Harry carry it to the honey house.

Helen kept the house hot to keep the honey flowing, by stoking up the portly little Dandy Perfection woodstove, but not so hot that the beeswax melted from the frames. She held the frame full of honeycomb upright with one hand and slid a hot uncapping knife upward across the comb with the other, to remove the wax caps that sealed the cells of honey. She removed all the caps on one side of the frame in a single sweep, taking enough wax to free the honey but not so much as to damage the comb. She then put the knife back into a pail of water on the stove, to keep it hot. It was dangerous work, and if she wasn't careful she'd lose a thumb to the uncapping knife. She uncapped both sides of the frames and handed them to Harry to insert into the honey extractor, two frames at a time. Then he turned the crank at the top of the extractor, spinning the honey out of the frames into a tub that was tapped at the bottom. When he was done, he turned the frames around and spun the honey from the other side of the comb. He turned slowly at first, while the comb was still heavy, then gathered speed as the frames emptied. Later Helen did the straining and bottling. When Augusta produced honey of her own, she would leave the honey house so sticky that when she took off her dress to wash up, it nearly stood by itself.

The kitchen was as hot as the honey house, as Augusta was canning that day. At one point she felt she'd suffocate from the heat, it was so stifling, and so she walked outside for some cooler air and a break from the work, wiping the sweat from her forehead with her apron. Why she wandered over to the honey house and peeked through the window she could only guess at now. Certainly she had her suspicions. Harry and Helen were both in there, laboring away. Helen had covered the floor in newspaper and would change the paper several times that day as it became gummy and difficult to walk over. Harry's smoky skin glistened in honey and sweat. Helen was stickier yet, as she was the one uncapping the comb. Neither of them saw Augusta peering through the small window in the far side of the room. Harry stopped turning the extractor for a moment and reached over to wipe a dollop of honey from Helen's lip, then licked his finger. Helen grinned at him, running her tongue over her lips. It might have been a scene from the Song of Songs. *Your lips, my promised one, distill wild honey.* Augusta didn't rush in to accuse her mother, or to backtalk as Joy did decades later. She turned on her heel and walked back to the house and went on canning plums as if she'd seen nothing at all.

"All that doesn't much matter anymore," said the Reverend. "It's all in the past."

Augusta bounced the rod up and down. "I had a premonition she would die. I saw her coffin. I told her so, too. She wouldn't believe me. Or maybe she did. She just didn't want to hear about it."

"I don't suppose she would."

She had told Manny about the vision first, as he had been right there in the garden when it happened. She thought now that he'd even been the reason she'd had the premonition. Manny went fishing by himself, now that Augusta was becoming a young woman, and when Augusta asked to go with him he said, "Stay here and help your mother." It seemed that the more she blossomed, the more he withdrew his affection. Hungry for it, she one day put on that pretty, childishly flowered blouse that almost hid her breasts, made

him coffee and a plate of butterfingers, and took them out to
the vegetable garden, where he bent hoeing between the
rows. She plastered sweetness on her face, willing the child
to the surface, the woman to submerge, hoping for that smile
of his that had edged away, hoping for his hand on her
shoulder in congratulation for this small effort of helpful-
ness. He smiled when he saw her coming down the row,
all right, then stretched and took out his red handkerchief
to dry the sweat on his forehead. "Putting on the dog
there, aren't yah?" he said. She looked down at her blouse.
"What're you all dressed up for?"

Augusta shrugged.

"Well, what you got there?"

"Coffee. Thought you'd be hungry."

"I am. I am." He took the cup and ate the cookies from
the plate as she held it, then handed back the cup, the handle all smeared with soil. He smiled his thanks and said,
"That's my girl." After taking the plate and cup back to the
kitchen and slipping them into the soapy dishwater in the
sink, she skipped back outside and wrapped her arms
around Manny's waist. He dropped his hoe, took her arms
in his two fists, and pushed her away. "What're the neighbors going to think?" he said. "You're too big for that! Go
on with you!"

She stumbled back. What did he mean? She must have
done something shameful to be punished so, but what? All
she'd done was wrap her arms around him in lovingness.
That was the shameful thing, it must be. She felt suddenly
dirty. The soil under her shoes—the garden, the sky—
whooshed away from her in all directions. She stared at her
feet, the only solid objects in all the swirling around her. For
a moment the spinning subsided and she was no longer in

the garden. There was a hole, a deep rectangular hole, in front of her feet. An open grave. She held something in her hand—rosemary, a clutch of rosemary. In the grave there was a simple wooden casket—whose casket? Her hand tensed, squeezing the rosemary so the air became thick with fragrance. Then the rosemary, the grave—everything— melted away in a whirl of motion, and when it finally stopped she found herself standing in front of her mother's huge rosemary mound, her hands pinching the buttons of her blouse.

She stared at the rosemary redolent in the warm evening air. Why was she standing here? Her father chopped into the soil right behind her. Her father. The cup of coffee. The plate of butterfingers. His hands pushing her away. "Mama's going to die."

"What?"

"She'll die."

She heard her father's footsteps coming toward her, but she couldn't move. She felt transfixed by the rosemary. Then his hand was on her shoulder and the spell was broken. He was angry. "What're you talking about? Who's going to die?"

"Die?"

"You said, 'Mama.' You said your mama was going to die."

"I don't know. I saw—I don't know what I saw. I saw Mama's coffin. There in the rosemary."

"You're talking nonsense."

"No. I saw it. Mama's going to die!"

"Stop that! Stop it!"

"I saw!"

"You shut up now. Quit your crying. You're working yourself into a fit. She's not going to die. And don't tell your mother about this. It would scare her."

But Augusta did tell her mother about the vision she had seen in the rosemary. She told her that very day, after pouring them each a cup of tea. She filled in details, the tan in the wood of the coffin (likely poplar, she thought), the gravel that surrounded the grave, the pungent smell of rosemary.

"And what is it that I've died of?" said Helen.

"I don't know."

"And when will this happen?"

"I don't know. I don't want it to happen."

"I doubt that it will. I believe you saw something. I'm just not sure we need to give it much credit."

"You remember when you knew Dad cut his hand on the mower? It was like that."

Helen flushed for a moment. She drank her tea. "Even if I believed you, what can I do? I don't know when I'll die, or how. I don't know any more than anyone ever does about their own death. I think it would be best if we forgot about it. And you understand you're to keep this within this house. You'll be thought balmy if you go off talking about it."

But she had told the Reverend and he hadn't thought her balmy. He had placed his fishing pole beside him and poured them both tea from the little ceramic teapot he'd brought. "That's a gift, you understand," he said, "from God. That you can see the future."

Augusta sipped her tea. "It doesn't feel like a gift," she said. "I should be able to use it, shouldn't I? I should be able to help people avoid things. I couldn't stop my mom from dying."

"No, it's not like that. You mustn't think you have the power to control things." He patted her hand. "You know what I think? I think you take too much on yourself. You worry too much. You need to get out. Be with some women friends. How about getting a job? The health unit in Kamloops is looking for women to help the elderly make meals or clean house, or to watch babies when their mothers go to the doctor."

"I don't have a car. Olaf wouldn't stand for it—me driving the truck into Kamloops every day."

"I've been thinking of getting a truck myself. It would be so much easier when we help a member of the church move. And there always seems to be something to haul to someone's home. Last week I took Lucy Guterson's old washer out to Mrs. Reed's because hers had broken down. I had to borrow Alfred Campbell's truck to do it. I'm forever borrowing his truck. Well, the upshot is, if I get the truck, I could lend you the Austin. Or you could have it, for that matter."

"Oh, I couldn't. That's too big a gift."

"I'll lend it to you, then, for as long as you need it. You need to get out. Be with other women. Get a little money for yourself. It's not healthy to be cooped up on that ranch all the time."

"I come to town Saturdays. I fish with you."

"That's not enough. You need women in your life. You need a little money of your own. They own you too much, that Olaf and Karl. I don't want to see you slide away as Mrs. Olsen did."

"What do you mean?"

"You know the story."

"No, I don't think I do."

"Why? What did they tell you?"

"That she died of cold. During a blizzard. She must have lost her way."

"There was no storm. She walked out into the night when Olaf and Karl were asleep and lay in the snow. Karl found her body in the morning. She went to sleep with her hands crossed over her breast and died of exposure. She was a romantic, locked away in that bachelor house. That ranch has a history of misery, for women."

"She killed herself?"

"Karl and Olaf must have had their reasons for not telling you. It was important not to say anything then, you understand. You know how this town talks. In any case, I'm certain she's gone to a better place. Death was a relief for her. But don't make her mistake. She had no women friends. She had no money for the little luxuries that feed a woman's soul. The house was as bare as any bachelor's cabin. No curtains. No pretty dishes. No music. No flowers. They'd pinioned her. Do you know that when anyone visited, she'd hide from them? You'd catch a glimpse of her looking out the window, and when you knocked you'd hear her scuttling away like a frightened mouse. She died a slow death. I saw it coming and I didn't take care of her. I let her slip through my fingers. I've never forgiven myself. I won't make that mistake again. Do you understand me?"

His earnestness surprised her, frightened her, pleased her. No man had ever paid her that much attention, not Karl, not Manny. It made her feel giddy to be held in such high regard by this important man, to be his friend. She felt chosen.

The Reverend's attention had given her the confidence to try for some changes on the Whorehouse Ranch. She nudged Karl's knee, and he cleared his throat. "Father, Augusta would like to spend more time with me, alone." When she nudged him under the table a second time, he rephrased it. "We need time alone together, when I'm not working."

"Well, you'll have to tell her not to expect so much. This is a farm. We've all got to pull our weight. You get plenty of time off in the winter."

Karl took Augusta's hand and glanced at his father. "But just Sundays off. Or one day during the week. Surely one day a week."

"One day you'll inherit this farm and you can run it as you please. But now it's my farm and I'll run it. If you don't like it you can go someplace else and get a job, but don't expect there to be a farm to come back to if you do. I can't run this farm by myself. It'll be in ruins if you leave."

"No one's talking of leaving, Father."

"Waiting for me to die, eh?"

"It's not like that, Father. No one wants you to die."

"You'd be happy if I kicked off tonight. You'd be celebrating."

"Father, please!"

"She'd be celebrating. And I'm only trying to work it so there's something to leave my son."

Augusta sighed. "I wouldn't be celebrating."

Olaf pointed his chin at their hands clasped on the table. "None of that here."

Karl pulled his hand away. Augusta slammed her fist on the table and noisily cleared away the dishes.

The old Swede lowered his voice, but he knew she was listening. "Some men have to spank their women," he said, "to get them to listen. I only had to spank your mother once. But some women, well . . ."

"Yes, Father."

After they were in bed and she'd scolded him for agreeing with Olaf, he whispered, "What was I supposed to say?"

"You could have said no, for heaven's sake! He was telling you to spank me, as if I were a child! He's got you wrapped around his finger."

"He's an old man. He's got old ideas. We've got to humor him."

"You're not humoring him. You're playing the slave to him! You do everything he says, at our expense. At *my* expense!"

"Shush! He'll hear!"

"I don't care if he hears." But she had lowered her voice.

"When I disagree with him he gets so upset," said Karl. "He's not well, you know. His heart could go at any time."

"He's healthy as you and me. And in any case he's had his time here."

"What're you saying?"

"We'd be a lot better off if he were gone, wouldn't we?"

"Augusta!"

"You don't even see it, do you? You don't see what he's done to you. He's made you small. He's made you afraid."

"Enough nagging!"

Why didn't she bang her fists against the wall, or flail on the floor at the injustice of her treatment, at her husband's unbelievable submissiveness to that small, ugly man. Why didn't she storm around the house breaking things, as she so often dreamed of doing?

She couldn't bear being thought a nag, but she couldn't stay silent for long either. Not a week after trying to get Karl some days off, she was at it again. They'd been talking of Karl's day in town. "Ronny Carver and Percy Martin came looking for a job today," said Karl. "I told Ronny no. I said Percy could come talk to you about lambing next spring."

Olaf snorted. "Good. Ronny's useless. His folks would have done better if they'd drowned him and raised a pig instead."

"You're not hiring Percy Martin," said Augusta. "He was the one who raped Shirley Matthews, just when we were engaged."

"Shirley dropped the charges," said Karl.

"A man can't rape a woman," said Olaf. "Ain't possible. A ram can't mount a sheep lest she wants it. She just goes running off. It's a thing women make up, so's they aren't to blame for messing around."

"You can't be serious," said Augusta.

Olaf glanced briefly her way and then addressed Karl. "Tell your wife she's going into town too much."

"She's sitting right here, Father."

"Tell her!"

"I heard what you said," said Augusta.

"Tell her to stop seeing that Reverend."

"Not this again! We're just fishing, for heaven's sake."

"Tell her to stop seeing that Reverend. She's dirtying our name."

"I'm doing no such thing."

"They're only fishing, Father."

"She's just like her mother, isn't she? For once in your life stand up for yourself!"

"Father, please!"

"What does he mean, I'm like my mother?"

The black bitch came out from under the table then, excited by the raised voices. She stood behind the old Swede's chair, yapping and barking so that Olaf had to shout over her. "I won't have it. No woman under my roof will behave like that!"

"Like what?" yelled Augusta. The black bitch leapt out from behind Olaf's chair and nipped at her skirts. She kicked at the dog, yelling all the while over the old man's insults. "You'd keep me locked up here, in the dark, with no friends, no money, no pleasures of any kind—"

"Shut her up!" hollered Olaf, and at first Augusta thought he meant the dog. But it was Augusta he wanted shut up.

"Augusta, please!" said Karl.

There at the kitchen table—with the bitch growling and the old Swede raging—Augusta knew the Reverend was right: this was slow death. Olaf would whittle away at her until there was nothing left, just as he had with his wife and his son. Well, she wouldn't let him. She'd find work. The Reverend would give her a letter of reference to take to the health unit in Kamloops. She'd make friends, earn a little money.

A school for the mentally handicapped—they were called "retarded" then—put an ad in the paper for someone to drive kids from Chase to school in Kamloops and back each day. Augusta sent in a letter of application and got the job. The wage barely paid for the gas, but through the health unit she could find work for the day in Kamloops. The Reverend lent her the old black Austin for these jobs, and she loved driving, lived for it; it freed her so. She could imagine herself hovering alongside the car, arms outstretched, hair blowing back, flying. She felt as if she could drive all day.

Every morning after she dropped the children off at school, she drove around to the health unit, where one of the nurses would have a list of people she could work for that day, doing housework for the most part. She worked for many of these people on an ongoing basis, daily or weekly. The first job she took on was working for Virginia, a widow who needed help to get in and out of the bathtub. Bathing her, Augusta saw what was to come. She tried not to stare as she helped the old woman wash herself; she tried to look at the ceiling, or the toilet, or the door, but her eyes were drawn back to Virginia's body over and over again. The woman's skin was surprisingly youthful and smooth; the skin on her upper arms and legs was not much different from Augusta's, though Virginia must have been eighty. Only the woman's hands and face had truly aged, and her posture, because she was bent over, and there was a slight hump at the base of her neck that always compelled Augusta to stand straighter. The old woman's underarm and pubic hair was as gray as the hair on her head. Augusta hadn't thought old women had pubic hair, or anything down there at all. In her mind they had been as hairless and smooth—and as sexless—as little girls. Yet as she steadied the old woman and helped her step, dripping, from the bathtub, she couldn't help but see that Virginia was still a woman. Although her breasts hung flat, the silvery bush at her crotch attested that if she didn't let her passion loose, it was only because she was tired, or without companionship.

Virginia slipped and fell while she was at home alone, breaking her hip, and died shortly after, not three months after Augusta took on the job.

Mrs. Stead, whose husband owned a freight company, had Augusta come by every Thursday morning to clean a house that was already practically spotless. One Thursday morning Augusta checked into the health unit for afternoon jobs and found one of the nurses fretting over a woman nearly nine months pregnant who already had nine children. The woman had a bad tooth, an abscess making her crazy, as if she didn't have enough to be crazy about, and a dental appointment she couldn't get to because there was nobody to look after her brood of young kids still at home.

Augusta phoned Mrs. Stead. "I wonder if you wouldn't mind if I came a little later this morning," she said. "There's a woman with a large family who needs to get to a dentist and there's no one to help her out."

"There must be someone else who can do it."

"No, ma'am. I'm the only one who showed today."

"Can't it wait? I have plans."

"She's in some pain."

"Well, what time will you be here, then?"

"I should be there by eleven-thirty. It depends on how long her appointment—"

"All right. But no later than eleven-thirty. I have to leave here at one."

"I'll try—"

Mrs. Stead hung up.

Augusta drove to the address the nurse had given her. It was a house too tiny for nine children and one more on the way, but it was the right house nevertheless. The same went for the woman who answered the door. She was too young and thin to be the mother of ten but there she was, pregnant as a woman could get; six of the nine children were clinging to her skirts. "The other three will be home shortly," she said. No *hello*. No *how do you do*. Augusta supposed that when you were in pain, and had that many children, you saved your breath for more important things.

The woman set out the makings for lunch on the table, in case her appointment ran long, and fled. Lunch was a loaf of bread and a can of jam, but no butter or margarine, and a jug of skim milk reconstituted from powder. Not much to feed nine hungry children. When the other three rushed into the house, all nine of them made a run for the table, though it was only ten-thirty. Augusta tried to settle them, make them sit down and eat properly, but the food was gone before she could create any kind of order. After lunch she got the kids playing hide-and-seek in the backyard and went about doing what she could for this woman, though she was only being paid to mind the children. She tidied up, swept the floors, did the dishes, and finished mending a few bits of clothing sitting in a basket by a chair. She got herself so wound up in her charity work for this woman that she didn't notice the time passing until it was nearly one o'clock and the pregnant woman was walking through the door.

Augusta turned down the dollar the woman offered her for her time and rushed off to Mrs. Stead's. She ran up the steps to the front door but the door flew open before she'd had a chance to knock. Mrs. Stead was furious. "Where have you been?"

"As I said on the phone, there was this woman—"

"You said eleven-thirty. Look what time it is."

"She was in a lot of pain. There were all these children. They needed lunch."

"You made me miss *my* lunch. I had a lunch date at the golf clubhouse with some very important people. Do you understand? People who shouldn't be kept waiting."

"But that poor woman—"

"I don't care what your excuse is. You made a commitment to clean this house every Thursday morning and that's what you'll do. I won't have you putting other people's work ahead of mine. I don't ever want this to happen again."

"But I couldn't—"

"Do you understand me?"

Augusta stared at the woman for a moment, then said, "Yes, ma'am, I do."

"All right. Get to work. I don't want to waste any more of my day on you."

Augusta slammed through her housework, vacuuming, mopping, dusting, waxing, and polishing. When she was done, Mrs. Stead stood at the door to hand her her wages. Augusta took the money but then threw it on the floor. "Why not give that to somebody who needs it?" she said. "Like that poor woman I worked for this morning? You can get yourself someone else to work for you." It was worth the three dollars and fifty cents she went without that day, worth every penny to tell her to shove off. She worried a little that news of what she'd done would get back to the nurses at the health unit. But Mrs. Stead said nothing about it, only asked for another girl who was more regular, and the nurse who had got Augusta working for the pregnant woman understood. Anyway, there were plenty of jobs where that one came from. Augusta was never without work if she wanted it.

Karl hated that she worked. He hated anything that upset his father, that heaped his father's condemnation on him. Out of the black of their bedroom he asked her, "You don't really have to work, do you? They'll say I can't afford to keep a wife."

"It's true, isn't it?" She shouldn't have said it, but there it was, and she just made things worse by trying to explain herself. "I can't keep begging from Olaf. We must have some independence. If you won't get it, I will."

"Then don't go fishing with the Reverend. Please."

"There's nothing for me here on this ranch. I have no friends. The Reverend's the only friend I've got. I'll go crazy if I don't see anyone but you and that old Swede."

"Shush!"

"You shush! He can't hear us. Listen to those snores. You'd think he was breathing his last."

"Surely if you take work you get out enough. You don't need to go fishing with the Reverend, too. It means so much to Father that you don't."

"I don't care what he thinks. The Reverend is my friend and I'll go fishing with him and you can be thankful for the trout we eat Saturday evenings."

In the dark she felt him pulling up his resolve. "You won't go fishing with him anymore."

"I'll do as I like."

"I said you won't go, and you won't."

"What right have you to say? You give me nothing. Look at the dresses I wear! I can't remember the last time you made love to me."

There was a long silence. Augusta felt her body taking shape in the black, pulling all out of proportion. Her feet and hands felt too large, her head too big. She was a cartoon figure. None of this was real. She couldn't be living this life. How had she got here?

"I'm tired," Karl said finally. "We work such long hours." "I found those magazines." He said nothing to that. After a time he rolled over, turning his back to her. "He's not going to kill me off like he killed your mother," she said. It was cruel, but there it was.

Karl sat up. "What?"

"You heard me."

"Where did you hear that?"

"I heard."

"He didn't kill her. She killed herself."

"Same thing. I see it now, how it happened. He killed her off in little bits. He took away her voice. Then he took away her hands. Then he took away her will."

"You don't understand. She was so sad. For years she was sad."

"I understand exactly. I understand he's doing that to you. And he'll do it to me. But I won't let him. You can stay here and die if you like, but I won't."

Karl said no more about the Reverend, and found ways to be busy most Saturday mornings when she drove herself into Chase. Olaf simply stopped speaking of her in any way. She might have been an unseen ghost rambling the house or, more to the point, a maid; after a day of work she still came home to make supper and clean house, but he didn't acknowledge her presence.

Augusta began taking her supper alone, after the men had gone to bed, or when they were out doing evening chores. While they men ate supper she busied herself washing the lunch dishes, or sweeping dog hair from the floor, or washing laundry by hand. It was a hard life in those days before modern appliances. Cooking meant splitting wood and making a fire. Washing meant hauling water. She didn't even have a toaster. In her early years of marriage she toasted bread on a contraption very much like a small oven rack, taking off one of the round stove lids and placing the rack. Even when she worked out of the health unit in Kamloops as domestic help, keeping house was no easy task. Not every house had electricity yet, and many were without phones. A woman had to be fit to keep a house then; she had to have muscle.

Each morning she made herself a simple bag lunch of buttered homemade bread, a piece of cheese, an orange or apple, and a thermos of tea. She ate it on the bench in front of the health unit. It never occurred to her to eat in a restaurant. She couldn't bring herself to pay what the clapboard outside the café next to the health unit advertised—a buck fifty for a bowl of soup and a sandwich that she could make herself at home. It was robbery. Yet one day she forgot her bag lunch and there she was, an hour's drive from home, with a couple of hours to kill before her next job. She had taken extra afternoon work, as school was out during the summer and she didn't have to drive the two handicapped children home. She'd have to feed herself somehow, and pass the time.

The café was nearly empty, as it was between coffee time and lunchtime. It was an adventure for her, going inside. She chose a booth large enough to hold several people, because it was near the window, looking over the bench on which she sat most lunch hours. She stared at this bench, suddenly shy, unwilling, unable to look around the café, until the waitress came by with the menu and a glass of water. The waitress said, "You alone?"

Augusta stared at the woman's apron. Her question felt like an indictment. Did she expect that Augusta was meeting some man? Or had Augusta missed a sign over the door, like the ones over the bars that said *Women Must Be Accompanied by a Gentleman*? "Alone?" she said.

"Is anyone else joining you? Lunch hour starts in about fifteen minutes. The place gets pretty crowded."

"No, no, it's just me."

"Well, you can sit here if you want, but if a big group comes in I might have to move you over to one of the smaller tables."

"I won't be long."

"Pardon?"

"I said I can't stay long. I have to get back to work."

"All right, then. Just so you know."

"I'll get a sandwich. What you have on the board outside."

"The soup and sandwich?"

"Yes, that's fine."

"All righty. Coffee?"

"Yes. No. Tea, please."

It was only then that she looked around at the place. It was a small café called the Silver Grill (later she found out from Joe that the locals called it "The Swill"). The whole place smelled of tomato soup and fried onions. Someone sitting at the counter on one of those spinning stools could watch as the cook grilled his cheese sandwich. Parallel to the counter and grill, one long line of high-backed red booths ran along the window. Augusta sat in one of these. In between the booths and counter was a row of small tables. The blue-green walls were bare except for a monkey calendar over the grill and a large, delicately carved wooden clock that hung over the door. It was like a large cuckoo clock except that, as the clock hit twelve and its doors opened, a stage emerged on which several brightly colored figures circled in and out of the clock, dancing to a lively music-box tune. The figures were little men and women chased by Death, a skeleton in black robes holding a scythe. Augusta was enchanted. She'd never seen anything like it. She watched the clockwork people, spellbound, until the music-box tune played itself out and the stage and all its figures retreated.

The place filled quickly with men and women from the offices around, and with workmen, many of whom still wore their army jackets or pants. The booths along the window were the first to fill, then the row of small tables, then the stools at the grill. She would have to move and she hadn't even finished her soup, or touched her sandwich. She spooned down the soup quickly, nervously, eyeing the waitress as she ran back and forth. Why had she come here? She could have bought some fruit at one of the grocers. Going hungry was better than sitting here waiting to be embarrassed. Then there they were, coming in through the café door: a group of women all dressed beautifully, or so it seemed to Augusta. They were office staff by the looks of them, working women. Sophisticated women. Laughing women. They glanced around the café, at Augusta all alone in the large booth, and then started to leave. The waitress caught them and directed them down the aisle toward Augusta. "You're going to have to move, miss," the waitress told her.

"I'm just about finished."

The group of office women stood around the table awkwardly, trying not to look at Augusta, tittering among themselves.

"I'm sorry, miss," said the waitress. "I warned you it would get busy."

"You can put my sandwich in a bag, then. I'll take it with me."

"I'll just move you over there, miss." The waitress took the sandwich and coffee over to the counter, and so Augusta was forced to fold her skirt beneath her and take the last swirling stool. It was all men seated at the counter. She felt the fool sitting among them, and was embarrassed that the laughing women who had taken her booth could surely see the hole in the calf of her stocking. The men at the counter had been talking heatedly and went silent when she took the stool in their midst. She was pretty in her way—sturdy and muscular from farmwork and housework—though she didn't know it then. Her skin was clear and rosy. The young man sitting to her left grinned at her, but she ignored him. She accepted the cook's offer of more water for her teapot and stared straight ahead, at the clothed chimpanzees on the calendar hanging on the wall. After a time the men went back to their conversation and talked around her back, as if she weren't there. They were using the kind of language that made her stomach turn and her muscles flinch as if she had been hit. She found herself hunching over her sandwich, holding her elbows close to her body.

Finally the man to her right said, "Hey! Cut the swearing. There's a lady present!"

She turned to him, to smile her thanks, and met a jangle of medals that hung over his heart. He was an older man,

Manny's age. Had he been an officer? Neither Manny nor Karl had fought; they were farmers and were needed at home. They were pretty, those medals, very impressive.

"Don't mind these," he said. "They don't mean nothing." He grinned and Augusta smiled right back. He held out his hand and she took it. "Joe. Joe Cumberland."

"Augusta Olsen."

After a time he said, "There's a table free now. Why don't we take it?"

"Yes," she said, surprising herself. "Let's."

What did they talk about during that first conversation? She didn't remember now. Likely about nothing at all, the weather and the cost of things, the meaningless chatter that lovers use to test the waters. What was said wasn't so important. How long the conversation went on was. The talk had to last until they agreed on each other. It was a dance they didn't even know they were doing at the time, and one where she took the lead. She brushed away her hair and he scratched his forehead. She touched her lips and he wiped his mouth with his napkin. Even if they didn't know it yet, everybody else could see it. Anyone sitting in the Silver Grill that day could have looked at Augusta and Joe and said, *Those two there, they're lovers, or if they aren't yet, they're going to be.*

Though their words said nothing, their bodies said everything, agreed on everything. And when the timing was right, her hand, moving almost of its own accord, reached over and casually brushed the sensitive hairs on his arm. If he didn't pull away, if he let the touch electrify the hairs on his arm, then the second dance would begin and it would be his turn to take the lead. Men generally forgot the first dance, Augusta thought, remembering only the part they played in seduction, and supposed that *they* were the seducers, the hunters, and women their prey. And yet it was her body that had opened the conversation and offered the first invitation, or Joe would never have been so bold as to take her hand or suggest a walk to someplace hidden away. But then, why should he remember? There was so much more ahead; the dance had only just begun.

− ƒïve −

Today, when the train stopped at Duncan, there was a girl overdressed for daylight standing outside a corner delicatessen across from the station. She was smoking a cigarette. A large handbag was slung over her shoulder, so she likely wasn't a clerk from the deli sneaking a smoke on her break, and in any case the clothes were a dead giveaway. An attempt to impress. An attempt to please. The girl was waiting on a man. There were several empty outdoor tables behind her, so she could have taken a seat and waited there. But no, she was nervous. She was smoking. What if he didn't show? Sitting down and waiting was a kind of risk; it said, *I really want this, I'll wait for you.* Standing and waiting was something else. It said, *I won't wait forever.*

In the first few weeks with Joe, Augusta had sometimes stood outside the café, waiting in such a manner, impatience pressed on her face, though she carried that little white pea of hope in her belly. Later, when she trusted that he would come, she was willing to sit with her cup of tea and plate of cinnamon toast, and wait. She even came to enjoy her few moments alone in the café, surrounded by the voices of the unemployed men as they argued up, up into obscenities on their twirling stools. The laughter of the office women at first frightened her and then later, when she came to trust that she was not the target of it, warmed her. Some of the women even gave her little smiles and nods—as if she were one of them—as they found their tables. But they wouldn't nod or smile if Joe was with her. They understood that he would take up her attention. So she came to enjoy waiting on Joe, watching the music-box clock. She sometimes even felt a sting of annoyance that he turned up so soon, because he would make demands on her; he would expect to be entertained and she had been enjoying her few moments of peace.

Just a day after that first coffee-shop dance, he walked her into a movie theater for a little cool relief. She had bathed for him that morning, standing in the steel tub and pouring water over her head, and had put on her good dress. She went to the café early, before eleven, and chose a table for two this time, facing the clock, so she could both see the figures dance at eleven, and watch the door below. She scanned the line of unemployed men sitting on the stools at the counter to make sure Joe wasn't among them. Then she waited.

Joe arrived at noon, dressed in his army coat, his medals flashing, because a man, even a punctual man, never thought to wait for a woman. He searched for her, and when he found her he sat at her table, not waiting for an invitation. She looked down at her hand stroking the handle of a fork, and then glanced at him, flirty, smiling as Helen had once smiled at Harry. "What say we catch a movie?" he said. "A matinée."

Walking from the summer sidewalk into the movie theater was a relief but a shock, too. From hot to cool, from white concrete light to bottom-of-the-river dark, she went with Joe into hiding. Hot outside, Lord, what a summer it was! The grasses along the fields at home were tinder ready to ignite. Karl's corn crop had leapt toward the sun and was now curling brown at the leaf tips from thirst. Augusta followed Joe into the theater, praying that he couldn't smell the sourness that heat and nerves had draped around her, praying that no one would see them, praying Joe would take her hand in his for the first time.

Joe was tall, a big man, and when she'd spent so many years feeling large and awkward beside Karl it was a relief for Augusta to feel diminutive, and protected. His eyes were dark brown, almost black, and he was balding and proud of it. "A man losing his hair has more vigor, if you get my meaning," he told Augusta. Although in private he was brash and playful in a way Karl would never be, he almost always showed his best manners in public. He stood when Augusta left the table to use the washroom, and took her arm as they walked down the street, as a Victorian gentleman might have.

At first they ate only in the café, or brought lunches to eat on the floor of the hotel room. But later, as they became braver (*brazen*, Augusta thought now), they sometimes took lunches into the park, where anyone could have seen them lying on the grass together or talking over the picnic table. One day a sudden thundershower engulfed their picnic and they were forced to take shelter under the park table until the rain passed, sharing canned kippers and giggling like teenagers.

They were reckless in their infatuation. Joe often drove Augusta out into the countryside, to the farm- and ranch-land surrounding Kamloops, where they waded into fields and chased each other through corn before hiding in it to husk and eat the unripened corn raw. One day they came across a number of hives a farmer had moved into an alfalfa field. Augusta climbed through a barbed-wire fence to raid the hive for a bit of honeycomb and to show off a few of her beekeeping skills. Joe watched her take off the lid and inner hive cover, pull out a frame of honeycomb, and shake off the bees. She cut out a chunk of honeycomb with Joe's jack-knife, and handed it to him as she put the frame back and closed the hive. They ran back to the car with their stolen honeycomb, laughing and licking their fingers. Joe took to calling her his "little honeybee" after that.

He was comfortable like the smell of soap, like clean sheets, like good coffee shared. While Karl blessed Augusta with quick, half-embarrassed pecks, Joe's kisses were a slow, involved exploration of her face. After lovemaking he combed her hair and kissed the nape of her neck. At other times he chased her naked around the hotel room, and tickled her on the floor.

There was that day in the department store when she stopped to run her fingers over a lipstick display. Knowing Joe was watching, she suggestively fondled the bright red plastic lipsticks placed there to demonstrate the color choices. Joe snatched one of the lipsticks from the display, slid off its lid, and said, "Look at me." He painted her mouth right there. The women standing around the makeup counter giggled and a clerk with a made-up face came over and said, "May I help you?"

Joe said, "No thank you. I'm already being helped," and kissed Augusta firmly on the lips as the crowd of women clapped and cheered him on. Then he stood back, recapped the lipstick, and handed it to the clerk. "I'll take this one," he said. Augusta was flushed. She was a movie star playing the part and he was her leading man. It didn't matter that she didn't know his middle name, and couldn't remember if he took his coffee black or with cream or if he preferred his steak well done or raw. Giddy from his attentions and the delight of the crowd, she tripped on the first step of the escalator going down to street level. Joe steadied her and turned to the two women behind them. "You'll have to excuse my wife," he said. "She's had too much to drink."

Augusta giggled and hit him playfully with her purse, but the thought that he'd called her his wife thrilled her. Was it possible? Could it ever be possible? "Do you think we could ever get married?" she said, once they were back at the hotel and both of them were lying naked on the bed, after lovemaking.

Joe turned on his side to face her. He must have seen how important it was that he go on playing the part, that he go on pretending. "If I weren't already married, if you weren't already married, we would."

She didn't push things. She knew so very little about him. She had no real idea what his life was like outside their afternoons together. He never offered the name of his wife, or even suggested whether he had children, though Augusta was forever complaining about Karl and Olaf and her life at the Whorehouse Ranch. In her turn Augusta never mentioned the Reverend. She knew it would be the Reverend, and not Karl, that Joe would be jealous of. When he had occasion to refer to Karl, he called him "the boy."

"Olaf doesn't pay Karl," she told him. "And he works him like a slave."

"If the boy was a man he'd stand up for himself." He grinned at his own small joke.

"I won't hold my breath waiting for that to happen."

"Why do you bother staying? Why not leave?"

"I'm not going back to my father's farm."

"There's other things you can do."

"The jobs at the clinic don't pay enough for me to go out on my own." She half hoped he would offer to help set her up in an apartment, so he could visit her there, but then what would that make her? In any case he didn't make any such offer.

"How about waitressing? Or secretarial work?"

Augusta shook her head. "I don't want to talk about it anymore."

One day she waited for Joe until a quarter to three, drinking too much coffee, reading the cook's newspaper. Having read everything else, she flipped to the obituaries and scanned the page. There was Joe's picture, labeled with another man's name. Augusta felt herself reeling backward, the walls and all the people of the café shooting away from her. Then, just as suddenly, she was shunted back to her booth, her coffee, the newspaper. She squinted at it. The picture wasn't of him; it didn't look anything like him. Why had she thought it was Joe? He arrived at that point, out of breath and sweating, apologizing for missing lunch but not offering any explanation. There was time for one kiss before they both ran to their separate lives.

She didn't tell him that she'd imagined she'd seen his picture in the obituaries. What was there to tell? But she did tell him about some of the visions she'd had. "Isn't that something?" he said.

"You believe me?"

"Sure, why wouldn't I?"

"Karl doesn't."

"There's plenty of things that we'll never see with our own eyes that are true nevertheless. I believe I've lived several lives."

"You have?"

"And you have too. Maybe we were husband and wife and our souls have met up for a little while in this life. Or perhaps I was your dog." Joe took everything lightly, even his own beliefs. It was something that annoyed Augusta, at a time in her life when she took things so seriously.

There was no phone on the Whorehouse Ranch and, though they hadn't discussed the issue, Augusta understood that she could never phone Joe's home. That would make for complications, suspicions. And certainly they never spent the night together. How could either of them possibly explain a night away? So it was an affair conducted in daylight. The closest they came to night was the half-light coming through the closed curtains of the hotel window. She never touched his face in darkness, or saw the change of color in his skin under candlelight. They made love in daylight; argued in the café in daylight; stopped in the middle of the street for a daylight kiss, comforted by the misconception that the city was large enough to hide them.

Now, so many years later, Augusta wondered how it was ever possible for the unfaithful to keep their secrets. If they did, it was only because their mates wanted to be misled. Rose had told Augusta that her husband had once come home with the smell of another woman in his hair, on his fingers. Rose had thought him stupid. A shower might have kept her from knowing what she had already guessed. She thought that maybe he wanted her to know, that the burden of his secret was weighing on him. Augusta wasn't so sure. Men weren't as skilled at picking up scent; they didn't understand the importance of smell the way women did. Perhaps they weren't equipped. She had read that women had keener senses of taste and smell, a side effect of child-bearing and child-rearing. Just as women knew their children, didn't they know their lovers as much by scent as by sight?

Augusta bathed herself, either at the hotel or at home, each afternoon after spending time with Joe. At home she dropped her dress and underwear to the floor and stood in the steel laundry tub in the kitchen, and used a washcloth dipped in water and lathered with soap to wash him from her body. One day Karl caught her like that, naked in the kitchen. He and Olaf were supposed to be out in the field or she would have bathed in the bedroom. She heard a scuffing at the door that she thought was Bitch, but when she turned Karl was standing at the doorway, staring at her, scratching the missing thumb. He didn't say anything at first, then, "Blade on the mower broke."

Augusta turned her back to him and slipped the dress over her head. "Hot," she said.

"You looked so pretty, Augusta." She turned around. It wasn't a thing he said. "We could go upstairs."

"We could."

He took her hand and led her to their bedroom and laid her on the bed with such tenderness that Augusta felt a little hope stirring in her belly. But then he only took off his trousers and underwear, leaving his socks and shirt on, and started to climb onto her.

"No, wait."

"What? You don't want to?"

"I want to."

"We can wait if it's your period."

"No. I wanted to touch first. Kiss a little."

Karl lay on his side beside her and pecked her cheeks: quick, darting kisses that surprised her, made her flinch. "What's the matter?" he said.

"I'd like to go slower. On the mouth, maybe." He tried but his mouth smelled of coffee and milk, his underarms of a morning's work. "You could touch me," she said.

"No, here."

"What?"

"Here." But his hands were rough, his callouses sharp, and his fingers too direct. For weeks he wouldn't even touch her. Now this. She jerked away.

"What's the matter?" he said.

"It hurt."

"Why does it have to be so complicated? Why can't we just do it?"

"Like animals."

"Yeah."

Augusta sat up on her elbows and pulled the skirt of her dress down over her knees. "Do you know I feel nothing when we make love? Nothing at all."

Karl stood and got dressed, and left without looking at her. How could he not know something was up? All the evidence was laid out there in front of him. Even the Reverend had his suspicions. She still met him at Deep Pool each Saturday morning, though she found herself talking less, guarding herself so she didn't let something about Joe slip out. But she couldn't hide the flush that swept over her when she thought of Joe, and she couldn't help thinking of him even as she sat with the Reverend. As she fished she caught herself smiling at the memory of something Joe had said, and once she giggled out loud as she remembered how he'd chased her around the hotel room. "What?" said the Reverend.

"Nothing."

"You seem different these days. Happier."

"I don't know."

"I think maybe Karl's finding a little time for you, a little romantic time?"

"No."

"It's just you've got that shine to you."

"I don't want to talk about it."

"Ah."

"What?"

"Nothing."

There was so much at stake for Augusta. All it would take was someone from Chase, in the city for a day of shopping, wondering who that man was that Augusta Olsen was holding on to. But the unfaithful were careless, and it was their bodies that made them so. Like bees on a mating flight, their bodies told them when to fly, and how high, and never mind the dangers of falling.

"I saw a man bungee-jumping today," said Augusta. She poured them all more tea, and offered Karl the plate of sandwiches.

"Fools," said Rose. "Paying money to jump off a bridge."

"I don't know. If my hip wasn't going on me, I'd give it a try." She wanted to feel again that thrill of sudden nothingness under her, the quick drop at Deep Pool. The bungee-jumping business she had seen today was a small building on an old train trestle over a deep gorge. It was parallel to the trestle they were traveling over, and the engineer stopped the train so they could get a good look at both the gorge and the bungee-jumper taking a dive. Esther leaned forward and watched with Augusta. "Imagine people jumping off that thing," said Esther, "with nothing but a rope tied around their foot to keep them from falling off the planet. I'll never understand why anyone would want to do a thing like that."

"Pardon me?" said Augusta.

"Bungee-jumping."

"Ah."

"They go naked sometimes, those bungee-jumpers. That outfit lets them jump for free if they do it naked. Last year an old lady, must have been seventy-five, jumped off that bridge naked, for some charity." Augusta's hand went to her bosom in remembrance of the ache she'd had there last time she'd attempted to run. "If I did that I'd have my boobs around my ears," said Esther.

Augusta grinned. "We got a letter at the seniors' center. They were making a movie about Doukhobors and wanted a bunch of old men and women willing to walk around naked in front of the cameras."

"No!"

"I couldn't believe it at first. But my friend Rose and I thought about doing it. You would be in a crowd of people, all naked. When would you ever be able to do a thing like that?"

"Did you?"

"No, of course not."

"Why not?"

"I don't know. What if my daughter saw? Or the people at church?"

"What if?"

"I couldn't bring myself to do it."

"It would've been a lot less dangerous than jumping off a bridge naked," said Esther. "You wouldn't have risked breaking your neck." The two of them watched as a young man leapt into the air with his arms open wide. Augusta felt the thrill of terror with him.

She and Joe had been nearly as reckless as that jumper, taking few precautions against either the possibility of pregnancy, or the chance of getting caught. One awful time Augusta pushed open the café door, smiled at one of the office workers she recognized, and saw Percy Martin sitting on a stool at the counter. He was gesturing as he talked to the man next to him; his feet just barely grazed the floor. Augusta backed out of the café and marched quickly around the corner, out of view of the café window. She was terrified. She wasn't sure whether or not Percy Martin had seen her.

She settled her heart down to a manageable flutter and went back around the corner to wait for Joe, with her back to the window. Looking back now, she wondered why she hadn't simply given up on lunch with Joe that day. Her actions made no sense. When Joe had finally arrived and wanted to go inside for lunch as always, she had come up with some excuse. She couldn't remember now what she'd said, so much had happened since, but she still remembered the emotions attached to that excuse: guilt because she was lying; fear that Joe would insist they go in; shame because the excuse was so transparent. Why didn't she tell Joe the truth? Why didn't she say, *There's somebody in there from my hometown, Joe. Somebody who could cause me a lot of trouble.* Why didn't she say that? Because she was still so young, and fear made her lie stupidly. Joe didn't push her, didn't insist on the truth and didn't make her go into the café. Likely he knew from the expression on her face what was up, what was at risk. He simply took her by the elbow, as a father might take the arm of a daughter, and they strolled down the street and around the corner before he stopped her dead on the sidewalk and kissed her so hard her lips pushed uncomfortably against her teeth. But that day didn't start a trend of meeting at some other place, as she had hoped, and for a long time after that she entered the café cautiously, and sometimes waited outside. Percy Martin didn't come back—not to the café.

At Christmas she and Joe exchanged small gifts—nylons for her, chocolates for him—things that wouldn't be noticed. His gift to her was accompanied by a card that she was forced to throw away before returning home. For Valentine's Day she was more inspired. That morning, before driving to Kamloops, she drove out to her home farm to collect honeycomb from the hive in the roof of the honey house. The whole way there, she fretted over what excuse she could come up with, in case Manny was home. But all the worry was for nothing; he'd gone into town, as he often did on Mondays.

There was a small access to the attic of the honey house, a square door at the apex. Armed with a lantern, a knife, and a syrup can, Augusta climbed a ladder to the access and wriggled through. The wild honeycombs hung from the rafters, one after the other, like the folds of a well-pressed party dress. Each comb was nearly heart-shaped, pointed at the bottom, rounded at the top, but without the cleavage. There were no bees on the outside combs; they were huddled in a ball, to keep warm, within the center combs. It was a simple task to cut the outside comb from the rafters and place it upright in the large syrup can. When she got back to the car she cut a V into the top of the honeycomb, so it was heart-shaped. After wiping her hands on a wet towel she had brought with her, she tied a red ribbon on the handle of the syrup can and attached a note that said, "From your little honeybee."

Joe was delighted. He took the honeycomb into the hotel room with them and smeared honey all over her, and himself. As he pointed out, they'd have to use it up, as he couldn't take it home with him that night. They licked honey off each other, and ate honeycomb until they were sick of the stuff. After lovemaking, they took a long, hot bath to scrub the honey off each other, and even after that Augusta found honey in her hair on the drive home.

Shortly after Valentine's Day, Karl came home saying Olaf had hired Percy Martin for lambing. "Not him," said Augusta.

"Why not?"

What could she tell him? *I don't want him working in case he saw me with Joe; in case he opens his big mouth.* Percy was a good worker, when he was sober. "I don't trust him."

"You won't see anything of him. We won't see him much. He'll be working the nights, once the lambs start coming."

But Karl was wrong. One morning, just as she was getting dressed to meet Joe, Percy Martin mounted the stairs to the second floor, smelling to high heaven of liquor. When she opened her bedroom door, he stopped his progress up the stairs for a moment and stared at her. At first she said nothing and stared right back. He was a tiny man with unnaturally short legs, a hairless bundle of bones, though when he walked he moved with the nervous, frightening speed of a rodent. He chewed something—tobacco? gum?— all the time; a film of saliva was always at the corner of his mouth. Under the stench of booze he stank the same high unwashed bachelor stink of the sheepherders Karl hired in the summers.

"What are you doing here?" she said. "Get out." She flung out her arm and half expected him to turn tail and run, but Percy Martin took one slow step up the stairs after another.

"Hear you're trying to get me fired."

"I have a right to my say. I don't want a rapist working on this farm."

"Don't get high and mighty with me, lady," he said. "I know you." Augusta took a step back. "You don't think I saw. But I saw."

"What?" said Augusta, but she already knew. "What are you talking about?"

"You're a fancy woman, ain't you? I seen you with that man in the city. And with the Reverend. Seems like you got men all over. I figure my money's as good as theirs."

"Get out of my house. Now."

He kept coming. "Is it babies you're after, then? I remember Karl got mumps when he was grown. He can't give you babies, can he? All's you had to do was ask. I can give you babies." He held out his hands as if to say, *Here I am.*

Augusta made a grab for the bedroom door, to shut it on him. But he leapt for her and pulled her by the waist toward him. She stumbled down to the first step and they wrestled there for what seemed like an eternity. She pushed one hand

away and another was there, grabbing at her clothes, rough-
ing her skin, pulling her hair. She gave one tremendous
push and suddenly Percy Martin was falling, arms and legs
flung up and over. He hollered as he hit the walls, the steps,
and landed on the floor at the foot of the stairs. She thought
him dead. She wished him dead. But he got up from the
floor and headed off outside. He didn't look back at her,
because she was already laughing from the top of the stairs,
laughing hard and high from someplace deep inside her;
laughing and laughing though her outsides trembled,
though damp fear stained her blouse.

Joe was waiting on her that day. "Where you been? I
thought something happened."

"A man came into the house, while Karl and Olaf were
out. A man who saw me here with you. He came right into
the house while I was upstairs and offered me money. He
thinks I'm a whore." Augusta started crying and began to
stand, to leave. "I can't do this anymore. I've got to get out
of here."

Joe grabbed her by the wrist. "Sit down," he said. "Here."
He handed her a napkin and she blew her nose. "Did this
man touch you?"

"He tried. I pushed him down the stairs."

Joe laughed. "You pushed him?"

"It's not funny. He scared me. And he knows about you
and me."

"Did you tell the boy about this?"

"No. He won't be back until this evening. I can't tell
him."

"You have to. This man is dangerous."

"He works for Karl and Olaf. He's one of the herders."

"Then you've got to tell him."

"What can I tell him? I don't know what to do."

Joe took both her hands in his. "We'll work this out."

"No. You can't have anything to do with this. Don't you see? You've got to stop coming here. If I deny things and then someone else sees us, that's it. Where would I go? What would I do? And what if they found out your name and they phoned and got your wife?"

"Oh, Christ. Who is this Percy guy? I'll punch him out."

"That would make things worse."

Joe released her hands as the waitress came by with menus and coffee. After she was gone, Augusta and Joe sat at the table in silence, staring off in opposite directions. "So you think we should stop seeing each other," said Joe.

"And neither of us should ever come here again, to this café."

"Too bad. It was growing on me."

"Yeah."

"I love you, you know."

"Are you ever going to leave your wife?"

"No, probably not."

"Then what good does it do telling me a thing like that?" They sat in silence for a few moments longer and then Augusta stood and, without even saying good-bye, fled the café.

She tried giving up her Saturday outings with the Reverend, but he wouldn't hear of it. "Something you're not telling me?"

"No. Nothing. It's just, Olaf gives Karl such a hard time about me fishing with you. He thinks the town will talk."

"I see."

"It's silly, I know. I just don't want you hurt."

"I think I understand."

Augusta saw that he did understand, that he'd guessed everything, or enough of it. Augusta looked down at her hands. "I'm sorry," she said.

"If there's something you want to talk about—"

"No."

When she got home from talking to the Reverend that afternoon, Olaf wouldn't talk to her. As they had little to say to each other at the best of times, she didn't really notice this until suppertime, when she offered him the bowl of peas. "Peas?" she said. She might have been talking to a wall for all the reaction she got. Olaf went on chewing and staring out the window.

"Peas?" she said again, louder, thinking he hadn't heard. But he had heard; he was ignoring her.

Karl took the bowl. "Father, Augusta asked if you wanted peas."

"I'll have peas," Olaf said.

"Whatever are you angry over now?" said Augusta.

Olaf chewed his peas.

"Father," said Karl. "Augusta asked what's the matter."

"She knows what she done. I'm not going to say any more."

It was at that point that she realized Percy Martin had got around to talking to Olaf. Olaf never talked to her again, not until their last big argument. Karl became interpreter between them, and it was a fussy business getting anything done that way. Augusta had to talk through Karl if she wanted anything of Olaf, and Olaf simply operated as if she no longer existed, as if she were invisible.

Things got very bad after that. Men who had once tipped their hats to her now took liberties as they would never have dared before. Other women's husbands rubbed their crotches into her backside as they passed by her in store aisles, or groped her as she stood in line waiting to pay for her groceries. Doing chores in town became a game of dodging; she was aware of each man's approach, and stepped off the sidewalk, onto the street, to avoid him. She shook her head away from exploring fingers and learned to fold her body into itself, to make it smaller than she thought possible, so a man passing by would have no excuse to touch her. But she found no defense against the women. The women threw hard stares at her. Some even spat at her feet as she passed them on the sidewalk. Their weapons against her were words, whispered to each other in coffee shops, in grocery aisles, in churchwomen's league meetings.

It was his wife, Lilian, who first brought the gossip to the Reverend's attention, gossip she'd heard at the churchwomen's league meeting. Likely it was Martha Rivers who started that ball rolling; she was a leading member of the league. "They're saying Augusta is soliciting," Lilian told him. "To make a little money, as Karl isn't bringing anything in. They've gone back to calling that place the Whorehouse Ranch, instead of the W. H."

The Reverend stormed into the next assembled meeting of the ladies of the league and, with Lilian dressed so beautifully in blue at his side, gave them hell. "I heard your talk about Augusta Olsen. I don't know who started it, or why, but I've never been so ashamed of the lot of you. She's stuck way up there, and who of you has visited her? Or paid her a kind word? Instead you make up stories about her. Making her life miserable. There are those in this room—in this town—whose minds are smaller than a thimble. I advise you to keep your mouths shut, unless you've got something worthwhile to say, and get on with your meeting."

The Reverend told her all about it at the next Saturday's fishing, his face flushed with excitement. Augusta interrupted him as he repeated the bit about their minds fitting into thimbles. "You shouldn't have done that."

"Why not?"

"They'll think you're involved. They'll read things into our fishing trips."

"I suppose they've done that already."

"But you getting mad like that won't stop the talk. It'll just inflame it. Now Martha Rivers and her gaggle will have another bit of gossip to hand around, how you defended me. They'll speculate on why."

"But Lilian was right there with me, standing by me."

"You don't know what it's like, do you? I could lose everything. Olaf could kick me off the ranch."

The Reverend laughed. "That would be the worst, wouldn't it?"

"This is serious. I'm afraid you've made things worse." And she was right. That was why those boys thought they could throw rocks at her the next Saturday, when she was all tidy for town. She was walking down the wood plank sidewalk by the train station, heading for the truck, when she heard the first stone land by the heel of her shoe. Then another. Then one hit her shin. She turned. Three boys ran off, stones dropping from their hands. They knew there was no one willing to protect her. The Reverend's defense of her had fueled the flames; if he did more he would be implicated, if he wasn't already. Karl would never say anything. Olaf would have picked up a stone and joined them if he'd been there. There was nothing she could do. She had put up with poverty and insults, and now rocks. She'd put up with a husband who didn't touch her for fear of disturbing his

father. Where would she go, she wondered, if Olaf saw fit
to throw her out of the house? Manny and the cold silent
farm were all that awaited her, and she doubted that he
would take her back in any case. She had made her bed. If
she chose not to lie in it, she would have to move to the city.
She would have to find work. All she knew in the world
was cooking and cleaning. And where would she find the
funds to set herself up in some other place? She didn't even
have bus fare.

‐ Ｓｉｘ ‐

When Augusta found she was pregnant she was, in turns, thrilled and terrified. She longed for a baby of her own, but she knew the child couldn't be Karl's. In the three weeks it took to find the courage to tell Karl, she brooded over the day Helen had told them she was pregnant. It had been a Sunday; there had been roast beef, scalloped potatoes, a layered jelly mold for dessert. As Harry Jacob was now back at the reserve, her mother took more time on their meals. "I'm having a baby," she said.

Manny stopped eating, his fork in midair. "A baby? We can't be having a baby."

"Well, we are."

Augusta wondered why Helen chose to tell Manny then, with her sitting right there with them. Shouldn't a wife tell her husband about a pregnancy first, privately, before telling the children? She felt as she did when, at night, she heard the rhythmic thumping of her parents' bed legs against the uneven floor overhead; she was listening in on something that shouldn't be overheard.

"We're too old for chasing around with babies," said Manny.

"Well, there's nothing I can do about it now, is there?"

"Isn't there some woman thing you can do?"

"A woman thing?"

"To stop it?"

Helen stared at Manny until he went red. He pushed his plate away from him.

"That's not going to do us any good. Here it is. We've got to accept it."

Manny sat back and crossed his arms. His nostrils flared as he breathed in. "It's mine, is it?"

"Whose else would it be?"

"Could anything go wrong?" said Augusta. "Could it make you sick?"

"Sick? Like what?"

"Like what I saw. Out in the rosemary."

"Enough with that," said Manny.

"Nothing's going to go wrong," said Helen.

"I don't mind there being a baby," said Augusta. "I'd like a sister."

"That's good, dear. You'll be a help."

Manny pushed back his chair, took down a gun from the rack, and stomped outside. "Go see what your father's doing," said Helen. "I want a bit of time in the house to myself."

Manny was walking the sorrel mare from the stall as Augusta reached the barn. Along with the gun he carried the bullwhip he used in training the horses. "What're you doing?" Augusta said.

"Taking her for a walk."

"Can I come?"

"You may not want to."

Augusta trailed behind Manny anyway, stumbling over wheat stubble, watching the rear of the sorrel mare sway and her tail flick at the flies. She licked her teeth, tasting the jelly dessert, thinking of Helen's jar of King George one-cent pieces she had counted and admired, once again, after church that morning. She thought of the flat, tart taste of those pennies. She expected nothing as she followed Manny and the mare to the benchland.

She stopped following when they reached the stubble of burnt fallen trees at the edge of the field several yards away from the old homesteaders' well. She knew now. Manny lifted the split boards away from the hole of the well and threw them to the side. "Why do you have to kill her?"

"She's too wild. She'll never be of any use to anyone."

"You could sell her back to the Indians."

"They wouldn't have her either."

"I'll have her. I'll tame her."

"You'd get yourself killed in the process."

"No I wouldn't. She's never thrown me. You don't have to do this. Please!" She started to cry.

Manny stared at her angrily, silencing her. "If you're not going to help, go home."

Augusta took several steps backward but stayed there, watching, crying silently. Manny took the halter off the horse and stepped the sorrel mare slowly backward, cracking the bullwhip to one side of her. She stomped and snorted, threw her head back, and whinnied. When her back feet met the hole, Manny threw his weight into her chest, pushing her backward. The mare snorted and shuddered as she lost her footing and her great body thundered down the neck of the well. Manny stumbled and almost followed her; Augusta's arm jerked forward as he fell to the ground, landing on his chest only inches from the hole. He brushed himself off and picked up the rifle, bouncing it slightly as if weighing, appraising, a piece he might buy. Then he lay back down on his chest, set the gun to his shoulder at an awkward angle, shooting down the well. Augusta didn't look away. There was nothing to see, only her father's back jerking suddenly as if he had just shot a gopher.

Later that evening, in the light from the Coleman, Augusta watched Manny take down his gun again, already loaded, from the gun rack.

"Now what are you doing?" she said. "You're not thinking of killing one of the others?"

"No."

"Where you going, then?"

"Out."

"Can I come?"

"If you keep your mouth shut."

She followed him to the field, where the wheat stooks stood silver in the moonlight. The wheat stubble crunched beneath his steps and she could see the ribs in the bottom of his boots, the moon was that bright. When he stopped and put his hand out for her to stop and leveled his gun, she waited, breathless, as three does and a buck came into view. She waited as he waited, and then breathed out as he sighed and lowered the gun. Together they watched the deer graze on the stooks until, scared by a twig snapping in the woods behind, the deer bounced off across the fields.

Manny thundered around the farm all that November and into December, hammering loose boards on the barn into place, fixing broken fences that wouldn't be used until the following summer, tearing down the old shed that for years had sagged under the weight of snow. Helen, for her part, busied herself by preparing her bees for the winter, fitting wood at the base of the hive to reduce the entrance against mice, and wrapping heavy black tar paper around the hives to protect them from the cold. Bees spent the winter closed into themselves, clustered into a ball, eating honey and doing the jitterbug. Those at the center of the ball were warm enough, but the bees on the outside were cold. They buzzed and jittered just as kids stamped their feet and rubbed their hands to warm themselves in the winter schoolyard. The agitation of these few bees spread to the bees one layer down, then two layers and three, until there was a cascade of excitement rippling through the hive. They all trembled and flapped their wings, generating heat that warmed the whole hive. As the temperature went up, the bees calmed down, until the hive cooled off and the frenzy of excitement started again.

That was pretty much how Helen spent that winter, too. She claimed an empty upstairs room as her own and often locked herself inside. She took few meals downstairs and instead ate plate after plate of cinnamon toast, then scrounged in the cupboards for the last cookie or piece of cake Augusta might have had time to make earlier in the week. Augusta would hear her pacing the floor overhead and when, a few minutes later, she went to take her mother a cup of tea, she'd find Helen limp in sleep in her chair.

Helen even hid when company came, and so did Manny; he simply walked away across the snow-covered field as if he hadn't seen the visitors coming down the road. Both of them would leave Augusta to turn their infrequent guests away. One day in December, Helen was standing at the kitchen window, nursing a cup of tea, when she said, "Oh, good gracious."

"What?" said Augusta. She was seated at the kitchen table, peeling apples for a pie. The whole kitchen smelled of them.

"I don't want to see those gossiping women."

Augusta stood and looked out the window with Helen. Martha Rivers was driving her mother, Mrs. Grafton, up the driveway in a truck. "You like Mrs. Grafton," said Augusta.

"Tell them I've gone to town."

"They'll see the truck is here."

"Tell them I skied, then."

Augusta laughed. "Skied?"

"I don't know. Tell them anything. Just make them go away." She fled upstairs to her room, forcing Augusta to greet the women and to tell them, stuttering, that her mother was sick and couldn't be disturbed.

That was a long, cold winter. When the soil finally warmed and the trees began leafing out, Helen, heavy in her pregnancy, unwrapped her hives to find half lost to starvation and disease. She could tell that two of the remainder had lost their queens. A hive that had lost its queen was frantic; the bees buzzed loudly around it in a restless, disorganized fashion, anxious and unsure. Helen might have been one of those bees, flying from one thing to another, starting chore after chore but never finishing anything, leaving Augusta to pick up the pieces behind her. Less than a month before she was due, all the craziness that had been building inside her blasted its way out onto a helpless wild creature that happened into the yard.

When Augusta was a girl there were porcupines everywhere, waddling comically from beneath stacks of hay in the fields as she forked the hay into cocks. Her father would go after them with a pitchfork, infrequently killing them, most often driving them into the bush or up a tree. On a Saturday when Manny was down at Deep Pool fishing, Augusta and her mother were hanging laundry on the line when a porcupine appeared in the yard. Helen gave a little shriek. There it was, within a rock's throw, moving in its strange rolling gait straight for them. The porcupine was no real threat but Helen wasn't thinking straight, or maybe some part of her had seen what was coming at her in three weeks' time and her fear bundled itself and took the form of that porcupine. "Get the gun," she yelled.

"It's all right," said Augusta. "I can scare him off."

"I said get the gun!"

"All right. All right."

Augusta made a dash for the house and took the .22 repeater from the gun rack and loaded it before running back outside. She aimed at the porcupine, which was still approaching the laundry line, but the little prickly thing looked so comical, so harmless in its way, that she couldn't imagine killing it. She let the gun drop.

Her mother said, "Give it here."

Helen was a terrible shot, even at this close range. While the porcupine tried desperately to waddle away, Helen fired and fired at it, kicking up dust around it several times before finally hitting it. With the very first shot, though, something in her manner changed. Blood crept into her cheeks and with each bullet her face darkened further. She looked at first angry, then furious, then enraged, and finally sinister. It was crazy behavior. She reloaded and went on firing at the porcupine, hitting and missing, until its body was a bundle of prickly red pulp. Then, perversely, she invited

Augusta inside the house for tea, leaving the body of the porcupine where it was for Manny to dispose of when he returned home. Helen was triumphant as she served them both tea in those rose-patterned teacups, but sat shame-faced as they ate their biscuits, and as she cleared away the dishes she looked sad.

The night Augusta told Karl she was pregnant was the only time she ever saw him close to tears. He didn't cry, but she could see the effort in his face to keep the tears back. All he said was "Yeah?" and then, grinning, "I wanted a baby too, you know."

It was all he could say in words, but what he didn't have words for he said in flowers. He hunted the hills and brought down bundles of buttercups and glacier lilies that blossomed right in the snow, cutting yellow swaths across mountain slopes. Then wild roses and wildflower bou-quets of yellow bells, shooting stars, bluebottles, and white mayflowers that bloomed together in hillside gar-dens so lovely that it appeared God had planted them Himself. He brought lupines, white daisies, pearly ever-lastings, fireweed, and handfuls of what he called "sun-flowers," which weren't a true sunflower but flannel root, which turned the hills above Chase and the South Thompson gold. Karl so wanted that child, and delighted in Augusta for giving it to him.

Pregnancy sat well on Augusta. People talked of women blossoming in pregnancy and that was just what she did. Her skin shone and her senses came alive. Colors were brighter, smells stronger, touch more electrifying, tastes capricious. It was as if she'd never smelled a flower before, never touched the fur on a kitten, never seen the blue in the sky or in Karl's eyes, or never tasted the salt in a pickle. Her body's craving for salt made a thief of her. The one indulgence that Karl allowed himself—that Olaf allowed him—was Hereford brand corned beef. Karl added a can to his little stock each trip to town, so there might be five cans of bully beef in the cupboard at a time. The craving made her take down a can and open it on the sly, all the time watching out the window in case Karl or Olaf came down from the mountains for the day. She ate half the can in one sitting, then wrapped the rest in wax paper, tucked it in a syrup can so Bitch wouldn't get at it, and put the lard can in the water trough, where Karl and Olaf would never look, ready for the next craving that came over her.

She was guiltily eating Karl's bully beef by the water trough when she heard Joe on the other side of the house, in the front yard. He was swearing for all he was worth, as if he'd hit his thumb with a hammer or banged his shin on the sharp edge of a board. Augusta dropped the last bits of bully beef on the ground, where one of the barn cats was sure to clean up the evidence, and wiped her mouth and hands on her apron as she ran around the house to see why he had come. What if Karl or Olaf came down with the horses to get supplies and salt for the sheep and caught him there? "Joe?" she cried out. But when she reached the front of the house she stopped short. There was no one in the yard. There were no tire tracks or footprints in the deep dust of the road. She trotted around the other side of the house, and then to the barns, and finally back inside the house, but there was no sign of anyone having been there.

Augusta's labor pains went on for twenty-six hours, so long that her doctor gave up on her and went home not once but twice. The nurses finally gave her a supper of roast beef, potatoes, peas, and rice pudding, and that meal must have done it, because not an hour after Augusta finished eating, Joy was pushing her way out.

It seemed at the time that the nurses swept Joy up before Augusta had a chance to see her, let alone hold her, but Augusta couldn't be sure, as her mind was still floating on a slurry of anesthetic. She didn't know if her baby was whole and well or somehow ill. All she knew was that she'd given birth to a girl. She wouldn't see her baby until nursing time. In those days a baby was supposed to sleep for four hours between feedings, and a mother was supposed to ignore her if she cried.

Augusta was left alone in the recovery room, for how long she had no idea. Under the hospital gown she was wearing the binder they put on new mothers at the time: a long, wide, elastic piece of material that was wrapped snugly around the woman and pinned into place with safety pins. It was thought that a binder kept the recovering uterus stable and in place. The baby got one like it, to prevent the hernias that prolonged crying was generally felt to cause. She lay half dreaming, half thinking over her choice of name. Early in her pregnancy she had decided on the name Joy if the baby was a girl—it was the name she had given to her own baby sister. During her mother's pregnancy, Augusta had closed the door to her room and wrapped her homemade dolls in towels, and one by one she had cradled them in her arms, cooing to them, tucking the towels beneath their sock chins. She could almost feel the weight of a real child in her arms, and smell the peachy sweetness of baby skin. She was delighted at the coming of this child, at the thought of having a sister, and of having a baby to care for, because she would surely care for the baby when her mother worked around the farm or went into town. It was as if she were becoming a mother herself. But now it seemed wrong to name her daughter after a dead child, and one who had caused so much trouble to boot. Karl had wanted to give a daughter a "real name," as he put it; he wanted to name her Blenda, after his mother. But Augusta didn't like that idea at all, and had been so set at the time on the name Joy that she wouldn't hear of any other. Karl had given in. Now the thing had been decided, and she would look like a fool if she changed her mind after making such a fuss.

The lights overhead were too bright; they hurt her eyes and made the white walls seem foggy and distant. Her body felt numb and sounds were magnified, distorted; she felt as if she were underwater, struggling to surface into wakefulness. The squeaky footsteps of a nurse's shoes came down the hall toward the closed door, then turned and receded. Another nurse's footsteps passed by. Then it was quiet for a long time. She closed her eyes and her thoughts drifted, slipped away. She could still smell the nail-polish-remover scent of the ether they'd used on her.

Out of the silence came two voices that seemed hushed and disembodied. Augusta opened her eyes. Although she thought the voices came from outside the recovery room door, she had heard no one approaching. She thought the voices must belong to nurses. "I've never had to do this before," said one voice.

"At least you don't have to tell her yourself. The head nurse gets that job."

"How does she do it? Does she just come out and say it? 'Mrs. Olsen, your father has drowned'?"

There was a pause during which Augusta imagined that the nurse shrugged or nodded in reply, and then the voices became indistinct. They didn't recede, they simply diminished. There were no footsteps walking away and Augusta began to doubt what she'd heard. She tried to move, to find out what all this was about. Her father drowned? But nothing would move; her body seemed caught in the moment of the young nurse's telling, frozen in it. She drifted in and out of the dream world the anesthetic had induced until the recovery-room door opened and Karl came in.

Augusta took hold of his arm and asked him immediately, before saying hello, "Is Dad all right?"

"Manny? He's fine. I saw him in town."

Augusta lay back on her stack of pillows. "I dreamed he drowned. Tell him not to go swimming. He takes chances, by himself."

"Manny's not going to drown. In any case you can tell him yourself. He's coming by tonight."

Manny did visit the maternity ward that evening, wearing the clothes he wore to milk his herd, smelling of manure and sour dairy, carrying a fistful of roadside daisies that he laid on the table beside her bed. He was looking old, tired. His clothes hung on him. She was glad none of the women in the ward were from Chase; his appearance shamed her. "You haven't been eating," she said.

"I eat well enough."

"You forget when you're alone. You forget to eat."

He scratched the back of his neck. "How you been doing?"

"Fine."

"A girl, eh?"

"Yes."

"What you call her? Joy?"

"Yes."

"Funny name. No name at all. Should have named her after your mother."

"She's my baby. I'll name her what I want." Then, "You didn't come for supper that time, like you said you would."

"Well."

"You could come. You could have supper with us. Sunday."

"All right. Sunday."

"You'll come?"

"I'll come."

"You sure you'll come? 'Cause I'm not going to go to all that fuss if you're not going to come. With the baby and all."

"I'll come. I said I'd come!"

Augusta pulled the sheets up over her chest. "I dreamed you drowned."

"What? Drowned? Crazy dream, that."

"It wasn't a dream, exactly. I heard these voices outside the door—afterwards, you know, when I was in the recovery room. I was alone and I heard these voices."

"You hearing voices, they better keep you in the hospital for a week longer, eh?" He grinned. He hadn't shaved that day, or for a week, by the look of him. Coarse gray hairs prickled at his chin.

"Promise me you won't go swimming like you do. You take chances on the river."

Augusta sat back in her pillows and Manny scratched his neck and glanced around the room at the other women in their beds. Then the nurse with a mole at her lip brought Joy in for her feeding and asked Manny to leave, and there wasn't another chance for discussion of the matter.

That was Manny's only visit. Olaf never came, never offered a word of congratulations. He had ignored her through her pregnancy, and would go on ignoring her, and Joy, once she brought the baby home. She half expected a visit from Mrs. Grafton, and dreaded one from Martha Rivers, but neither woman turned up. The Reverend was her only other visitor, and he dropped by for a few minutes carrying a little crocheted blanket that Lilian had made for Joy. "How's the mother?" he said, grinning.

"All right."

He looked around the room at the other women and lowered his voice. "Guess you won't have much time for fishing for a while."

"No, I don't suppose so."

"I'll hold your spot. It's no fun fishing without you." He turned the hat in his hands. "Pass my congratulations on to Karl."

"Sure, sure I will."

He leaned down and kissed her cheek. "Don't worry," he whispered. "It'll all blow over."

He turned and walked out without saying good-bye, though he stopped at the doorway and glanced back at her briefly. She spent the rest of that week in the ward with nothing to do except brood over the dream—or vision or hallucination—that she had had in the recovery room. She came to doubt she'd heard anything at all.

Augusta and Rose cleared away the lunch dishes. "Karl," she said, "do you remember me telling you my father was going to drown?"

"Something about it."

"What do you remember?"

"You said you had a dream or something like that, and you thought he was going to die."

"You remember when I had that dream?"

"You were in the hospital. The week Joy was born."

"And then he did die."

Karl nodded. "Why're you asking?"

She'd half hoped that she'd remembered wrong, that she'd had that vision of Manny's death after the fact and somehow remembered it the other way around. It would have given her less reason to believe in the odd dream pointing to her own death that she'd had on the train earlier in the day. But that vision of Manny's death must have happened the way she remembered it, and she remembered it all so clearly.

She had been packing her things, getting ready to leave the hospital, when the young nurse, all starched cap and apron, came into the ward, looking so concerned that Augusta immediately asked, "What's wrong with my baby?"

"It's not your baby."

"What, then? What's happened?"

"The head nurse wants to see you."

This was when Augusta knew that the voices she had heard in the recovery room were right. "You haven't done this before," she said to the nurse.

"Pardon?"

Augusta didn't say another word. She felt drowsy or drunk as she followed the young woman to the head nurse's office. The room felt familiar though she'd never set foot in it before. There was a monkey calendar on the wall, exactly like the one at the Silver Grill. On the nurse's desk were a white ceramic coffee cup holding pencils and pens;

a photograph of two red-haired children, a girl and boy; several file folders; books; a telephone; and a bouquet of white daisies in a blue glass vase. Augusta turned to the head nurse and watched the nurse's mouth tell her what the disembodied voices had told her the day she had Joy.

There were times, like this one, when she felt she was simply walking through the moment, knowing every word, every sound, every motion. Life was a joke heard for the third time, the punch line long ago given away. Living wasn't living at such times; it was acting. She felt distanced from her own life, dead to it. How many more times would she take these same steps, speak these same words? She was walking the same life over and over until, like an old carpet in a hallway, its fibers wore away and she could see clear through them.

That day, the day her father drowned, Karl drove Augusta and Joy home down the highway that followed the South Thompson, the river that had claimed Manny. "I can't believe it," she said.

"What?"

"Do you remember what I said, about Dad drowning?"

"Of course."

"Did you tell him?"

"No."

"I told him. He went anyway."

"That was his choice."

His irritability stopped her from saying more. She stared at the deceiving calm of the South Thompson. It looked so lovely, hardly capable of taking a man's life. It wore the wide infinity of the sky, and made her believe that if she sank into those waters she would come out in some other place, a mirror to this one. Manny had once told her that the Indians living on the other side of the river believed a whole other world existed on the underside of the water, populated by fish and other creatures who acted like humans. Maybe this was where her father had been heading when he'd stepped into the South Thompson and been swept away. Maybe some small craziness inside him had known that the other place was there, underneath all that flowing water, and was bound to discover it. His soggy body had bounced against rocks and surfaced, but maybe the part that was truly her father had come up again in that place where the fish had souls, and it was human beings who were the myths and legends, mere stories told to fish children.

Augusta refilled all their teacups and took a cookie for herself, then carried her cup over to the balcony again. Rose followed her, and together they looked down at the hive in the garden below. A loose ball of bees still hovered in front of it. "Did I ever tell you there are undertaker bees?" asked Augusta.

"No," said Rose. "Surprisingly, I can't recall you ever telling me that."

"Most bees die outside, while foraging. But some die inside the hives. The undertaker bees carry the dead body through the hive and deposit it outside the opening. They leave it there a day or two until it's dried out a bit, so it's lighter. Then one of them collects the dead bee and flies into the sky, away from the hive, where it drops the body. Isn't that a fitting funeral for a bee? A sky burial."

"A hell of a lot more exciting than the funerals we go to," said Rose.

Augusta nodded and ate her cookie. It seemed they were always going to somebody's funeral, a man or woman from the seniors' center, someone they had played cards with the week before. Augusta couldn't say that she had ever got used to it, exactly. On the other hand, funerals were social events at this stage of life, a chance to catch up with friends still living. They were dry affairs. The funeral home and crematorium in town were plunked down in the center of a treeless cement parking lot and were surrounded by seniors' housing complexes. (A cunning bit of development there, she thought. The law of supply and demand in sublime action.) The services were getting to be repetitive. They were made to sing all the old favorites: "Abide with Me"; "The Lord Is My Shepherd"; "Rock of Ages"; and "In the Garden" ("He walks with me, and He talks with me, and He tells me I am his own"). Augusta didn't want anything so dour sung at her funeral. She'd have them sing "Morning Has Broken." None of this sulking around her dead body as if that were all there was left of her.

Death hadn't been handled by strangers when her mother had passed away. When Augusta came home from school to learn that her mother had just died giving birth to a dead child, she struggled right along with the ladies of the churchwomen's league as they carried the body from the bed downstairs to the parlor. She stood behind them as they wiped her mother down, and she cut that good navy dress clean along the back so her mother could be buried in it. She helped lower the body into the wooden casket, and combed out her mother's long hair so it spread over the white lace pillow she was laid to rest upon. She was seeing death through. At just fifteen years old she was asked to do it, and she did it, even if her father could not.

Her father had been there when she came home from school. He had been sitting at the kitchen table—sitting perfectly still amid the sea of busy churchwomen. He hadn't shaved that day and was wearing the grimy plaid shirt he'd done chores in that morning. Augusta had wrapped her arms around his neck, but he'd taken her wrists in his hands and yanked her arms away and whispered, *hissed*, "What will the women think? Get away with you!"

Then he'd stood and left the house and sat on a stump round back of the barn, staring off into space. He didn't lift a finger to help with any part of the funeral preparation. He left it all to the women of the church. But Augusta had to be useful, Martha Rivers made sure of it. "See to the baby, will you, Augusta?" she said.

The other women went silent for a moment. Some of them glanced at one another with knowing smiles. Augusta wondered what they were up to. Were they testing her mettle? Seeing if she'd touch a dead child? "What do you want me to do?"

"Just clean the baby. Wipe her off. Wrap her in something. Did your mother have a christening gown for her? Well, a blanket will do then. You'll need a knife, to clean up the cord."

Augusta filled the washbasin with warm soapy water, and carried it and a towel and knife upstairs to the bedroom where her sister still lay in the wooden cradle that had once been Augusta's. For no good reason Augusta could see, the women followed her, Martha Rivers in the lead. The baby's face was covered in a crocheted blanket, and when Augusta lifted the blanket away she got her first look at the dead child. Her sister was so unbelievably tiny. She was a blue doll, caked with blood and white stuff collected around her neck. Her hair was black, black as an Indian's.

"She's so dark!" Augusta said, turning to the door. The women were crowded there, huddling in the doorway. They were a dizzy bunch, staring at her like that, especially Martha Rivers. Why on earth was she smiling at such a time?

"Yes, she is dark, isn't she?" said Martha Rivers. "Nothing like your mother. Or your father." One of the women covered her mouth to suppress a giggle and pushed her way out of the group. "What?" said Martha Rivers. "Have I said something?" But she never lost that smile.

Augusta felt her blood rising. She caught Martha Rivers' meaning. She knew now what her mother had done. "My grandmother was dark," said Augusta. "Italian." Though her grandmother was as British—as fair and blue-eyed—as the rest of the family.

"Yes, of course," said Martha Rivers. "Well, then, you know what to do." She turned and took most of the women back downstairs into the kitchen. Mrs. Grafton was the only one to stay. She came into the room and put a hand on Augusta's shoulder. "I'll clean the child. There's no need for you to do it. You've been through enough today."

"No," said Augusta. She shrugged away Mrs. Grafton's hand and fought nausea to wipe the baby clean, to wrap her in the crocheted blanket her mother had made. The baby's joints were as loose as a Raggedy Ann's; her lips looked as if they'd been drawn on with a pen. Her tiny fingers were perfect and her long fingernails showed the blue of the skin underneath. Her hair was silky black, and even in death her little head carried the sweet smell that assured she would be snuggled and loved. Augusta wanted to hold her and never let her go; she wanted to rock the child as she rocked her cloth dolls. When Mrs. Grafton finally went downstairs and left her alone, she did hold her; she held her grief as she would have held her sister in life, close to her chest, her cheek against the baby's soft black hair. Up to this moment she had felt nothing but irritation and anger—at her useless father and the stupid ladies of the women's league; at the disruption to her routine. It all seemed her mother's fault. Helen in her selfishness had gone away; she'd hid and left Augusta to handle things yet again. But here, holding the weight of that child in her arms, baby love like a stone in her throat, Augusta cried. Her sister didn't have a name. She would never have a name except the one Augusta gave her right there. She called her baby sister Joy, because that was exactly what Augusta did not feel.

Augusta finished the last of her cookie and glanced at the bird feeder that hung beside her on the balcony. Karl had kept it stocked with birdseed and suet, but they had only managed to attract a few common birds—towhees, chickadees, sparrows, and juncos. The old man down the road appeared to have enticed most of the more interesting birds to the feeders in his garden. She'd seen varied thrush there, and Steller's jays and occasionally a few California quail sneaking in and out of his bushes. There, for much of the season, birds had twittered and swooped like angels around the cathedral spires that were his trees. Dozens of hummingbirds had buzzed around the flowers in his garden until midsummer, when they'd left for the fireweed blooming in the mountains.

A hummingbird had flown up to Augusta's window on the train that morning, showing off its green iridescent neck plumage before shooting off. It was late in the year for a

hummingbird sighting, she thought, although they sometimes flocked in late August after coming down from the
mountains. But they rarely stayed more than a day or two
before flying south.

When Augusta had been a girl, birds had been as abun-
dant as the food they fed on. Every farm in the valley had
several pairs of bluebirds, sweet, trusting little birds that
nested in birdhouses farmers nailed to fence posts, and
blackbirds that sang out their territory in the marshes.
Crows followed along behind her mother, plucking up the
Lincoln Homesteader peas as she planted them. Gold-
finches clung to the stems of bobbing cosmos and took their
dinner right from the flower heads that had gone to seed.
Birds pooped on the laundry hung out on the line, and generally made themselves so available that Manny went out
with the shotgun each morning of the garden season to shoo
them away.

Even Helen's funeral had been besieged with birds.
Augusta had been fifteen at the time. So young! She
couldn't remember much of the service now, of what the
Reverend had said about her mother. What she did remember, she recalled with such clarity that it was as if she were
there now, standing by the grave, staring down at her
mother's casket. It was a plain wooden box, built by Mr.
Rivers, Martha Rivers' father-in-law. He built all the coffins
for the congregation. She had brought rosemary to toss in
the grave, a promise that she would never forget her mother
or her baby sister, and she squeezed this bouquet so tightly
that the sweetness of rosemary drifted around her. She must
have cried during the service because standing here, looking down at her mother's grave, she tasted the saltiness on
her lips.

A crowd of people stood behind her, mostly women. The women who had known her had brought dishes of food for the meal that followed. The few who didn't know her mumbled among themselves at the unfairness of a God who would make childbirth so heavy a burden. They didn't talk about the questionable paternity of the baby, not here at the funeral, though by then all of them must have known. Certainly that was why it was so well attended. For them the funeral was a carnival of sorts; they came to see how she and Manny would react. They watched so they would have something to entertain themselves with later. Nevertheless, each of the women carried flowers to throw into the grave.

Where was her father? He wasn't standing with her and she hadn't thought much about it until that moment, but it was strange that a girl should stand alone at her mother's grave. She glanced tentatively at the crowd, but turned quickly back to stare down at her handful of rosemary. There were so many people watching her. She tossed the rosemary down into the grave, onto her mother's casket. Then the others threw flowers into the grave; delphiniums and foxgloves, Indian paintbrushes, bundles of bachelor's buttons, sweet-smelling snapdragons, marigolds and calendulas, wild roses and handfuls of Shasta daisies. The casket was completely covered in flowers, so that no wood showed through. It could have been a pit full of flowers, and like a child leaping onto a bed of leaves she could have jumped into the flowers and landed softly.

Martha Rivers came over to Augusta at the luncheon that followed, and pulled her outside by the arm and made her stand on the steps of the church. She put an arm around Augusta and despite herself Augusta calmed a little under her touch. Martha pointed at the trees around the church, and at the rooftop, and at the air above them, because the trees, the church roof, the air was thick—black—with crows. Augusta held her ears against their chatter. "Crows don't flock together this time of year," said Martha. "Those are angels, come to take your mother. Most times when people die, they get themselves just one angel to come help them over to the other side. But when a baby that young dies, then a whole chorus of them comes, to help that little soul along. Your mother and your sister are lucky, to have all that help. It's not always easy to get there. Look at that!" The whole flock took to the air then, shocked into flight by some passing car, and they quite literally darkened the sky. Feathers lost in flight or from their short-lived airborne battles drifted down.

Manny shook Helen's bees out of their hives the evening after the funeral. It was a European tradition to force bees out of their hives on the death of the beekeeper. Bees couldn't belong to anyone else, and in some way they aided the ascent of the beekeeper's soul. Maybe that was so, because one of the hives collected in a great ball against the kitchen window that Helen had spent so much time looking out of. They stayed there until sunset, then, catching the last of the light, flew off in a glittering golden-red globe that moved through the sky as if guided by a single mind. Swarms rarely flew far. Augusta watched as this swarm, attracted to the lingering smell of honey, found a knothole in the honey-house roof and took up residency in the rafters. The descendants of Helen's bees lived there for decades afterwards.

Augusta saw Harry Jacob in town about a month after Helen's funeral. She paid for her grocery order at Colgrave and Conchie's, picked up her two bags, and turned to see Harry walking in the door. He stopped when he saw her glaring at him. He was all slicked up for town, likely pursuing some new woman, she thought. The anger must have shown in her face because his eyes darted around the room as if he were searching for escape. Finally he turned on his heel, jogged down the store steps, and headed off toward the train station.

After the funeral Augusta went numb all over. She slept and slept. Then, when nothing was getting done around the farm because grief had hit her father in pretty much the same way, something clicked inside and she worked herself to exhaustion. She filled her days to fill her mind and keep her mother out of her thoughts. Even so, the grief snaked up and rubbed itself against her when she was thinking of some other thing: were these pickles still good? Should she count on a late summer and plant another row of peas? Did the floor need washing? And suddenly she'd be weeping. Grief invaded her lungs and left her short of breath. It leapt into her heart, bringing its skip-beat panic. It wound itself around her neck and tightened against her throat; it pulled at her hands, making her drop the pickle jar to the floor. It slid into her belly and squeezed her stomach so she had no desire to eat, and then it fingered its way into her mind and stole names—names of people she had known for years, names of plants she had known from her mother's garden. She forgot why she had entered a room and would have to retrace her steps. And she walked in her sleep, as she'd done since seeing that rosemary vision of her mother's death, except she didn't run around the house. Now she'd wake and find herself out in the garden, or standing in the barn, with a hazy notion that she'd been hunting for something she'd lost. But once she was awake, she couldn't think what it was she was searching for.

Shortly after Helen's death, Tommy Thompson was killed. Somehow he'd got himself enlisted during the war, despite the fits. He must have lied to get in. But why, wondered Augusta. He must have known that anywhere, anytime—driving a truck or shooting across a muddy patch of ground at some German soldier who was shooting back— possession could take his soul up and out of his body and replace it with a thrashing, incoherent demon. At home he'd been avoided because of his fits. He'd been called "wild man" and "savage," as if he were an Indian, though not by Augusta. Were the seizures in some way to blame for his death? Did the possession take him during some crucial time, on some battlefield, leaving his body without the wits to defend itself? She never found out. She could never bring herself to ask his parents when she saw them in town, although she had written to them after she saw his death announced in the newspaper.

The letters she sent to that boy's parents were strange, and unsigned, and they shamed her still. It must have made their grief more intolerable, to be reminded of it weekly by this stranger, because she had written every week for nearly four months. The letters rambled on about how she had loved him, how brave he was, how considerate and kind, how unfair the war was, and how unfair death was; she went on about the sorrow that nearly ripped her apart, the nightmares that plagued her, her inability to sleep or eat, the weight she had lost over his death, the sadness that made it impossible to carry out the most basic daily chores. All this about a boy she barely knew and had hardly spoken with. The letters were nutty, and Augusta blushed when she thought of them.

Augusta led Karl and Rose into the living room, where they took their seats. "Would you want to know when you were going to die?" she asked.

"No," said Karl.

"Absolutely," said Rose.

"Why? Why would you want to know?"

"So I could prepare."

"How could you prepare for something like that?" asked Augusta. "I'd worry to death."

"I'd get my affairs in order. Plan my funeral."

"That'd be a waste of time," said Karl. "Leave that to the living, after you're gone. It's one less thing to worry about while you're alive."

"What would you do, then," Augusta asked him, "if you knew you were going to die?"

"I already know I'm going to die," said Karl. He laughed, but Augusta didn't. She couldn't bear the thought of it. She had known when she married Karl that she'd likely be widowed at some point. Women generally outlived men, and there was such an age difference between her and Karl. She should count herself lucky to have him with her now, she thought. Even so, living without him was a prospect she shunted to the back of her mind.

When Manny had died, grief hadn't hit Augusta right away. She had kept herself busy setting things straight at his farm—Augusta's farm. She had to sell most of the animals and some of the equipment to pay off his debts, and then they rented out the house and farm to Martha Rivers' younger brother, Teddy Grafton, so he could be close enough to help out his parents. The rent brought in a little money; not much, but it was regular, and Augusta and Karl could call it their own and stick a little of it away each month.

The baby made the gossip that much worse. One day Augusta had Joy in the pram and was walking with her from the train station, where Karl had parked the truck, to Colgrave and Conchie's. Karl was already at Yep Num's, having walked there as Augusta settled Joy into her carriage. Augusta saw Martha Rivers approaching from the direction of the store and speeded up her walk, but Martha ran to catch her. She caught up with her out of breath and placed her body in front of the pram so Augusta had to stop to avoid running into her.

"Well!" she said. Not even a decent hello. "Let's see!" She bent over the pram and took a perfunctory peek at Joy sleeping there, but she hadn't really wanted to see. It was only an excuse to say it. "My, doesn't she have her father's eyes?" Then she smiled, turned heel, and walked briskly back to the store. Joy didn't have Karl's blue eyes. Joy's eyes were turning brown, as brown as Joe's. Anyway, Martha Rivers hadn't even seen her eyes, as Joy was sleeping.

Augusta walked with the pram a little distance toward the store and then turned a wide arch away from it. If Martha Rivers knew about Joe, then the men who haunted the café knew about him. The old men without the strength to work. The bachelors, like Percy Martin, and the men without jobs. They would all know by now. She stood there, on the wooden platform of the train station, at the point where the platform turned into a sidewalk that led to the café. Harry Jacob left Colgrave and Conchie's and crossed the street. When he saw her standing there he stopped and tipped his hat to her, before going on his way. It was a gesture of what? she wondered. Respect? No man tipped his hat to her in that town anymore. Even he must have heard the gossip. Then *that* was why he tipped his hat. They were equals now. Some time later Karl left the café, and when he saw her standing there, he came over. When she said she hadn't done the shopping, he didn't ask why. He left her in the truck and bought his supplies alone. If he had heard anything about Joe in the café, he didn't say a word. Not then. Not ever.

After that Augusta stopped going to Chase for supplies altogether, and made Karl pick up mail or pay bills. It was the city of Kamloops she lingered in, where she shopped and visited the Silver Grill café for a cup of coffee and a bit of sweet reminiscing. On days when she could leave Joy at home with Karl, she sat in the café for hours, watched by the questioning eyes of the cook, trying to look calm as she drank coffee and ordered pie she couldn't eat so she could justify sitting another hour, but Joe never did turn up.

Around this time she dreamed she was dressed in rags and walking alone down a lonely road. A car pulled up beside her and the driver was Joe, dressed in his medals. She felt awkward because she was dressed so poorly and because she was homeless; she felt lost and ragged. Even so, she got into the front seat beside him, and as they drove along she started to feel better, and her clothes began to change from shabby to fashionable. They went on driving down the road with no destination in mind. Joe happily whistled "Fascination."

She tried phoning him once. She parked herself in the phone booth near the café and found his name and number in the phone book and forced herself to pick up the receiver. But that was as far as she got. If his wife answered, what would Augusta say? If Joe answered, would he really want to talk to her? She stood in the phone booth, holding the receiver, until a man wanting to use the phone tapped on the door.

After that, she began searching for Joe along the streets of Kamloops. She'd walk for hours, pushing Joy in the pram, haunting the pretty window displays full of things she couldn't afford, hoping she might bump into him. Once she thought she had seen him turning a corner, and ran after him, only to find it was some other man. Another day she stepped out of the pharmacy and was standing on the fan-shaped imprint in the sidewalk that said "Rexall Drug-store," tucking her wallet back into her purse, when she looked up to see not Joe but Manny passing by and walking down the street. Was this one of her visions? Was he a ghost or had she really stepped backward in time?

She called, "Dad!" and ran after him, and took him by the shoulder. When he turned he wasn't Manny at all, but some stranger. "Oh, I'm sorry," she said. "I—"

The man smiled and tipped his hat to her and walked on. She stood in the center of the sidewalk for some minutes, bumped and jostled by passersby, watching her father walk away.

"I saw Gabe walking around Nanaimo today," said Augusta.

Karl looked at her and blinked. Rose said, "What?"

"I saw him walking around, as if he weren't sick or lying on the operating table."

"A vision?"

"Not exactly. I thought it was him, but then it wasn't. I was so sure I'd seen him."

"That's encouraging, don't you think?" asked Rose. "Maybe some part of you is saying he'll be up and walking around in no time."

Augusta didn't tell Rose the rest, about how she had been so convinced it was Gabe that she'd called out his name. But still she'd been groggy, half asleep. She'd been dozing as the train pulled into the station. Esther had woken her. "Is this your stop?" she said, shaking Augusta's knee, shaking her awake. "Hey, are you getting off in Nanaimo?"

Augusta grunted groggily and looked around. The train had come to a stop and somehow she had remained asleep as the three young men and the rest of the passengers left the train. Had she slept through the conductor's call as well? She must have. "Where are we?" she said.

"Nanaimo," said Esther. "Are you getting off here?"

"Nanaimo?" said Augusta. "No, no, I'm staying on to Courtenay."

"You want something, then? Something to eat? They have a snack bar here. We've got fifteen minutes."

"Yes, maybe."

Augusta slipped her fingers under her glasses and rubbed her eyes as Esther took her massive basket with her and left the train. When Augusta followed, the conductor was leaning against the station, smoking a cigarette. The Nanaimo station was much like the others, although this one had several planter boxes in which maroon chrysanthemums had been planted. Its platform connected with a back alley on one side and a sidewalk leading to shops on the other. A snack truck selling coffee, doughnuts, and chips was parked in the back alley, in front of the station building. Esther stood beside the snack truck, talking to the woman who ran it. She laughed a shotgun laugh, sending the crows on the roof of the station flying off in all directions. Crazy birds, thieves, Augusta thought, they'd snatch any shining thing that caught their eye. She had seen them swoop down to pick up bits of glass glittering by the roadside, had yelled at them as they pinched new penny nails from Karl's barn-side workbench. She watched one crow fly over—its wing tips transparent in the sunlight—then followed its shadow as it slid across the platform. Several people were walking by, in a group. One of them, a man in his late forties, turned and Augusta saw that it was Gabe. She took a quick painful step forward and called, "Gabe!" but when he turned he wasn't Gabe at all. The man looked away as he would from any stranger, and continued walking with the group of people.

Esther went on talking to the woman who ran the snack bar, and the conductor went on smoking and staring off into the sky as if nothing had happened. Perhaps they hadn't witnessed her folly. Why on earth had she seen Gabe? she wondered. What was her mind telling her? That he would pass on? Or maybe that he would make it, he'd be walking around in no time? Sometimes her premonitions were vague like this. She could tell what they meant in hindsight. When the event was over she could tack on meaning to the gut feelings she'd had when she knew something was wrong, or to that strange dream that had meant nothing at the time. Other times she knew what her visions meant at the time she had them, like when she saw her mother's death, and her father's.

The night Augusta saw Manny on the street in Kamloops she woke suddenly and began to cry. Karl sat up beside her in the dark. "What is it? What's the matter?"

"Dad's dead. He's dead."

"That was weeks ago!"

"I saw him. I thought I saw him today in Kamloops. Then it wasn't him at all. Now I just saw him again. I dreamed he was here in this room. Talking to me."

Joy, sleeping in the crib next to their bed, began to whimper. Augusta picked her up and, seated on the edge of the bed and still crying herself, rocked her back and forth. Karl was bewildered by her sudden grief. She wished he would put an arm around her, or fix her a glass of hot milk, or ask her what she was feeling, listen to her. Instead he got dressed. "Where are you going?" she said.

"Out. Might as well get a start on chores. I can't sleep with you going on like that." She had been angry at him then, but understood now, so many years after the fact. He'd no more witnessed that sort of crying and carrying on than Bitch had smelled a woman's skirts, not since his mother had walked into the snow, at any rate. No one had taught him how to hold a woman and in that way share the grief and lessen it; no one had taught him the words to say. He didn't know how, and his lack of skill made him fearful, and the fear made him angry.

Angry or scared then, but later in the day he was sorry. He brought her a kitten from the barn to make up in some way for his behavior of the night before. Karl was so shy giving his presents. Red-faced, he held out that little offering in his big hand as if he was sure she'd reject it, and him too. But she took it and kept it in a box in the kitchen while he returned to the barn. She'd have to take it out again before Olaf came in for dinner. It was just another kit from a barn cat's litter, a fearful, desperate creature always shrilly mewing. On and on, it never shut up. Joy had been crabbing all that day too; nothing would please her. She lay crying in the Indian basket on the kitchen floor as Augusta tried to bake bread. The kitchen was hot from the oven. Sweat slid down Augusta's nose, and Joy's and the kitten's shrieks pierced her ears. Suddenly the lid inside Augusta blew clean off. She picked up the kitten and shook it, and when that only made it mew harder, she threw it at the wall. For the briefest of blessed moments Joy stopped crying. Then she started again and the kitten was there on the floor, dead. Augusta had killed it. That was precisely what her hands had wanted to do with her own baby girl. Not kill her, no— not that. But shake her and make her stop, make the noise stop, make the demands stop. Augusta stared at her hands, at the fists they had become. Then she fled the kitchen, leaving Joy crying in her basket, and ran around to the far side of the house, where she slid down the warm wall and held herself.

Out in front of her, the sheep pastures stretched on and on. Beyond them the poplars still held a few leaves. If it were winter she could walk out into those fields and lie down in snow and find cool comfort. But it was too warm now for dying, and she had Joy to think of.

Then suddenly it *was* winter. The fields had turned to white and the day to evening. Wind scattered fine snow across pastures so white they seemed to be lit from within. And there was a figure out there, a woman walking away from the house. Augusta called, "Blenda?" But the woman went on walking and then, so far out that Augusta could have mistaken her for one of the black poles of bare poplar if she hadn't been moving, she lay down and became part of the field. Augusta stood to follow her, to find her, but as she took her first step it was a warm autumn day.

In the dark of their bedroom, after she'd rocked a restless Joy to sleep, she said to Karl, "What are we still doing here? Why are we renting out my farm to someone else when we could be living there, farming for ourselves?"

"Shush. You'll wake Father."

"No. You tell me. Why are we still here?"

"Father needs help. I can't run both farms."

"Your father can hire more help. If you think he doesn't have the money, then you're a bigger fool than I've been. Don't you see? You can farm for yourself. You can get out from under his thumb. I can get away from him!"

"I don't have the money to set out on my own."

"I'm going to die here. You understand? I will die."

Of course she knew Karl would do nothing. She'd have to do it herself. The following morning she scrawled her demands on brown wrapping (as Olaf had not allowed her the luxury of writing paper) while sitting on a stump outside. Then she took a stout stick and marched into the house, and when the black bitch snarled and leapt to bite her, Augusta brought the stick down hard on the mutt's nose and sent her yelping outside. She slapped her demands on the table, and yelled them in case her suspicions that Olaf couldn't read or write were true. "We're moving to my farm. You're going to give Karl thirty percent of this year's lamb sales so he can set out on his own. You owe him at least that for all the work he's done for you."

Olaf's nostrils drew together, and he pursed his lips. He nodded and went back to drinking his coffee. Augusta stood there, waiting for some reply. "You agree?" she said finally.

"Yes. Just get the hell out of my house." He put a sugar cube in his mouth and sucked coffee through it, making a slurping sound that he knew Augusta hated. Augusta went outside, and when she saw Bitch waiting by the side of the house, growling, she whacked the dog on the nose a second time. The dog fled.

Looking back, Augusta wondered why she had ever stayed so long or put up with so much. No woman would now, now that she had some choice in life—somewhere to go, and the means to get there. But then, well, a woman put up with more because there was no way out. The same could be said of a man, in some cases. Divorce was rare among farmers, practically unheard of. Where was there to go? Whoever walked off the farm walked away with little or nothing. Husbands and wives were married to the land as much as to each other. A different sort of love arose from that kind of necessity; it wasn't romantic or lustful, but it was steady. It was a love they manufactured each day, so that they could carry on.

-Seven-

The apartment was much neater than Augusta had left it three weeks before, though it was still chock-full of stuff; they never had enough storage room. The floor was vacuumed, the side tables were dusted, the kitchen counter was cleaned off. Everything was in order, despite the efforts of the cats. Two of the kittens sat amid the clutter of ornaments on the shelves. Another sat between plants on the windowsill, eyeing the birds. A fourth purred in Augusta's lap and the rest chased an empty orange plastic container, from inside a Kinder Egg Surprise, around the room.

"You've done a nice job of cleaning up," she said to Karl. "Much better than I've ever done myself." It was true. He had always been tidier than Augusta. Even before she went into beekeeping full time, she found herself embarrassed, when visitors dropped in, by the slut's wool gathering in the corners and the stack of dishes soaking in the sink. She found herself apologizing for yesterday's breakfast crumbs still littering the floor under the table. Nothing much had changed; if anything, her housekeeping skills were worse than before, because she was often unable to reach a crust of toast that had fallen from her lap to the floor, and the vacuum was too heavy and awkward for her arthritic hands. Karl did the vacuuming now. She tidied the apartment when the spirit moved her, which was less and less often these days. She made the bed when she got around to it, sometime in the afternoon, after she and Karl had had their nap. There was no use making it twice in one day. Housework would never be her crowning achievement, the life's work for which she'd be known: *Here lies Augusta. She kept a tidy floor.*

Joy, on the other hand, got herself all wound into a knot over housekeeping, even though their house was never finished. Gabe had built the house with the help of Joy and whomever he could bribe into wielding a hammer. Seven years after he'd started the house, the kitchen cupboard was still on the floor, not nailed to the wall, and one wall of the living room was unfinished plywood. The floor of the guest room was uncarpeted and the doors of Joy's walk-in closet lacked the mirrors he had promised to put up.

But though the house was unfinished, it was not untidy. Joy kept that place spotless. Gabe complained that it was uncomfortably clean. Before he'd gone into the hospital, she had spent much of her time at home picking up the Polar Bear socks, the blue underwear, the denim overalls, the red longjohns, and the crocheted hippie hat that he insisted on wearing, and tossing them into the empty basket she had set in each room expressly for Gabe's dog piles. As she pointed out, only the socks were truly dirty. If he would just put his clothes away in the evening, she wouldn't have to do so much laundry. She had been trying to break Gabe's habit of dropping his clothes on the floor since she'd married him. Joy hung her clothes neatly in a closet she kept fragrant with lavender potpourri. She did the wash every evening immediately after work and ironed clothes in the early morning. She told Augusta it was peaceful doing her chores then, in the hours before Gabe awoke. She could get a handle on things; she could get the house under control before he woke to make his messes.

Augusta could guess at the source of her daughter's obsessive tidiness. All through her growing-up years, Joy had been too embarrassed to bring her schoolmates home to their messy house. Well, once she had done so. She had invited Jenny Rivers, Martha Rivers' daughter, home to show her the newborn kittens nested in the empty calf stall. When she brought Jenny into the house for Kool-Aid and cookies the girl said, "Your house is a mess. You live like Indians"—even though Augusta was standing right there in front of her.

Joy said, "We do not!" But Augusta could see that she perceived the kitchen, the house, her mother, in a new, stinging light. Supper was never on time, dishes were always in the sink, because Augusta spent her days outside on a tractor, or shoveling manure, or loading the stoneboat with rocks that were magically and frustratingly manifested by frost each winter. The kitchen smelled foul, of the compost rotting in a bucket on the counter, and of damp mildew from the basket of dirty laundry still sitting in the corner. The floor was gritty because it hadn't been swept for days. Augusta smelled faintly of manure, obscenely of sweat, of labor, of work. Her hands were rough, a man's hands; they had never seen nail polish. Augusta had few occasions to put on a pretty dress or paint her lips red, and fewer reasons to bathe in bubbles. She seemed too lazy to care, or to tidy up on a day when she knew Joy was bringing a friend home. That was how Joy judged Augusta. Although Joy

said nothing then, Augusta could see it in the embarrassment and anger in her face. Augusta, for her part, had put
the blame firmly on Jenny Rivers. The girl was just like her
mother.

Karl hadn't helped matters. He was forever making
Augusta feel bad about her poor housekeeping habits. One
day he came home from Chase with a set of stainless-steel
pots. He'd run into a wandering salesman, likely while having coffee and a game of crib at Yep Num's café. He didn't
say anything at all about the pots, not at first. He set them
down on the kitchen table and sat to take off his boots.

"What's this?" said Augusta. Delighted, she fingered
the slick surface so like a mirror that it reflected everything
in the kitchen: the cupboard with its few dishes, the brown
jug on the windowsill, the stack of dirty pots soaking in the
sink, her own smiling face stretched all out of proportion.
How wonderful to have stainless-steel pots after years of
wrestling food off the chipped enamel. "They're wonderful," she said and tried to hug Karl. But he stood and shook
her off. "When you slept in this morning I couldn't make
porridge," he said. "I couldn't find a clean pot."

Augusta stared at the pots as Karl climbed the stairs to
the bedroom. His words had taken away the shine on those
pots and left them looking cheap. What was more, Joy had
been playing in the parlor and had heard them. She stood in
the parlor doorway, staring at Augusta, *accusing* Augusta.
Then she ran to her room and slammed the door behind her.

Joy, in her more anxious moments, still sometimes went
into a cleaning frenzy when she visited Augusta. Not a
month before Gabe fell to the seizure, she had come for a visit
and promptly started scrubbing the bathroom. She had gone

to use the toilet, but when Augusta went to check on her as she'd been gone so long, she found Joy on her hands and knees, wiping the base of the toilet with a washcloth. "Oh dear, you didn't come here to do housework," said Augusta.

"No, I want to," said Joy.

"Come have some tea."

"Let me do this. I've got to do this. Do you have a brush? To clean the floor? I've got to clean this floor."

"I suppose. Yes. Under the kitchen sink."

Joy glanced at Gabe and he got up and went to the kitchen to retrieve the cleaning supplies. Joy pulled up her sleeves, put on rubber gloves, and, on hands and knees, scrubbed the bathroom floor. Gabe pushed a rag around the bathroom sink until Joy backed into him and shooed him to the living room. When the cats came to wind themselves around her, she hissed at them and pushed them away over and over again. "Do you really have to have so many cats?" she all but yelled.

"It's only temporary," said Augusta. "Until I find homes."

Joy moved on to the bathtub, the sink; she polished the mirror, which had been spattered by weeks of Karl's shaving. Once the bathroom was done she cleaned the kitchen, scrubbing the grime from under the microwave, and pushing the stove and fridge to one side to clean beneath them. She vacuumed the living-room rug and spent the rest of the afternoon dusting the many figurines and teacups, bears, and milk jugs that cluttered the shelves. "Do you really need all this stuff?" she said, and her face was red in anger. But how could the apartment be anything but cluttered, Augusta wondered. Her space had shrunk from that huge drafty old farmhouse down to two rooms and a bathroom.

Manny's house—Augusta's house—had been huge compared to Olaf's bachelor cabin. There were four bedrooms upstairs, although two of the rooms were left empty for the first few years they were in the house as they didn't have furnishings for them. The front door led into the kitchen, as it did in most farmhouses. Off the kitchen were two rooms: a large, dark parlor that she rarely used, and a sitting room that had been her childhood bedroom. This room was brightly lit by day by three long windows with slide-up bottoms that let the fresh air in. The windows were curtained with drapes made of paper; they were soft, almost velvety, and covered in a floral print.

She and Karl had sold much of her parents' furniture to pay Manny's debts, so the sitting room, like the rest of the house, was sparsely furnished at first. She had a camp cot that functioned more or less as a couch on which she napped or laid Joy down to sleep. There was one chair, and a rug that Helen had made by pulling strips of fabric through a hemp feed sack with a wooden hook. It was quite a pretty thing; Helen had been skilled at rugmaking and had fashioned a rose design into it. In the corner of the room, Augusta kept the silk parasol the Japanese girl-bride had given her. The only other bit of furniture was the old treadle Singer sewing machine that had belonged to Helen and that Augusta still used. Augusta had breast-fed Joy in this room. Much later, after Joy had grown up and left home, she and Karl watched television here.

The kitchen was a small, dark room and yet it was the center of the house, the heart. It was where she, Karl, and Joy ate, where Augusta cooked and canned, where they took their morning coffees together, and where Augusta and the Reverend visited after fishing. The linoleum on the floor was well worn; its flowered pattern had disappeared in spots and the edges were ripped. But it was a lot easier to clean than the wood floor of Olaf's kitchen. They had kept the big wooden icebox that had belonged to her parents. Karl put blocks of ice a foot by two feet into the top portion of this insulated box, where the ice lasted for up to a week. He hauled the ice from Pillar Lake in winter, and stored it, covered in sawdust, in a pit dug into the ground under a small shed on the north side of the house. The icebox was a treat after they'd gone so long without one at the Whorehouse Ranch. Augusta could again make the Spanish creams and layered jellies that her mother had created.

The Grafton boy had left behind a kitchen cabinet, a hutch atop a base of cupboards. It had been painted cream at one time but the paint was worn from years of use and the wood showed through. In here Augusta kept the dishes: tin plates Karl refused to give up, and Helen's rose-patterned plates, cups, and saucers. Beside the cabinet there was one tall window that faced the fields and the barns. Sometimes out of this window she'd see a bear with cubs far off in the field, or a coyote trotting through the hay. The window was curtained with plastic drapes, ugly things but cheaper than fabric—cheaper, even, than the paper drapes. A wooden table stood in front of the window. Other than the calendar and her mother's cups and saucers, the only decoration in that kitchen in those first years was a brown jug that had come as a sales gimmick in a bag of flour. She kept this, filled with wildflowers, on the windowsill.

As time went on, the house was slowly filled with the Reverend's gifts: the calendar he gave them each year, the pretty milk jug he bought for Augusta's birthday, the sturdy bedside table he made her one Christmas, the framed needlework and doilies Lilian made herself and sent along, the hooked rug the Reverend bought at a church bazaar, and a framed painting he did himself of the South Thompson River at Deep Pool. He brought good, practical gifts, like a secondhand radio when the power line finally stretched as far as the farm, an electric kettle, a toaster.

Now that Olaf wasn't around, Karl was demanding in bed, or as demanding as he could be. He turned to Augusta almost nightly with his head down, smiling shyly, and Augusta let him climb aboard. It was over quickly; it took less time than sweeping the kitchen floor or doing a sinkful of dishes. She might have been a ewe chewing her cud as the ram mounted her and went at it; her role was to stay put. He gave her no time to warm to the idea. Afterwards he thanked her, several times, as if it were a particularly difficult chore for her that had pleasant results for him, as if she had spent a July afternoon sweating over the stove, canning the jars of strawberry jam he loved so. He made no attempt to arouse her; it was as if he didn't understand that she, too, could be occupied by pleasure, as if he didn't know that she, too, had the hot tongue and taste buds necessary to enjoy a good strawberry steeped in syrup.

Harry Jacob came by the farm looking for work not long after they moved. She was upstairs changing the sheets on the bed when she heard the knock on the door. By the time she made it downstairs, he was walking between the outbuildings, heading toward the barn. Presumably he was searching for Karl, though Karl was in town that day. As Augusta stepped into her gum boots, she watched through the screen door as Harry slid between the granaries and headed toward the honey house. He'd cleared a hole in the dust and was peeking through the honey-house window as she made her way through the grass to catch up with him. "Hello, Harry," she called out.

He startled and turned. "Augusta," he said and extended his hand. When she wasn't quick to take it, he slid his hands into his pant pockets. "I was just—I was looking for Karl. He around?"

"In town."

"Oh." He stared down at his boots. He appeared older than his years. His hair had gone completely gray. He had a bit of a belly on him.

"Something I can help you with?"

"I was thinking he might have some work for me."

"I don't think so. Karl hasn't been hiring since we moved off the ranch. We haven't been going up on the mountain in summer, so we've been doing all the work ourselves." It was the truth. Karl didn't have the money to hire help. "Heard Alice died," said Augusta. Karl had brought the news home from town two winters before. One of the herders having coffee at the café had told him Alice had come down with the flu and had never pulled out of it. She had finally died of pneumonia.

"Yeah."

"I'm sorry."

"Yeah, me too."

"How's your wife?"

"Good. Good. She's living with her cousin now."

"Ah."

"What did you do with all your mother's bees?"

"Dad shook them out and put all the hives inside. One colony found a home in the attic here; another one lives in

the wall of the barn. We don't know where the others went.
They're probably all over the farms around here."

"You ever going back into honey?"

"I don't know."

"You could sell that equipment of your mother's, you
know. I'd buy it."

She shook her head. "No."

"Well. If you need any help, you let me know."

"Sure."

"All right, then." He nodded and put his hand up in a
wave as he passed by her. Augusta watched as he cut across
the field and jumped over the fence to get on the road. He'd
walked all that way to ask for a job, likely stopping at every
farm in the valley. She thought about giving him a ride back
to town. But what if Sara McKay or Martha Rivers saw him
in the Austin with her? He turned to look back at the farm
and waved when he saw she was still standing there.
Augusta waved back and went into the house.

Augusta *had* thought of making honey, starting an apiary. Helen's bee boxes and honey extractor were still in
good shape, as Manny had carefully stored them in the dry
honey house. She would fill glass jars with liquid amber
and attach pretty labels: *Augusta's Honey,* or *Sweet Clover
Farm Honey.* Jars and jars of honeyed light. But then where
would she sell them? she wondered. During the war honey
had replaced sugar for canning, sweetening tea and coffee,
and making cakes and cookies. Now that the war and
rationing had ended, the market for honey had bottomed
out. Augusta herself had dumped her honey-canned fruit
once sugar was available. Everyone was hungry for sugar
then, and sick and tired of honey.

So Augusta chose to go into eggs. There was little investment and not much work, as Manny's chicken coop was in decent shape, and Augusta and Karl needed eggs themselves. Augusta begged change from Karl and bought hens from whomever she could—from Mrs. Grafton, Sara McKay, and even Martha Rivers—and started out with thirty-six chickens in all. A henhouse that size needed only one rooster, two at most. Too many roosters and the chickens wouldn't lay eggs.

Augusta put her hand on Karl's arm. "Karl, you remember that couple living beside us who bought a rooster for every chicken they had?" Karl laughed.

"What?" said Rose.

"These two bought an acreage next to the farm just before we left," said Augusta. "They were city people, and figured now that they were out in the country, they needed to produce their own eggs. They thought chickens were monogamous, like geese. The roosters were so busy raping the hens and clobbering each other that the hens gave up laying from the stress of it all."

They all laughed. Manny had called a city dweller that useless a *cock's egg*, after those first malformed eggs of the laying season. Living that long on concrete, eating food that they had no hand in producing, led to a naiveté most city people weren't aware they possessed.

Eggs bought in a supermarket were most often white, perfectly shaped, thin-shelled, anemic-yolked, tasteless things. That was what most people thought of now, when they thought of an egg. But those were factory eggs—laid by battery-house chickens kept overfed, immobile, and cramped—chosen for shape and size. The yolks of eggs from chickens allowed to run around the yard weren't pale yellow; they were almost orange and had a sharp, unmistakable smell. The eggs Augusta collected had brown shells and came in all shapes and sizes. Some chickens consistently laid huge eggs with two or even three yolks. Sometimes these big eggs cupped one very large yolk. On the other hand, pullets laid tiny eggs, some with nothing inside but the white, or with just a marbling of yolk. The first eggs of the laying season were often misshapen. The shells were thick and rippled or appeared corrugated; occasionally there was no shell at all, only a soft external membrane.

Augusta sold her eggs for forty-five cents a dozen. Hardly big money, and later on, when Joy was in her teens, the price she got was barely worth the cost of keeping chickens. Even so, almost all the farm women in the area sold eggs, to bachelor neighbors who didn't keep chickens, to town people, and to Colgrave and Conchie's. Martha Rivers put her eggs in pails and carried them down the old Shuswap Road shortcut to Chase. It must have been a four-mile hike. It wasn't that the Rivers didn't have a truck; it was that driving the truck to town would have taken all the profit out of selling those eggs. Augusta only took eggs to town on days when they were going anyway, as it was much too far to walk from their place.

A week or two after she'd begun selling eggs, Augusta walked into the kitchen to find Karl raiding her supplies. "What are you doing?"

"Thought I'd take Dad some eggs."

"He can pay like everybody else. I'm not giving him eggs."

"For Pete's sake!"

"He never gave us anything he didn't work us for."

"It's just a dozen eggs."

"Then you pay for them."

"You want me to pay for my own eggs?"

"They're not your eggs. They're mine. My chickens."

"That you bought with my money."

"You're farming on my land."

"Ah, Christ!" Karl dug into his pocket and slammed two bits on the table and walked out of the house with his dozen eggs in a basket. Augusta, feeling childish and stupid, sat down in the kitchen chair with her coffee. When the anger and embarrassment of the argument wore off, she contemplated what she'd buy with her egg money: new paper or plastic curtains, maybe a new oilcloth for the table. It didn't cross her mind to buy anything as extravagant as a new dress. Egg money wasn't much to begin with, and it went back into housekeeping and the farm. What that money did do was provide a woman with a little buying leverage, much like the money she'd earned working in Kamloops. A woman knew her man couldn't begrudge her a tin of sockeye salmon or a bit of chocolate if she was providing the two dozen eggs that covered the cost. Although more forceful women like Martha Rivers, who did save their egg or cream money for themselves, were often well turned out in new blouses. Women like that—women who had no trouble finding pleasure for themselves and figured they deserved it as much as their husbands or children—made Augusta angry. They were selfish. She probably would have been better off if she'd joined them in the fun of a little indulgence. As it was, her resentment surfaced in odd places, like in a basket of eggs for a lonely old man.

It wasn't a week after Augusta made Karl pay for Olaf's eggs that the Reverend arrived on the farm doorstep with a half-dozen fresh trout and invited himself in for supper. Augusta was embarrassed, as she wasn't dressed for company; she wore a ratty old housedress. She cleaned and cooked the trout as the Reverend and Karl drank coffee together at the kitchen table. The Reverend did most of the talking. Karl bounced Joy on his knee and answered questions about his plans for the farm and how was Olaf getting along, but he didn't offer much, didn't help the conversation along. They ate the fish and when Augusta stood to clean off the table, the Reverend helped dry dishes. She was uncomfortable about this. He was a guest, she the hostess, and no man had ever done dishes in her house. When she was done washing and had pulled the plug on the sinkful of water, she realized her engagement ring wasn't on her finger. "My ring!" she said. Then suddenly she was living the moment of her wedding vision: her hands searched in soapy dishwater along with the Reverend's, and his hand met hers underwater.

Augusta didn't see Karl watching them search for the lost ring at the time; she didn't know he'd seen a thing until they were standing together watching the Reverend drive down the roadway with two dozen of her good eggs. "You don't have to look so tragic," said Karl. "He'll be back."

"What?"

"I thought you were selling your eggs, not giving them away."

"They're my eggs and I'll give them to whomever I want. Don't you think we owe him something? He lent me his car so I could work. He brings us things we can use."

"I don't want his things. I don't want any of it."

Karl marched back to the house and Augusta followed him into the kitchen. "I do. It makes my life easier. We couldn't afford those things."

Karl shoved a chair so it scraped loudly across the floor. It was as much anger as he ever showed. "Don't you think I wish I could afford them?" he said. "Don't you think I want those things for you?"

"I don't know what you want. The only things I ever get, I've got to fight for myself." It was true, or partly true, but the moment she said it she wished she hadn't. Karl gave the chair a final push and went upstairs to the bedroom.

The Reverend had never been Augusta's lover, not in the way Karl and half the town likely thought, though once, as they were sitting on the rocky beach at Deep Pool, he had taken her hand and said, "If I were thirty years younger, if things were different—" But that was as far as he went, and a little hand-holding and the occasional chaste kiss were as far as they took things. They fished off the bank, and sometimes fried the fish they caught right there, in butter, in the cast-iron pan the Reverend kept in his truck. They built a fire in a circle of stones on the beach and kept it lively by adding twigs and branches from time to time between casts. Usually it was rainbow or Kamloops trout they caught (Karl said they were the same thing, both pink-fleshed fish that tasted the same). Along with the fried fish the Reverend made strong tea in an old kettle that was blackened from many campfires. Other times they'd bring hot dogs that they cooked on maple sticks and ate with crusty rolls and hot English mustard. And always Augusta brought the Reverend his sweets. He was so like a bear, feeding on the butter tarts and jelly rolls and cake she baked each Friday evening. Fatter and fatter he grew, until she supposed no one could suspect licentiousness of him, because, with that belly in the way, how could it possibly be accomplished?

Joy took a shine to the Reverend, at least when she was very small, as he was there every Saturday offering her sweets and little toys. When she was about two and a half, he finally convinced Augusta to come back to church each Sunday. "Courage," he said. "Show them what you're made of." And she did sit through his services, alone in the front row with Joy on her lap, as there was no one with whom she wanted to sit. She never stayed for coffee afterwards. Once during a service Joy wriggled off her lap, and before Augusta could catch her she scurried to the pulpit with her arms held up to the Reverend, clearly wanting to be picked up. The Reverend, laughing, scooped her up and sat her on the edge of the pulpit and finished his sermon with one arm around her. Augusta was sure that incident got Martha Rivers' gums flapping.

Augusta wasn't sure what Joy's childhood memories were. Joy changed the subject or turned away whenever Augusta brought it up. Augusta remembered the Easter eggs they had dipped in pickled beet juice to make them pink, or boiled in orange rind for orange, or soaked in slightly stewed nettle or lamb's-quarter for green or in caked laundry blueing for blue. She remembered helping Joy wrap the eggs in crisp brown onion skins and string before boiling them to create a delicate, mottled, multicolored pattern.

She remembered how she and Joy had jumped up and down in the huge wool sacks held upright in wooden frames, to pack the wool down for shipping. How they could both fit into that bag together, holding each other's hands and jumping as if on a trampoline, sweating and giggling, the wool so full of lanolin that even Augusta's garden-cracked heels softened.

She remembered taking Joy out to watch the sheep in the top field when Karl was working elsewhere on the farm. The field was fenced on three sides, so there wasn't much to watch for except coyotes. Augusta packed a lunch of cheese sandwiches, cookies, and milk, and a bag of toys for Joy, and together with a dog named Jack they walked through fields of grass and alfalfa. Joy didn't like "girl toys," as she called them. She wanted cars, trucks, farm sets, and, above all, horses. Together they built miniature farms in the field as they watched the sheep. From sticks they made tiny barns, shearing sheds, cabins, houses, and fenced-off pastures filled with toy cattle and sheep. Augusta made Joy a wagon one day, from a large matchbox and four empty thread spools. They plowed tiny fields, and planted gardens using moss and the previous year's dried berries and rosehips for vegetables and fruits.

There was the Christmas she was too busy to help Joy learn her lines for the pageant, and when the evening for the pageant came around Augusta had to sit in the front of the church with the poem in hand and coach her along. Every child in that church had a part, and Joy's recitation came at the end of the program, when everyone had had quite enough; people were beginning to mill about at the back of the church, where women from the league were serving hot cocoa. Joy stood on stage, uncertain, and began mumbling, then stopped short. She looked down at Augusta, terrified. The few other children still on stage giggled. Those few people still listening in the audience coughed. Rather than waving Joy off stage and giving her some sign that it was all right, she gestured for her to go on, and mouthed the words of the poem to her. Joy went on mumbling, her bottom lip trembling, as Augusta fed the poem to her line by line. The event shamed Augusta now. But somehow at that moment it was important that Joy finish the thing, so no one from the women's league could say her girl was stupid, or a quitter. Instead, in all likelihood, they talked of how poorly her child did, how pushy she herself was. Joy finished the poem and, to a paltry hand of applause, ran off stage crying.

Karl seemed to have a way with Joy, at least when she was still a young child. In winter he often boiled her a pot of toffee, then drizzled it onto a clean bed of snow, sometimes forming the letters of her name with the thick sweet stuff. It cooled quickly and hardened into candy that broke into sticky shards when she bit into it. In spring and summer he scrambled around the house on all fours, a horse for Joy to ride on. He threw her into the air and caught her over and over again, until they were both out of breath from giggling. Out in the yard he put down his tools and swung her around in a game of airplane anytime she wanted. He built her a swing, too. It was a sturdy rope swing with a wooden seat hung from the big maple that stood beside the house. Augusta remembered the day he put up that swing with such clarity that when she thought of it she wept. She had put on coffee and was waiting on it, enjoying the warm heady smell, when she happened to look out the kitchen window. There he was, way up on a ladder propped against the stout arm of the maple, the red in his jack shirt and his crop of carroty hair on fire in the evening sun. Augusta found herself watching him, struck by the strength in his back and arms, amazed all over again at the largeness of his hands, farmer's hands that had grown huge from a lifetime of work.

Karl didn't expect conversation from Joy, as Augusta did, and Joy was a help to him, handing him tools as he worked on the tractor, or carrying empty buckets behind him. It seemed so important to her that she did help. She followed him like gosling after goose. He was always giving her some little thing to do to keep her busy, but he seemed to think Joy was a puppy, born with the sense to avoid danger, not the helpless child she was. Once, as he was shoveling out a stall, a horse kicked Joy in the small of her back and Karl didn't even notice. Augusta came out carrying coffee and found Joy sitting on dirty straw in the horse's corral, dazed. She asked Karl what had happened but he only shrugged and went on shoveling. Augusta packed Joy off to bed for a nap and it was then, as she was undressing her, that she found the red, perfectly shaped hoof mark on the girl's back. Only by the grace of God had the horse missed booting Joy in the kidney or in the head. Another time the big ram butted Joy down again and again as Karl sheared sheep nearby. Karl, engrossed in clipping, didn't hear the screams, but Augusta did, and carried the terrified girl off to the house. Joy was only bruised, but how much worse could it have been? Augusta worried Karl over that until he snapped at her. "She could have been killed!" she said.

"She's all right."

"You've got to watch her."

"I watch her."

"She doesn't always know to get out of the way."

"I said I watch her."

"Especially when she's around the animals. You've got to watch her with that ram."

"Quit nagging."

No matter what she said, he would go on working as he always had, in his own way. So Augusta worried Joy with her complaints. "Your father takes too many chances. You must be careful around the animals. You could so easily be hurt. You watch what you're doing." On and on she went, worrying, nagging, pleading with the girl. Somehow she believed that if she only said the words *be careful*, then Joy would; they were a blessing of sorts, and would protect her. If Augusta didn't say them, well, all manner of catastrophe would happen.

All the years Joy was growing up, Augusta would have nothing to do with Olaf. She hadn't set foot on the Whorehouse Ranch once since they'd moved out. She'd seen Olaf only infrequently, when she happened on him in the streets of Chase. In all those years they hadn't spent one holiday with him, and that suited Augusta just fine. Karl went to see him, though, often with Joy. Over the years Olaf seemed to accept her as a grandchild, and sometimes even sent her home with candies or oranges. Karl took Olaf presents and the food hampers Augusta might think to put together, and he spent a little time with Olaf during Easter Sunday or Christmas afternoon. Augusta imagined these visits as dreary affairs where they sat together at the kitchen table. Olaf hadn't the knack for celebration. They might smoke pipes together, but there would be little in the way of conversation. They seemed to have no need for talk.

Then, at some hidden signal, Karl would decide it was time to go home, and he'd say his good-bye.

The night Olaf died, Augusta dreamed that she saw her own father, Manny, wearing snowshoes and standing, of all places, in the snow of a pasture on the Whorehouse Ranch. It was night in the dream. The sky was black. But the snow was so white it seemed to glow, reflecting whiteness into Manny's face. He smiled, but he didn't wave or say anything. He did the awkward kicking dance of a man turning on snowshoes, and then shuffled away across the snow into the black.

Augusta woke from the dream with a start. The room was black. Karl snored. Why, seven years after his death, was she dreaming of Manny? And what was he doing at the Whorehouse Ranch?

The next morning at breakfast Karl said, "I'm thinking of going to see Father."

"Say hello for me."

"I suppose you don't want to spend Christmas at the ranch."

"If he wants to come here I won't put up a fuss."

"Well, I'll tell him, then, that he's welcome for Christmas."

Karl still wasn't home from the ranch by suppertime. Olaf had no phone. It was the only time in their long lives together that she had no idea where Karl was. Finally, at nine, she made a thermos of tea, bundled up Joy and herself, and drove the Austin to the Whorehouse Ranch. The whole scene had the quality of a dream: a bed of sparkling white stretched out into the darkness on all sides of the cabin and outbuildings. The trees around were loaded down with snow. There had been traffic on the road; she could see many tracks leading to and from the farm. The cabin was so much smaller and shabbier than she remembered it. Icicles hung from a roof so heaped with snow that she wondered how the structure could support such weight. With Joy carrying the tea behind her, she creaked open the cabin door and was relieved to find Karl sitting at the kitchen table, in his father's chair. A lit kerosene lamp sat on the table beside him. There was no fire going in the house; it was bitterly cold.

"They've come and gone already," he said.

"Who?"

"The police and ambulance. They took him away. He's dead."

"Who?" she said again, stupidly. Karl didn't reply. Of course he meant Olaf. All she could think was, *Finally the old man's gone.* It wasn't happiness she felt at his death, just relief. She was almost surprised that Karl felt differently, that he felt sadness or grief. "Where's the dog?" she said.

"The dog?"

"The black bitch."

Joy tittered and put a mittened hand over her mouth.

"She died after we left."

"Oh. I didn't know."

"Don't you want to hear? How he died?"

"Yes, yes, of course."

"I found him out there." He pointed at the front door. "I found him where I found my mother. He laid himself out there and crossed his arms like she did and let himself die." Karl drew in quick breaths but he wouldn't let himself cry. He leaned on his knees and put his head in his hands.

"I'm sorry, Karl," she said. But she made no motion to touch him. He looked so forlorn sitting there, head in hands, in his father's red chair. The house was freezing. She sought out one of Karl's red handkerchiefs from her pocket and wiped her nose, then took the thermos from Joy and poured them all a cup of strong tea, black the way Karl liked it. Joy held the cup up to her nose to warm her face, but didn't drink from it. The house was deadly quiet. Their breath floated ghostly against the black behind the lantern. Augusta found herself humming, then singing quietly. Her voice echoed around the bachelor cabin. *Won't you come home, Bill Bailey?*

Joy said, "Did something happen to Grandpa?"

Karl showed his grief with little energy. He picked at his food; Augusta had to dress it up with gravy to get him to eat. Sometimes she'd wake to find he wasn't there in the bed with her, and when she went to find him, opening the downstairs door because he was nowhere in the house, she'd see him standing out in the half-snow, half-mud field. She worried for a while that he might join Olaf and Blenda out there, so she spent some sleepless nights watching that he came back in. He always did, tucking himself into bed with limbs so cold she'd have to rub them to get the life-blood going.

Joy didn't seem to miss Olaf much; she was out making snowmen in the yard an hour after they got back from the funeral. Augusta felt a little sadness for not being kinder to the old man but, since he'd been dead to her those past few years anyway, she felt little else. In fact the years following Olaf's death were good years. They had some extra money from the sale of the Whorehouse Ranch—not much, after the farm bills were paid off, but enough that she could buy those extras she'd been missing: a few dresses for herself, a set of pretty plates. Karl got his flock up to the number and quality he was after, and there were toys for Joy. Augusta went a little overboard, filling the girl's room with toys she had always wanted for herself—dolls and stuffed animals. She once bought Joy yet another teddy bear and gave it to her in the store. Joy wasn't impressed.

"A teddy bear? I'm too old for that."

"No you're not. It's adorable!"

"I don't like it. That's for babies."

"I've bought it for you."

"It isn't mine. You bought it 'cause you like it."

Augusta glanced toward the counter to see if the clerk was watching this performance. She was. She stuffed the bear into Joy's arms but Joy wouldn't hold it. She let it drop to the floor. "Pick it up!"

"No!"

"Everyone's watching."

"I don't care." Then Joy ran out of the store, leaving Augusta standing there with the teddy bear on the floor and everyone staring at her. She didn't look at them. She retrieved the bear and stormed out after Joy, grabbed her by the arm, and forced her across the parking lot into the car, slamming the car door behind her.

Now, thinking of that day, Augusta felt the chill of embarrassment. Why had she forced that bear on Joy, and then punished her for not wanting it? She was such an independent child who almost never seemed to need Augusta. When she was ten the country school down the road she'd been attending burned down one night. It was a shock for her, the loss of the familiar. Nevertheless, Augusta remembered the incident with warmth, because for once Joy needed comforting. She cried, huddled next to Augusta, as they drove past the black, smoking debris the next day. She cried for the loss of her desk and her books and the picture she'd drawn the day before; she cried for the unhatched chicks in the faulty incubator that the school board later announced was the likely cause of the fire. But even then Joy had Karl's practicality about her. After she had her cry, she said she was thankful that she'd brought home her new skates from school the night before.

After that fire Joy was bused to school in Chase, with the rest of the children from the valley. Both Native and white kids attended the school now; the Indian children were no longer forced into separate schools as they had been in Augusta's day. The family of one of the girls Joy went to school with turned up at the farm one day. Charlie Samson drove his Fargo pickup up the driveway with his daughter Patsy in the cab beside him. A number of adults rode in the back of the pickup. Presumably they were Charlie's brothers and sisters, and perhaps cousins. They all piled out when Charlie parked in front of the house.

He knocked on the screen door, then stood back a step and waited. His daughter stood behind him. The rest of the group waited at the foot of the porch, on the pathway that led from the vegetable garden to the house. Augusta opened the screen door. "Hello?"

"I'm Charlie Samson. This is my daughter Patsy." He examined her face. "Your daughter goes to school with Patsy."

"Oh, yes."

"Can I come in?"

"I don't have enough chairs—"

"That's all right. They can all wait outside."

He nodded at the rest of the group and Augusta stepped aside to let him and his daughter through. She glanced at the group and closed the screen door.

"Is your daughter here? I've come to talk about your daughter."

"Yes. Have a seat. Joy? Can you come into the kitchen, please?" Then to Charlie she said, "Do you want some coffee?"

"No thank you."

Joy rumbled downstairs from her room and then, when she saw Patsy, stopped short at the doorway. "Come on," said Augusta. "Sit." Joy slouched in a kitchen chair and stared at her foot scuffing against the table leg. "Joy, do you know Mr. Samson? He's Patsy's father." Joy nodded. Augusta turned to Charlie. "Maybe you should tell me what this is about."

"The other day at school Joy called Patsy a *squaw*. I don't want anyone calling my girls that."

"No. Of course not. Joy, did you call Patsy that?" Joy didn't say anything. Her chin trembled. "I can't believe Joy would say something like that. I don't know where she got it from."

"You don't, eh?"

Augusta's face grew hot. "No, I don't. And I can promise you it won't happen again, will it, Joy?"

"No."

"No, what?"

"It won't happen again."

"Say you're sorry."

Joy glanced at Augusta and then started to cry. "I'm sorry," she said, and ran back to her room.

After Charlie and his kin had streamed back into the truck and left, Augusta went up to Joy's room and sat next to her. The bed was strewn with crumpled tissue. She was still sobbing. She blew her nose.

"We've never used words like 'squaw' in this house, have we?" said Augusta. "Karl never called a woman that, did he?"

"No."

"Then I don't understand," said Augusta. "Why did you say it?"

"It wasn't just me. Everybody was doing it. She started it. She was calling me names."

"Names like what?"

Joy shrugged. Augusta couldn't get anything more from her. When she tried to hold Joy, the girl shrugged away, then ran downstairs and outside. Augusta sat for a while in silence, thinking of Alice and how she'd called her *Siwash*. She thought of the names the Grafton boys had called her after her mother died. The five pale, white-haired Grafton boys had caught her alone on the schoolyard one day and danced circles around her, pretending they were Indians dancing around a fire. "Indian lover!" one of them sang out.

Then another: "Your mother was a squaw!"

"Hey, halfbreed! Who was *your* dad?"

"Augusta is a bastard, bastard."

"I am not," she said.

"Your mother was an Indian lover."

"She was not!"

"Your baby sister was a redskin."

"She wasn't. *She wasn't!*" Augusta pushed her way past the boys and ran off. They peppered her with rocks as she fled, and hurled names at her. *Indian lover. Halfbreed. Bastard.*

Her father was seated in the kitchen, drinking coffee. "You're home early," he said.

"I'm quitting school."

He put down his cup and examined her face, deciding if she was serious. "Your mother wouldn't like it," he said.

"Well, she's dead, isn't she?" It was a stupid thing to say and she wanted to pull the words back and swallow them, but there they were, in the air between them. He didn't say anything for a time. Finally, when she took a step forward to pour herself coffee, he said, "Well, if you're not going to school, you're sure as hell going to get to work around here."

"I won't do any more farm work than I'm already doing. I spend all my time here. I never get out. I'll get a job."

"What job? Who's going to hire you?"

Yep Num, the Chinese man who owned the café in Chase, was known and liked for his habit of giving out sweet ginger, lichee nuts, and Chinese lilies at Christmastime to his few lady customers. Perhaps he thought Augusta pretty. Whatever the reason, he hired her with no experience and no references. It was a small café and waitressing there should have been easy but she had little talent for it. Manny drove her to work. She was dressed in the white uniform Yep Num had supplied and she felt stiff and awkward in it. She had no real clue of what was done at the café. She could count on one hand the number of times she'd been to a restaurant. Shyness made her stomach tie up in knots, so she hugged it and lurked at the back of the café, hoping to make milk-shakes all day. But she was scared, too, of the milkshake machine. Yep Num had to prompt her to serve customers, and more than once she caught him and the crib-playing patrons gaping at her and shaking their heads. What were they saying? Were they talking about her mother in the way the Grafton boys did? At the end of the day Yep Num told her she wasn't suited to the job, and the expression on his face told Augusta that he thought her lazy. Well, she wasn't lazy. What did that Chinaman know? Shyness made her muddled and stupid, and if he'd given her a week to get used to the place she might have excelled as a waitress, as Joy did so many years later. Maybe then she might have gone on to something more than marriage and mothering. But what did it matter now? Things went as they went and there was no changing them.

The Saturday after Charlie Samson's visit, the Reverend placed his hand on Augusta's as they sat having coffee. Joy happened on them as she passed through the kitchen on her way outside, and stopped dead in her tracks. "Let go of her!" she shouted.

"Joy, he's only—"

"Let go!"

"Joy!"

"It's all right," the Reverend said, and withdrew his hand. "Your mother and I were just talking. I wasn't hurting her."

"You're a liar," said Joy, and she ran out of the house, the door banging behind her. The Reverend stood to go after her.

"Wait," said Augusta. "Let her cool off. She doesn't like company when she's angry."

"I should talk to her," said the Reverend. "Explain."

"Something else has been bothering her. I think the kids at school have been giving her a hard time." She told him about Charlie Samson's visit. "She won't talk to me," said Augusta. "Maybe you could take her out for a drive or something? See if you can't get her to talk?"

The Reverend gave Joy his bamboo fishing rod to use and took her fishing at Deep Pool that afternoon. Joy stood near him, facing toward the reserve village, trying to cast as he had instructed. Out of the blue she said, "Was my grandma an Indian lover?"

"What?"

"Jenny Rivers said my grandma had a baby with an Indian."

"You're going to have to ask your mother about that."

"She did, didn't she?"

The Reverend reeled in his line but said nothing.

"Are you ever going to marry Mom?"

"Why would I marry your mother? I've already got a wife. And your mom's got your dad."

"But you love her, don't you?"

"There are a lot of ways to love somebody."

"Are you my father?"

"No! Wherever did you get that idea?"

Joy shrugged.

"Karl's your dad, and he's a good dad. Why would you want another one?"

The Reverend didn't say anything more, but he told Augusta about the conversation. "Maybe you should talk to her about it," he said. "All of it."

"I will if she asks."

"I think she has a right to know."

"I said I will if she asks." But Joy didn't ask, not then.

-eight-

The Reverend passed away in 1969, in his bed, asleep. He had never retired, never left the church he so often complained about. He'd preached into his seventy-fifth year. The whole town turned out for his funeral. Lilian took Augusta's hand as she and Karl stood in the condolence line, and in front of all those gossiping people of Chase she kissed Augusta's cheek. "You were such a good friend to Gavin," she said. "I don't think he would have stayed in this town if he hadn't had you to talk to. And I didn't want to move. You made my life so much easier. Thank you, my dear."

So there it was, Augusta supposed, forgiveness, though perhaps there was nothing to forgive. Karl took Augusta's hand then, and led her from the church to the truck. It was the first time she could remember him taking her hand in public, in front of all those eyes.

Augusta took Karl's hand now, as they sat side by side in the apartment. The skin on his old hand seemed almost transparent, and papery in texture. She cupped his hand in both of hers, and stroked the bumpy, scarred skin where his thumb should have been. "Do you miss this thumb?" she said, realizing, as she said it, that of course he would.

"It doesn't feel like it's gone," he said. "Sometimes I think I could pick up a pen with it, but of course I can't. When I put on my shirt, I can feel the material of the sleeve sliding over it, as if it were there. When I wash my hands, I feel the water on it."

Rose and Augusta glanced at each other. "Really?" said Augusta. Karl nodded and blushed, as if he had given away a great secret. Augusta lifted his hand and kissed the air where his thumb would have been. "Feel that?" she said. He smiled and nodded. When she brushed her lips over the phantom thumb again, he giggled. "Tickles," he said, and wrapped both his hands around hers.

She couldn't help but think now that a little more hand-holding just after the Reverend died might have brought about a resurrection of their marriage if money had been less tight and if Karl had been wiser about her grief over losing the Reverend. If only he'd asked what might please her, and after a time courted her a little; offered her a little tenderness. As it was, he was clumsy with her. He made sheep's eyes at her in bed the night of the Reverend's funeral, but she put her arm out to stop him. "Is it your period?" he said.

"No, it's not my period."

"What, then?"

"Good God," she said, and then, because it felt like too much work explaining her grief, "I don't want to."

"Why not?"

"I just don't."

"All right, then."

Oh, God, she thought. How was she going to survive the loneliness and drabness of the farm without the Reverend's companionship and the little niceties he brought her? The bit of money from the sale of the Whorehouse Ranch that had smoothed things over was gone. She'd be fighting Karl's cheeseparing all over again, and she'd be living the rest of her life without the pleasure she'd known during those few months with Joe. The Reverend had made that loss bearable; the sweetness of his company had made her feel that longing less.

She thought she might go back working for the health unit in Kamloops. Joy was older now, nearly seventeen, and could help out by making meals if need be. The money wouldn't be much, barely enough to pay for the gas, but it would get her out of the house. She still had the ancient Austin. Maybe she could get work that was a little steadier, something that filled the whole day to make the drive worthwhile.

She took a drive into Kamloops to find out. "You have any bigger jobs?" she asked the nurse. "Something that makes a little more pay?"

"Nothing but piecemeal work right now. Except that one live-in. But you won't want that."

"What's the job?"

"An old man. Needs somebody there just about round the clock. Usual housework and meals. He's looking for somebody to be there should he fall or take sick. He's nearly eighty-five but won't leave that house. He has no kids to look out for him. Never married, as I understand it. Pay isn't great, but it's steady. He's got a nice room for his help—I've seen it—and he pays board. He wants someone who doesn't mind doing a little fix-up work. Not heavy stuff. Just painting, that sort of thing. He'll take just about anyone. He's getting a little desperate for some help. But like I said, it's a live-in."

"I'll think about it." But she wasn't thinking seriously about taking the job. There was Joy to consider, and she didn't like the thought of leaving the farm and the garden. Still, it was a tight time for them. The winter had been cold and they'd run out of feed and had to buy it. It would be May before the wool check came in. They wouldn't starve—they were never short on meat or eggs, as they were right there for the taking—but they had little money left for the extras they didn't grow themselves, or even staples like coffee, sugar, and salt, and as they had run up such a large bill at Colgrave and Conchie's she was ashamed to go in there.

Thinking that they were completely without money for groceries, she put ham stock into a pot for split pea soup and realized that they were even out of dried peas. She lifted Karl's town pants from the hook by the door and felt for his wallet, hoping for a bit of change to buy some peas, and found a fifty-dollar bill. He'd seen her desperate scrounging for meals and had kept this money from her—from them. She was so angry she didn't hide the wallet or the money when she heard him scraping the mud from his boots on the porch. She waited for him—rather theatrically, she thought now—with the wallet in one hand and the fifty-dollar bill in the other, and looked him straight in the eye when he came in. He glanced at her, the wallet, the fifty, then turned his back to her to hang his hat and scarf on the pegs by the door. The backs of his ears were red. He took his coat off slowly and hung it and shuffled to the table without looking at her.

"Well?" she said.

"Well, what?"

"You were keeping this from me."

"I was saving it."

Augusta threw the wallet and money down. "Saving it? For what?"

"Emergencies."

"I think we're having one. This should be going on our grocery bill. Buying some food."

"We're not starving. We're getting by."

Augusta pressed her knuckles into her hips and stared down at him. He glanced up and away, scared, she thought. *He's scared of me like he was scared of Olaf.*

"I've got to get out of here," she said. She ran upstairs and pulled out her suitcase from under the bed and started filling it. Some time later Karl followed her up.

"What're you doing, Augusta?"

"I'm taking a job. A live-in job."

"Where? What job?"

"I'll tell you when I know the job isn't filled already." She swung the suitcase off the bed and marched downstairs and out of the house. Karl trailed behind her.

"Are you coming home tonight? Augusta! Are you coming back?" She didn't answer. She got in the Austin and sped off. She was at the Kamloops health unit before it was time for Joy to arrive home.

She knew as soon as she arrived at the old man's house that it was a mistake, a stupid decision made in anger. What had she been thinking? Joy was just sixteen; she wasn't old enough to go without a mother. She already missed her so much. Even so, she called Sara McKay, a neighbor with a phone, and asked her to tell Karl she'd taken the job and would be staying there. She spent much of that first night away from home crying and jerking awake from some unfamiliar noise. She hated the steady clamor of the city streets, and missed her bed, and more than anything she missed Karl, who warmed her hands at night. It was the first time she'd been away from home since she'd lived on Olaf's ranch.

The old man had a bachelor's nature and kept to himself. As he had few needs and didn't make much of a mess, Augusta found herself coming up with busywork to fill her day. She rearranged the kitchen cupboards to suit herself, washed curtains, and went through the old man's clothes searching for things to mend. After supper she tried to entice him into a game of crib and a bit of conversation, but he wasn't interested. He answered her questions with a terse yes or no and didn't offer anything more. He read a book in his chair as she washed up the supper dishes, and went to bed at eight o'clock.

A few days into her new job, she phoned Sara McKay again and asked her to ask Karl and Joy to come to Kamloops the next day, Saturday, and meet her at the Silver Grill café. Once they had ordered their meals, she regretted the choice of café. She didn't like having Karl there, in the place she still thought of as hers and Joe's. She felt nervous that Joe might walk in the door and discover her sitting with her husband. Joy slouched angrily in the corner of the booth beside Karl and only picked at her food. "Can we go now?" she said.

Karl ignored her. "You'll clean house for him, a stranger, but you won't come home and straighten things for your own husband and daughter."

"It's a job," said Augusta. "I get paid."

"If it was income you were after—"

"You'd pay me a wage for keeping the house?"

"Well, no. But we could have come up with something for you."

Augusta glanced at the couple sitting beside them, at one of the tables for two, and lowered her voice. "Don't you see that all I want is a bit of independence? I've never had anything to call my own."

"You've got the farm, don't you? You keep reminding me it's yours."

"But you run it. You decide what's to be done. You're the one taking in and laying out the money." The waitress came by with the bill. "I'll pay for my lunch," said Augusta. She put her purse on the table and searched it for change. The bill was only a dollar seventy-five. She must have enough. But she came up two bits short. "Karl, could you loan me a quarter for this, until I get paid next week?"

Karl picked up the bill. "Keep your change," he said, and stood.

Joy got up after him. "Oh, you're independent all right," she said.

"Wait," said Augusta. Joy turned but Karl, not hearing, walked out the door. "I miss you." Joy looked down at her feet, turned, and walked out under the music-box clock.

Augusta collected the change she had counted out on the table. Enough for a few cups of coffee. All she had until the old man paid her in a week's time. What was she doing? She gave her notice to the old man that night, and packed her things and left for home after making him lunch the next day.

When she arrived, Sara McKay's Mercury Comet was in the yard, though the International was nowhere around. The kitchen door was open. Sara was at the sink, cleaning fish. She was short and portly, matronly, though she wasn't much older than Augusta. "Sara, what are you doing here?"

The woman jumped. "Good Lord, you scared me."

"What are you doing?"

"What does it look like I'm doing?"

"Does Karl know you're here?"

"Of course he does. He's the one who hired me."

"Hired you?"

"To keep house. Make meals. I'm staying in that room there." She pointed at Augusta's sitting room. The door was open and all the furniture had been moved around. Augusta's silk parasol was hanging upside down from the roof so the lightbulb shone through it. "We got to talking the night I came over to give him your message. I'd been looking for a job."

"What about Roger?"

"I left Roger. Kind of funny, eh? You left Karl, then I left Roger to come here."

"I didn't leave Karl."

Sara snorted. "You say so. Karl will be back shortly. Joy will be home from school in about ten minutes. Are you staying to dinner?"

"What did you do to my cupboards?"

"I arranged them so they make sense."

"They made sense before."

"You say so."

Sara didn't have the skillet out. Only a pot of water sat on the stove. "Aren't you going to fry those?" said Augusta.

"Karl doesn't like his fish fried. He likes them boiled, like I do them."

Who did she think she was, telling Augusta what her own husband liked or didn't like, as if she knew better? That night Augusta, Karl, Joy, and Sara ate a silent dinner of bland, tasteless fish. Sara kept glancing at Karl, but he

didn't seem to notice. He was intent on his plate and the fish
he ate hungrily; he'd never eaten Augusta's fish with that
much energy. When he was done he patted his belly and
smiled at the woman and said, "That was good." Augusta
looked at Sara, and at Karl, and at Sara.

"What's going on here?" she said later, after pulling
Karl outside.

"What do you mean?"

"Sara McKay, that's what I mean."

"Joy and I couldn't keep up school- and farmwork and
the house besides. So when she offered on Friday night, I
hired her."

"I thought you were broke. That's why I went off to
bring in a bit of money. Now you pay that woman to keep
house when you'd give me nothing."

"You're my wife. I can't expect a stranger to work for
nothing. That's slavery."

Augusta groaned and threw her hands in the air. "What
do you want from me?" said Karl. "You left. I made the best
of it and now you don't like that either."

"What I want is some respect. What I want is some
income, something I can call my own, a reason for getting
up in the morning. I need to get out, to have some friends."

"You've got all that here. If money's what you're after,
we can work something out. Not much, but something."

"It'd still be your money, not mine."

"It's my money I give to that woman, and she seems
happy enough."

"It's not your money she wants."

"Now, what do you mean by that?"

"Don't you see how she's looking at you?"

"Don't go off—"

But Augusta wasn't listening. She stormed off into the kitchen, where Sara was washing the supper dishes. "You're fired," she said.

Sara wiped her hands on a dish towel. "What?"

"Out. Get your stuff. In fact, I've got a job for you. A live-in situation. Just perfect for you."

"You can't—"

"Yes I can. This is my house. My farm. I own it. Karl doesn't own any of it. Did you know that? Only the sheep and machinery, and the bank owns half of that. If you thought you were working yourself into a cozy situation, you were sadly mistaken."

"I didn't—"

"Go on. Get packed."

"What does Karl have to say about all this?"

"That depends," said Karl. He was leaning against one side of the doorframe. "That mean you're coming home?" he said to Augusta.

Augusta sighed. "I guess," she said. "If you'll have me."

Sara threw down the towel and marched into her room—Augusta's room.

"She'll need to be paid."

"You know where my wallet is." He nodded at the pants hanging on a coat hook by the door, then turned and walked off into the cornfield, which was nothing but mud right then as the snow had just that week melted. Augusta shook her head at his naiveté. He'd trust that woman and leave his wallet any old place. But she herself should have been watching Sara as she packed her things into burlap bags, because the silk parasol the Japanese girl-bride had given Augusta so many years before went missing for good.

Augusta spent days after that cleaning the house, re-arranging the kitchen, putting the furniture back in place, erasing all evidence of the other woman's presence. When she'd set the kitchen to order and washed all the floors, she started work on the dark, hidden-away places, the top cupboards and the pantry, the attic and beneath the beds. Karl's old suitcase was under the bed, where he always kept it. Augusta slung it onto the bed and opened it, already angry, yet hoping he'd thrown out the filthy magazines. He hadn't. He'd added to the collection, but along with those magazines there was also a book in the suitcase, a book unlike any she'd ever seen him read, called *How to Love a Woman*. It was a lovemaking manual with tasteful, instructive drawings, not smut, and chapters on courting a woman, assessing her likes and dislikes and the ways she might like to be touched, and commenting on things that should never be done. Had he been thinking of her, that she might come back? Or had he been thinking of Sara McKay? Surely not Sara.

Augusta put the book and the suitcase back under the bed, then went downstairs and left the house. She wrapped her sweater around her. It was past noon and still a fog hung over the valley, draping itself over the barn and out-buildings. Hoarfrost gently snowed down from the birch and glistened on the bare lilac bushes near the house. There was still a bite of winter in the air, though they would begin seeding in less than two months' time. It was so very quiet. Even the occasional bleating of a lamb for its mother was hushed by the heavy mist. She headed toward the barn, thinking she'd check for newborn lambs. But there was someone ahead of her, walking among the outbuildings—a dark figure masked in fog. "Hello?" said Augusta. Karl was in town and Joy was at school. Neither of them would be back before four. "Are you looking for Karl?"

The figure kept walking, slowly, as if he hadn't heard her. "He's in town," Augusta called out, then regretted it. She shouldn't be admitting that she was home alone. She retrieved a shovel Karl had left propped against the implement shed and, carrying it between her hands like a shotgun, made her way past the many granaries and sheds toward the barn. The figure had disappeared. Had he slipped between the outbuildings? She walked slowly, checking each of the passageways between the buildings. "Hello?" she called out. "Can I help you with something?" A chill went through her. Why hadn't she thought to put on a coat? "I've seen you, you know." Maybe it was some kid out to scare her. Or maybe it was one of Joy's many boyfriends sneaking around. "If you're looking for Joy, she's not here."

Augusta turned to walk between two granaries. Whoever it was must have gone behind the outbuildings. She turned the corner at the back of the buildings and there was the figure, trotting off into the fog. Was it a woman? "You there," she said. "What do you want? What are you sneaking around here for?" Augusta followed the figure, heading toward the honey house. She couldn't see the building at first, it was so hidden in fog. But she heard the rusty squeak of the hinge on the door she hadn't opened in years, and then the door slammed shut. There was no way she was going inside. The window she'd spied her mother and Harry through all those years ago was filthy, covered in fly specks and dust. She pulled the sleeve of her sweater down over the heel of her palm and rubbed a circle in the grit. The inside of the honey house was pretty much as Helen had left it: the

Dandy Perfection woodstove and the honey extractor, the rows of honey jars on the shelves above. And there was Helen, standing with one hand on a stack of beehive boxes, smiling. Her dark hair was loose around her shoulders; she was wearing the dress Augusta had cut down the back to bury her in. She patted the hive box.

"Mom?" said Augusta. "Mom!" She ran around to the door and scrambled inside, but there was no one there. Just the many empty hive boxes, and all her mother's equipment. Augusta sat on a stack of hive boxes and hugged herself. "Mom?" A few lambs bleated in the barn, the sound so muffled by fog that they seemed to be a great distance away. She looked around at the equipment in the dim light, then stood to inspect the extractor, the bottles, the boxes themselves. Except for a layer of dust they were all in good shape. The boxes only needed a few nails and a fresh layer of paint.

"I'd like twenty dollars," said Augusta.

"Twenty? What for?"

"It's a surprise."

"You know we're low on money."

"You were willing to give Sara McKay money; I think you can spare me a little."

"All right, all right. But I'd like to know what it's for."

"Bees," said Augusta.

Joy looked up from her plate. "Bees?"

The bees came in the mail, buzzing away in a wood-framed screened box. Honey was popular again, as everyone was suddenly concerned about eating natural things, wholesome things, when all through the fifties it had been sugar they'd wanted. She could get as much as thirty pounds of honey off each hive at first harvest, and she'd put the honey in bottles with pretty labels. It wouldn't be that much extra work. A beekeeper needed to make only eight or ten visits to each hive a year, checking for problems like raiding by other bees or wasps, covering the hives come winter, feeding sugar-water syrup to help them along, examining the hive to see that the queen was alive and well and that there was lots of brood, and adding supers as the hive grew. If she didn't give the bees enough room, half the hive would turn emigrant on her and swarm off to find a new home. But if she could catch swarms from wild hives, or swarms that had taken off from other beekeepers, early enough in the year she could put them into new hives. The swarm, like immigrants, would be much more productive than the established hives.

Augusta had Joy help her retrieve Helen's hive from the honey house. It was relatively easy, just a matter of climbing into the attic and cutting the combs down one by one. But the bees were more active this time of year, and they didn't take kindly to having their home moved. Augusta dressed Joy in overalls, gloves, and a bee veil, and had her stand at the base of the ladder as Augusta handed down honeycombs to her. Joy then put the combs in bee boxes that Augusta had made ready. All was going well until a few bees made their way inside Joy's veil and she ran off shrieking, trying to yank the veil off. Augusta climbed down the ladder and ran after her, trying to get her to stop, but she couldn't keep up with her. Finally she stopped and watched Joy run around. Joy eventually ran back to Augusta, with one glove off and the veil half off her face. Augusta calmly removed the veil and inspected the few stings the girl had received on her face. She took her into the house and put a poultice of baking soda and water on the stings.

"If you don't panic, they usually don't sting even when they get inside the veil," she said.

"I hate bees. I'm never helping you again."

"Oh, come on. Do the stings hurt anymore?"

"No."

"When you're thrown, the thing to do is get right back on the horse," said Augusta. She took Joy's hand and led her back outside.

"Where are we going? I don't want to go near those bees again."

"Don't worry, we're not going there."

"Where, then?"

"You'll see." Augusta led her around back of the barn, where one of Helen's old hives had built a home inside the barn walls. It had grown over the years and had swarmed many times. There was a swarm now that had landed in a clump only a few feet from the original colony. It clung to the wall at about shoulder height. Joy stood back, but Augusta reached up and ran her hand over the bodies of the bees, petting them as her mother had. A few bees flew off and hovered around her, but none seemed interested in attacking. "Come, try it," said Augusta.

Joy tentatively held out a hand, touched the ball of bees, then quickly pulled away. "Slowly," said Augusta. "Like this." She showed her again, and Joy followed her example, grinning at the wonder of it.

In late April, Augusta drove from farm to farm in the valley, putting out the word that she'd give ten pounds of honey at fall harvest to anyone who alerted her to a swarm she could capture. When there was a dramatic change in the weather, from a cold winter to an early, warm spring, as there had been that year, hives were sure to swarm in May. The only farm she didn't stop at was Sara McKay's. (Sara had worked only a month for the old fellow in Kamloops before she was back with her husband on the farm.) Augusta left her name at the police and fire stations too, in case they got a panicked call from somebody in town about a swarm. It was good thinking on her part, because she ended up with twice as many hives from swarms as from the mail-order bees.

Most swarms landed on bushes or the limbs of trees in one big clump. All she had to do was carefully cut the branch away with pruning shears and shake the bees, like so many tiny dried leaves, into a burlap bag. She tied the bag tight and drove home with the bag of bees buzzing away in the backseat of the car. Once home, she simply spilled the bees at the entrance to a stack of empty supers— the bee boxes—and the bees, attracted to the smell of honeycomb on the frames inside, quickly ran into the hive by themselves. Occasionally the swarm landed on the ground and she had to scoop the bees up with her hands. If they were calm enough, she often went without gloves. A handful of bees felt for all the world like a handful of warm black currants, and when she gently dropped the handful into the burlap bag a few still clung to her hand. Bees always walked uphill. They walked the length of her sleeve, up to her shoulder, before flying to rejoin their sisters in the bag or on the ground.

She found beekeeping meditative, relaxing. It was work that involved her completely; she lost herself in the concentration required to handle the bees, and soon learned that if she entered into the work fearful or upset, the bees would smell it on her, and read it in her suddenly clumsy actions, and sting her. But if she worked in a calm manner, keeping her movements slow and deliberate, she was stung much less frequently.

That first summer of beekeeping, she collected a hive from Mrs. Grafton's barn. It wasn't a swarm, but a hive that had made a home for itself between the studs inside the walls. Protected by a bee veil and overalls and wearing Karl's work gloves, Augusta took a crowbar to the siding of the barn and opened the hive to the sky, then pulled the honey and brood comb from the wall with her hands, only using the knife to loosen the comb from the wall. She put the comb into the boxes she'd brought with her, covered them, and left the new hive by the barn for a week, so bees out foraging when she had collected the colony would make it their home.

When she returned for the hive it was late evening. Martha Rivers was visiting her mother. She came out as soon as she saw Augusta in the yard. She was looking a little tired, but was still a handsome woman. "Come in for a visit?" she said. "I see you at church, but then we never get a chance to talk after."

"It's getting pretty late. I'd like to get these guys set up tonight."

"So you're starting up the beekeeping, I hear."

"Yes."

"Using your mother's equipment?"

"Haven't had to buy anything but the bees and foundation."

"Well, you've got your first customer."

"*You'll* buy my honey?"

"Sure, why not?"

"I'll give you five pounds free if you find me a hive to capture."

"I thought you promised my mother ten."

"All right, then. Ten."

"It's a deal." Martha offered her hand and grinned.

Augusta hesitated and then shook it. "I should get going," she said, and squatted to lift the super containing her new hive.

"Here, let me help."

"You could get stung."

"Nah. What if I do?"

Together the two women loaded the hive onto the back of the International. "Look, no stings," said Martha.

Augusta got into the truck and waved her thanks. "Don't be such a stranger, eh?" Martha called out as she drove off. Augusta looked back at her in the truck mirror. Overtures of friendship from Martha Rivers, of all people. But unexpected friendships jumped up everywhere that summer she went into bees. When she went around asking about swarms, she was invited into kitchens by farmwives who, she discovered, were as lonely as she had been. And when she went around again selling that first harvest of honey, she found the women not only willing to buy her pretty jars but hungry for conversation, too. She could count on at least an hour's visit for each farm she stopped at. More often it was two. When she visited Mrs. Grafton's farm it was three hours before she left, whether Martha Rivers was there or not. She'd been suspicious of Martha during those first few visits, scared she'd bring up the past. But Martha was on to other gossip, other women's affairs, other women's misdeeds, and Augusta found herself caught up in the gossip, reveling in it, passing it on. All those years she had thought that she was the only one starving for companionship, that somehow the town's talk over Helen's death and Joy's birth had marked her as an outcast no one would welcome into her kitchen. But now it seemed that much of that had been forgotten or, if not forgotten, put aside. It was that summer that Augusta and Karl finally got a phone on their place; they were the last in the valley to get one.

The society of other women was a side benefit she had never guessed would come of beekeeping. Or maybe it wasn't a side benefit at all; maybe it was the point. Maybe it was conversation, more than independence, that had driven Helen to sell honey hand to hand all those years ago, and maybe company, not charity, had been the reason she carried syrup cans of stew to Mrs. Grafton.

Rose and Karl dozed in their chairs. Augusta sat with them, watching Rose sleep. Rose's face was relaxed. Her cloud of white hair, pushed up against the chair back, formed a nimbus around her head. She could be a decrepit angel, Augusta thought, wings tattered from too many years of good deeds, grumbling and complaining as she lent a hand. She wished she could tell Rose about the dream premonition she'd had on the train that day; she needed to talk about it, to work it out. But she knew she couldn't. Its meaning was as plain as the forewarning Augusta had had of her own mother's death. It would scare Rose, just as it scared Augusta. Would she die today or tomorrow, she wondered, or would it be a year, two years, five years from now? She felt suddenly alone, with both Rose and Karl sleeping. She shook Rose's knee and Rose startled awake. "What? Did the phone ring?"

"No. No. I remembered that I hadn't told you about the boys on the train."

Rose yawned. "Couldn't it have waited?"

Augusta took another cookie from the plate on the coffee table. "Remember how we stopped that kid who tried to steal your purse?" A boy on a skateboard had scooted behind Augusta and Rose that past spring as they walked along the street in broad daylight, and grabbed Rose's purse by the shoulder strap. But she and Rose had been quick-thinking. Rose felt the tug on her purse strap and clutched it, so the boy had to stop and try to wrestle the purse out of her hand. That gave Augusta enough time to hook him behind the knee with her cane—just as Karl had once caught sheep by the leg with his crook. She gave one good yank and the boy lost his balance and down he went, losing his grip on Rose's handbag. He scrambled up and took off, but without the purse. That afternoon Rose and Augusta got pink and tiddly on a sweet, bubbly wine.

Rose laughed. "Yeah. Grannies' revenge!"

"Well, I got revenge again today. There was a boy smoking on the train and I gave him heck."

"He quit?"

"You bet he quit. I threatened him with my cane!"

Rose laughed but didn't press Augusta for details. She stretched and yawned and closed her eyes. In a few moments she was snoring her own particular snore, a low whistle that vibrated her bottom lip. Just as well, thought Augusta. Rose wouldn't have liked hearing about Esther again.

The train was a dayliner, two cars long. The seats were upholstered with red striped fabric. There were "No Smoking" stickers everywhere and yet the car smelled deeply of stale smoke.

The boys who had sniggered at Esther sat in seats that faced each other, like those Augusta and Esther sat in. She could see their gestures, their laughing faces when they turned, but because of the noise of the train she couldn't hear their conversation. One boy had on the most ludicrous hat she had ever seen. It was made of fleece but was shaped like a crown, like that cartoon character Jughead's hat. In her mind she called him that: Jughead. The other boy wore a hat that looked for all the world like an old sock. She christened him Sockhead. She gave the third boy the name Spitter because he chewed sunflower seeds and every few moments he spit the shells onto the aisle floor. He had the jittery, jackrabbit moves of a person trying to quit smoking; every few minutes he smelled the yellowed tips of his index and forefinger.

Augusta had been sleeping when the train horn sounded several times, startling her awake and leaving her ears ringing. Then the train lurched to a stop, sending her cane clattering to the floor. The Spitter stood and looked out the window. "Hey, wildlife!" he said. The other two boys stood to take a look, and they all laughed. A deer? What wildlife? Augusta gripped the arm of her seat and heaved herself up. Esther bent over to retrieve Augusta's cane, and together they made their way to the other side of the train. There was no deer, no wildlife by the tracks. A young, drunk Indian man stumbled along beside the train, slapping the car with his hands as he might slap to get a horse moving. Jughead pretended he had a rifle and was shooting the man. "Let's go hunting, eh?" he said, and they all laughed again.

Didn't they see that Esther was Indian, she wondered. How could they be so crass? She thought Esther might turn on the three—she had every right to—but she didn't. She watched with Augusta as the frizzy-haired conductor jumped down from the first car and talked to the drunk man. "I lost a son like that," she said.

The drunk man stumbled back, away from the tracks, as the conductor pulled himself up into the first car. Augusta and Esther held onto the seats to steady themselves as the train began to move again. Augusta instinctively raised her arm as the man fell so close to the tracks that she thought the train was going to hit him. The train sped on and the drunk man crumpled beside the tracks disappeared behind a forest of arbutus and blackberry bramble. Augusta and Esther returned to their seats and sat heavily. Esther slipped her glasses down to rest on her chin, and rubbed her eyes.

"You said you lost a son," said Augusta.

"Well, he wasn't a true son. I didn't give birth to him. But he was like a son, my nephew. He was my little sister's boy. She died when he was, oh, fifteen, so I took him over. But he was already gone by then, wild and drinking. He killed himself like that, on purpose. Got drunk and walked right in front of a train."

"We should have got off, maybe."

"Yeah, two old women with bum hips fighting a drunk man. Why didn't these three strong huskies here stop to help?" Augusta looked away, at the boys. She couldn't think of anything to say. Young punks. No regard for anyone but themselves. They were young Percy Martins, the lot of them. Spitter pulled out a cigarette and lit it. *How dare he?* Augusta grabbed hold of her cane and banged it against the floor of the aisle. "You!" she said, surprising herself. "You put that cigarette out!"

The boy exchanged a look with his companions. Sockhead poked his head over the seat to glance at Augusta, then turned back. She hoisted herself up and steadied herself against the seat, and Spitter pointed his chin at her and blew smoke into the air. "Put it out!" she said. He took another drag and stared out the window in defiance. Sockhead and Jughead were watching Augusta now, along with the other passengers. She clung to the backs of the seats and made her way to them. As she reached them she lifted her cane over their heads and pointed at a "No Smoking" sign over their window. "Don't you see the signs?"

The Spitter said, "What's it to you?"

Augusta pounded her cane hard on the floor between their feet. The three of them flinched. "Put it out now or so help me God I'll smack it out of your face."

Jughead said, "Put it out, man. You can smoke later."

"Old bitch can't tell us what to do," Spitter said quietly.

"What?" said Augusta.

"Don't be stupid," Sockhead said to Spitter. "You don't smoke if it's bugging somebody else. Get some manners."

Spitter said, "Fuck!" but he tossed the lit cigarette to the train floor between their feet and put his foot to it. He crossed his arms and stared out the window.

"Thank you," said Augusta.

Sockhead said, "Sorry about that."

Augusta nodded at him and made her way back down the aisle. She caught Esther grinning at her as she lowered herself into the seat, and laughed at her own improbable behavior. Although she could smell the fear on herself—she was sweating in it—it felt good to give those young goats heck. She felt triumphant. And silly. She suddenly had to use the washroom.

Augusta washed her hands and looked into her bathroom mirror. She'd developed a cold sore over the course of the day, a reminder of the stress of the last three weeks. She pressed a finger to the sore as she passed Rose and Karl sleeping in their chairs, and made her way to the kitchen. There she spooned a little honey from the jar and dabbed it on her lip. It soothed and coated the hurt, a sticky kiss. It was the antiseptic ointment of past ages, the salve warriors had taken into battle to heal their wounds. The ancients used it to embalm. They immersed the bodies of infants who had died during birth in vats of honey, preserving their bodies for all eternity. She would like to be buried that way, encased in honey, like the bee suspended in amber that she carried in her purse.

Joy had admired that brooch one day during Augusta's stay with her. Augusta was hurriedly putting on her makeup in the bathroom, as Joy was waiting for her in the kitchen. She had her makeup bag in the bathroom but, as she called out to Joy, "I forgot my comb in my purse. Could you bring it, please?" Joy obliged but misunderstood her request, and rummaged in the purse for the comb, instead of bringing the purse to the bathroom. She happened on the brooch.

"What's this?" she said, bringing it and the comb to the bathroom.

Augusta took the comb and looked away as she combed her hair. "Oh, I treated myself to that after we sold the farm."

"I've never seen you wear it."

"Never had the occasion, I guess."

"It's beautiful. I've never seen anything like it." She held it up to the light. "So lovely! It's like the bee was caught in its own honey." She took it back to the kitchen with her, and when Augusta came out of the bathroom she was still admiring it.

Augusta sat at the kitchen table, tasting the honey on her lips and watching Karl as he slept, chin on chest, in his chair. A single white hair stood up defiantly at the top of his bald head, silhouetted by the window behind him. It made her smile. Perhaps it was no coincidence that her love affair with Karl had begun, so many years after their wedding, when she started producing honey. It had been an ointment for her soul, a source of self-assurance and fun, but perhaps it had also been a salve for the many old hurts between them.

Augusta gifted Karl with the first cake of honeycomb she produced on her own. She cut it from the frame in June and carried it on a plate to the garden, where he was hoeing and plucking weeds from between rows of sugar peas and sweet peas. The honey was yellow and sharp with the flavor of dandelions; even the comb itself was bright yellow. The honey ran liquid from the cells, quickly filling the shallow plate and running onto her fingers, down her arm. When she reached Karl his hands were caked in garden soil, so she let him taste the honey from her sticky fingers. He ate the honeycomb she held up for him and, laughing, licked the honeyed palm of her hand. Her bees, which had been flitting from sweet pea to sweet pea, flew up to the scent of honey, alighted on her plate, hovered around her sweet fingers.

Gabe had once brought a recipe to show Augusta. It was literally a recipe for whipping up a batch of bees, which he had found in Virgil's *Georgics*. He gave her a copy. It was now dog-eared because she loved it so:

> *How often in the past the putrid blood*
> *Of slaughtered cattle has engendered bees . . .*
> *A bullock with two years' growth of curving horns.*
> *Both nostrils and the life-breath of his mouth*
> *Are plugged, for all his struggles. . . .*
> *They abandon him shut up, with broken branches*
> *Under his flanks and thyme and fresh-picked cassia . . .*
> *Meanwhile the moisture in those softened bones*
> *Warms and ferments, and little animals,*
> *An amazing sight, first limbless, then with wings*
> *Whirring, begin to swarm, and gradually*
> *Try the thin air, till suddenly, like rain*
> *Shed from a cloud in summer, out they burst. . . .*

Marvelous. Terrible. It had made Augusta laugh. Likely what they took for bees were some sort of golden fly. The people who wrote the Bible thought the same thing, that bees rose from the bodies of the dead. Didn't Samson scrape honey from the carcass of a lion on the way to his wedding? *Out of the eater, something to eat; out of the strong, something sweet.* Augusta had seen the eggs and larvae of bees growing inside the hive or she might have believed it herself. She liked the idea that for generations folks went around thinking they could whip up a batch of bees, create life from herbs and a carcass of an animal they had killed with their own hands, and have the sweetness of honey arise out of that. Maybe they had it partly right, she thought—the sense of the recipe, anyway—because wasn't that how some marriages went? The ones that seemed, at least from the outside, as if they could go on forever? Somewhere along the road something knocked the life breath from the marriage; some turn of fate—the death of a child, a lost job, or more likely an affair—killed it dead. Oh, it struggled on for a while, but anyone looking at a couple at that stage could see that the marriage was dying. The partners' movements seemed at odds with one another. Suddenly they were crashing into each other in the kitchen, stepping on each other's toes. The dance they had once done effortlessly became a chore that left them both irritable and hateful. But after that stage, after the kicking was over and the breath was gone, they passed by each other like strangers on the street; there was an agreement there, all right, but of another kind.

But that was where the magic, the recipe for bees, came in. Because occasionally something fermented inside the lifeless carcass of a marriage, something began to stir, limbless at first, then with wings whirring, trying out the thin air, till suddenly, like rain from a summer cloud, it burst out with a force that drove old lovers to do things no one, not even they themselves, thought they were capable of.

A couple of weeks after Augusta took that weeklong job at the old man's home, Karl started bringing her eggs. The first eggs of the laying season, eggs laid when the light was just strong enough to pull them from the young hens. Tiny eggs, eggs without yolks, eggs with rippled shells, or soft, rubbery eggs without shells at all. She'd seen them all before; these first marvelous eggs of the season were nothing new to either of them. Yet Karl hunted for them in the secret nests young hens made in the long grass around fence posts, nests the hens lined with down and feathers they plucked from their own bodies. He presented the eggs like gifts, some so fresh they were still warm and moist. "Look here what I've got. You ever seen anything like it? Look how small." And they'd look together, both amazed at this small, soft-shelled thing they passed between them.

She had the habit then of taking her evening coffee outside, by herself, as Karl and Joy finished off their supper plates in the kitchen. Most times she sat on a stump Karl had placed at the foot of the garden, and from there she looked over the field, imagining the young corn that would sprout there, rolling the day over in her mind, finding pleasure in sitting that no longer required a fishing pole to justify it. Then she'd just know he was there, and she would turn and find Karl standing on the porch watching her. At first he bloomed pink and all but fled back into the house, but gradually, evening on evening as the corn seedlings sprouted and took on their leaves, he stood a little longer, ventured a smile now and again, until he stood so long, watching her with such sweetness, that it was Augusta who blushed and turned away.

One day Karl came home carrying a single precious calypso orchid, a fairy slipper, a flower he had to have been searching for because it never grew out in the open, but off the road, in places of magic where a rotting log lay among evergreens on needle-covered ground—a cool, mossy place—only there. So he'd been looking for it, hoping to please her. When he walked up as she worked over a hive in the orchard, and held the orchid out to her, there, that had been his apology and his forgiveness. Of her, for taking a lover all those years ago, and of himself, for not knowing how to be that lover.

Joy saw her silly old parents courting in this way. After Karl had gone out to do the evening chores, while she and Augusta were finishing up the dishes, Joy said, "Why do you have to act like that? You should act your age."

"And how's that?" said Augusta.

"You've been all over each other. It's embarrassing."

"I should think you'd be happy to see us getting along. And anyway, I hardly think a little hand-holding qualifies as being all over each other."

"It's sick."

"Sick?"

"I know about you. I know about you and Reverend Lakeman."

"And what do you know?"

Joy paused, then said, "Nothing."

"No. You tell me. What did you mean?"

"I said, nothing!" Joy didn't say any more. She went on wiping dishes. And Augusta didn't press further because she was suddenly lacking the heart necessary to speak. Her hands shook as she sank them again and again into the dishwater.

What was it, two weeks, three weeks later? She had taken Joy into Kamloops and dropped her off to shop by herself after making plans for them to meet at the Silver Grill. It was much the same as in her days with Joe. The high-backed booths were the same, though they'd been reupholstered, and the fascinating old clock was still on the wall. She bought a newspaper and sat down at the same window table she'd taken that very first day, and ordered coffee and pie. Blueberry pie. The pastry was soggy but the berries were fresh, and whipped cream could make up for most anything. She took a second bite out of the pie and looked out the window. There was the young Augusta walking down the sidewalk toward the café. She was wearing a pretty blue dress, sandals, and her hair spilled over her shoulders. Somehow time had skipped backward all those years. Was she coming to see Joe? Her heart pounded at the thought. Was it possible? Would she see Joe, sweet Joe, again?

But then there were men talking in the booth behind her, talking about this phantom of her young self approaching on the sidewalk. "Hey, look at her!"

"Man, isn't she something?"

The young Augusta dissolved into Joy. It was a shock to see her self disappear like that and to have this other young woman walking in her place. Until that moment she hadn't realized just how much she and Joy resembled each other, at least from a distance. She wondered if men had talked like that about her when she was that age. She had thought herself an ugly duckling. Likely Joy was more resourceful when it came to men. Times were changing, and Joy had gone on dates as Augusta never had. No man came to court her, not with marriage in mind, or even serious lovemaking, in the old sense of the word. For Joy it was play, a form of entertainment. Shaggy-headed boys in strange theatrical costumes took her away for the evening in shining cars shaped like fish. She put on smiles for these boys as she never would for Augusta; she was some other girl getting into their cars. For them she had a skip in her step, an alertness, even a giggle. She hardly ever laughed at home, and her natural quietness had been tuned to a practiced muteness with this onset of womanliness. Between Karl and Joy, suppertime was frustratingly quiet. That was why Augusta

left them to finish their meal and took her coffee outside—
to get away from that lack of talk. Yet, off the farm, Joy
seemed to be some other creature entirely. Even here in the
city with her mother, she could be chatty when she wanted.

Joy came into the restaurant and joined her at the table.
She'd just sat down—not even a hello—when out she came
with it. "Who's my father?"

It was a punch in the stomach. "What?"

"My father. Who was my father?"

"Lower your voice!" Augusta hissed. She could feel the
red rising in her face. Certainly these men behind her would
be listening.

The waitress came, carrying coffee and offering Joy a
menu, but even with this interruption she wouldn't let it go.
"Well?"

"Well, what?"

"Who was he?"

"Karl is your father."

"You were having an affair with Reverend Lakeman all
those years. I saw you."

"What did you see?"

"You holding hands. I saw you kiss him once."

"Oh, for heaven's sake! Is that what this is about? That's
as far as it went. We were friends. Good friends. I never hid
the fact that I loved him. He stood by me through some trying times in a way your father was incapable of."

Joy was quiet for a moment, then she said, "Was he my
father?"

"The Reverend? Heavens, no!"

"Jenny Rivers told me Dad wasn't my father."

"Well, Jenny Rivers is a stupid, gossipy girl."

"Why do I look so different? Why am I so tall?"

"All you have to do is look at me. Your grandmother was tall."

"Jenny Rivers said there was talk after I was born. That Dad wasn't my father."

Augusta stared down into her coffee cup. "Yes, there was talk. How on earth did you come to be talking about such things?"

"They used to make fun of me, you know. At school. When I was a kid. They called me a bastard. They called you things."

"What did they call me?" Joy slouched farther down into the booth. "Karl's been a good father, hasn't he? He never made you feel less than his daughter, did he?" Joy shrugged, then shook her head. She stared at the table. "Karl is your father. That's the truth. You understand me?"

The day after Joy asked who her father was, Augusta made a trip into Kamloops on her own and forced herself to find Joe's number and to dial. She was nearly faint with relief when it was he who answered.

"Joe?"

"Yes?"

"This is Augusta."

He didn't say anything for a moment, then "Just a minute." She could hear him covering the receiver with his hand, and his muffled voice saying, "Why don't you take the coffee into the living room. I'll just be a minute," and to Augusta, "Hello?"

"I won't keep you. I wondered if we could meet, at the café. Today. I've got something I need to talk to you about."

"All right." Then he laughed a little nervously. "Is it a matter of national security?"

"Not quite."

"How about two, then? At the Swill?"

Joe was there at two. As he sat across from her he said, "Hasn't changed much, has it?" Although he had. He'd been in his forties when they'd spent those afternoons at the Plaza Hotel, and he'd have to be sixty now. He had much less hair and he'd lost some of the height and breadth that had made him seem so protective to Augusta during their affair. But then Augusta supposed she'd done a fair bit of changing herself. She'd put on weight and changed her hair color. She wore glasses now.

"You're looking good," he said.

"You too."

"You want lunch?"

"No, coffee's fine."

"What's so urgent?"

"No *how've you been*?"

"Got my curiosity up," he said. Augusta fiddled with her coffee cup. "Come on, out with it."

"We've got a daughter."

Joe grinned. "Really?"

"I thought you'd be mad."

"How could I be mad at a thing like that?"

"She's seventeen and asking questions. Why she doesn't look like Karl and so on. There was some talk—there was a *lot* of talk—and I guess she heard it. I told her Karl's her father and I think she believed me, but I thought it was time I told you."

"Why didn't you tell me before?"

"I tried phoning once. And I came here. For a while I kept thinking I'd see you on the streets."

"Chickened out, eh?"

"It would've complicated things, wouldn't it? If I told you? Would you really want to know?"

"What's her name?"

"Joy."

"Pretty name. She's seventeen? It's been *that* long?" Augusta nodded. He shook his head. "I suppose I should give you some money, shouldn't I? To help things along. Is she going to college?"

"Then I'd have to explain where the money came from."

"You could say you found work in Kamloops. Then maybe we could get together sometimes, here."

"I've already gone through the gossip once. I'm not going through it again. You don't know how it was. Besides that, taking money from you would change everything."

"You going to tell her about me?"

"You want me to?"

"I don't know how I'd explain some kid turning up on my doorstep."

"That's just it, isn't it?"

"And wouldn't the boy have a hard time with it?"

"I guess. I think Karl likely heard along the way. His father did. But I don't want to dredge it all up again."

They sat in silence for a long time. Then Joe said, "Best to let it lie, then."

"Yes."

"You got a picture of her?"

"Yes, of course. Here. That's this year's school picture."

"Ah, look at her."

"I should have brought more photos. I don't know what I was thinking."

"What is she like? Does she have hobbies? Is she good at school?"

"She does pretty well at everything. No A's this year, but she's not working hard either. She used to do a lot of horse-back riding, but she seems to have given up on that now. She's not much for baking or canning or any of that sort of thing, and Karl can't get her to help out with chores. To tell you the truth, I'm not sure what her interests are now. She just seems to hang around with her friends. She has a lot of boyfriends. When she comes home she locks herself in her room and listens to music. She likes to shop for clothes."

"Sounds like a regular teenaged girl to me."

"I suppose. We fight a lot."

"I came looking for you too, you know."

"Not the days I came."

"Right after you said we should stop, I came to this café every day. I figured you'd change your mind and turn up. But you didn't. Then I sort of gave up. I didn't come after that. But that's all water under the bridge now, isn't it?" He took both her hands in his. "So tell me, how've you been?" Augusta pulled her hands from him and glanced around the café. "Sorry," he said.

"We moved back onto my home farm. I've got my own honey business. Here, I brought you a jar." She took the small jar of honeycomb from her purse. "Sales are pretty good. I meet a lot of people that way."

"Look at that."

"One day I heard you outside the house. I thought for sure you'd turned up and Karl would catch you there. I ran to find you, I was so sure."

"What was I saying?"

"You were swearing. Like you'd hurt yourself."

"Could have been any number of days. I'm always whacking my thumb, bumping into things."

"I can't stay. It's a long drive back and Joy will be home soon. I told Karl I'd be there to make supper."

"I understand. Can we get together again sometime? Just for coffee?"

"I don't think that would be a good idea."

"Are you happy with the boy now? Has he been good to you?"

Augusta nodded. "I think so. He's a good man. He tries so hard. And I love him."

"Yes, of course."

The waitress came by with more coffee, and after she was gone they both stared in opposite directions for a while. "I should be going," said Augusta, finally.

"Are you sure we couldn't have a coffee now and again, as friends?"

"I'm not willing to risk everything I've built. Not anymore."

"Then I guess you better be on your way."

Augusta stood and put on her coat. "Are you staying?"

"Yes. I'll buy."

"We're agreed, then? I won't tell Joy?" Joe nodded and squeezed her hand before she left the café.

Augusta never did tell Joy about Joe. She thought she'd set her mind at ease, convinced her Karl was her father. As she so rarely spoke her mind openly and she was hardly ever home, Augusta was never quite sure what she was thinking. On graduating Joy took jobs, any job she could find. Baby-sitting, housekeeping. She even waitressed at Yep Num's café, though now it was called the Chase Café and was filled with loggers and layabouts. Yep Num had long since returned to China, and the café had passed through the hands of many owners. Joy was good at waitressing; she seemed to find a smile when tips were at stake. Or perhaps it was only for Augusta that she couldn't find one. Augusta hated to think so. For all their difficulties, Augusta was proud of her. She was self-reliant in a way Augusta had rarely been. Yet Joy had no specific plans. There had been no talk of college. Boys came and went, picking her up and depositing her. The bit of time Joy spent at home, she spent closeted in her room.

Then Augusta found the piggy bank, a large ceramic pig with a slot in the top that Augusta had bought and painted herself. Joy had seemed to like it. She had kept it on the nightstand by her bed. But one day Augusta found it broken open and lying on the ground around back of the barn. In the midst of the cracked pieces she found a penny. It was a shock, that was all. She'd put so much patience and effort into painting that pig, and here it was all bashed apart. It hurt. She went into the barn and told Karl about it. "Maybe she dropped it," he said. "By accident."

"Oh, I don't think so. It was deliberate."

Karl's face closed and he went back to shoveling, and Augusta knew that Joy was there behind her, listening. She turned to her. "I saved nearly two hundred dollars," Joy said. Augusta said nothing. Stupidly she found her eyes watering. Joy would only think her sulky. "It was *my* piggy bank," Joy said.

"I don't see why you had to break it."

"It had no hole in it, to take the money out."

"Well, you should have thought of that before you put the money in!"

Augusta knew even then that they weren't just arguing over the piggy bank, but some other thing, some larger thing. Joy was readying herself to leave, and that was what hurt and angered her mother.

"You control everything I do!" Joy screamed. "I can't turn around but you're on me, nagging me! Telling me what to do! You never shut up!"

Augusta closed her eyes. Joy knew she couldn't bear being thought of as a nag. And here was Karl shoveling behind them, hearing every word. She and Joy listened for a moment to the chunk of the shovel in the packed manure. Then Joy said, "I'm leaving!" and stormed off into the house.

Joy packed her few things and marched off into some boy's car—a friend, she said, just a friend—for a ride to the bus depot. She'd got herself a waitressing job and an apartment to share with a girl in Kelowna. Not so very far away. But she was already distant getting in that car. Crying, Augusta tried to hug her good-bye, but after giving Karl a kiss on the cheek Joy gave Augusta only a shoulder and pulled away. She was steely-faced, closed as a banker's door.

It was nearly harvest when Joy left home. The cornstalks were blushing crimson and the base leaves were curling brown. Augusta and Karl herded lambs through the corn to graze on the weeds growing between the rows. That day was so hot that the crows had given up flying and instead paced in the dirt with their mouths open, panting like dogs. Augusta was irritable, mean with the heat. The huge leaves of the corn prickled and scraped against her face and arms; they made a rasping sound as she moved through them. The whole world was corn, a great golden-green sea of it with tassels like the tips of waves pointing to heaven, and beneath them the fluid roll of deep, shining green betraying the lay of the land. Augusta's honeybees were everywhere, flying from tassel to tassel collecting pollen. There was nothing beyond but blue sky and shimmering air and the sun on their heads. She was glazed with sweat; Karl was drowning in it. Halfway down the field he took off home for some relief. "I'm getting some water," he said. But when he came back he carried no jug or even a tin cup for her, only his red handkerchief wound in a knot. *Look at that*, she thought. *He gets himself water and brings me nothing. I could die of thirst and heatstroke for all he cares.*

But when Karl reached her he took her wrist and turned it, exposing the tender underside, and placed his water-soaked handkerchief on her hot skin. It was ice-cold; he'd tucked bits of ice into his handkerchief to cool her. She pulled her hand away. She said, "What are you doing?" It was a shock, cold on skin that hot. But Karl took her other hand anyway, and bathed this wrist in cold. She gritted her teeth and let him, not understanding at first, not letting the cool soak into her. She watched his face slip from red into pink and then into no shade of embarrassment at all. His shyness melted away in all that heat. Wondering at this, Augusta found her own body relaxing, easing under his touch. She closed her eyes and felt the wet cloth on her face, wiping away the meanness, smoothing away the maddening heat. She bowed her neck and let him wash the sweat from her shoulders. With her eyes closed she still saw the sun and the corn before it, rows and rows of corn, silks streaming. She would become silk, she would bow in the breeze like tassels. She would lie in the sweet earth of the furrows between these rows and sleep.

All at once she realized that he was undoing the buttons of her dress. She opened her eyes to watch him. The redness was back in his face, but so was determination. Where had he found the courage? He looked once full into her face, and then back at his hands at work on the buttons. She wanted to say, *What are you doing? Not here!* And to take his hands and make them stop. But they were sheltered by corn, and there was no one to see but the bees, and the cool air he let flow on her breasts was a blessed relief. She let him slip the dress off her shoulders and down to the furrow at her feet. She let him unhook her brassiere and slide her panties down her thighs. And when this was done she let him bathe her. He wiped the sweat from her cleavage and then lifted each breast and wiped the sweat from beneath it. He wiped the shine off her belly and cooled her thighs and relieved the hot places behind her knees. He bathed her, there in the heat in the cornfield, with his old red handkerchief, and when he was done he left her, just left her standing there, eyes closed and naked, and kept on walking the lambs down the rows. The shock of his leaving was worse than his first cold touch. She wanted more and he knew it. There was a hint of triumph in the set of his shoulders. It was so unlike him, not a thing she could imagine Karl doing. Had he planned this, Augusta now wondered, or was it something he had happened on, like a shell-less egg in a hen's hidden nest? Had it taken him too by surprise?

− n ⁶ i n e −

That one summer was all Augusta and Karl needed to practice their dance; the time it took for corn to sprout and turn crimson was long enough for them to get back into rhythm. Long enough that Karl gave Augusta a new engagement ring to replace the one lost to dishwater, a diamond this time, and a gold wedding band to match it. He presented the rings to her wrapped in a series of boxes, one inside another, so at first she thought he was giving her a vacuum cleaner. But then, as soon as they weren't bumping into each other in the kitchen or grouching at each other over the don't-matter-much things, old habits put to the side during this second courtship slipped back into their days; not all the old habits, but most.

Like the way Karl wouldn't buy Augusta sanitary napkins, no matter how large she wrote the words on the shopping list or how many times she circled them in red. Or the fact that when he cooked a meal it was always the same: boiled beef ribs loaded with fat and served with unleavened dumplings. He'd make a sort of stew out of the stuff, four meals' worth, and it must have reminded him of his bachelor days because in winter, rather than scrape out the pan and put the stew in the refrigerator, he'd put the lid on the pan and sit it out by the doorstep to freeze, as he had in the old days at Olaf's cabin. Or the way he got cranky if Augusta was too chatty during a meal. He'd say, "Well, let's get this meal eaten before it gets cold." And she'd feel obliged to sit and eat with him in silence where, before Joy left, she might have taken her cup of coffee and gone to sit on the stump.

He went on bringing her flowers too, like the moccasin flower that only he knew where to find, someplace down on the edge of the ravine; the bunch of wild roses he brought her as soon as they were in bloom; or the pearly everlastings he brought her every year on their anniversary. And if she wanted to do something nice for him, she'd bake a lemon pie.

Augusta kissed the smooth skin on the top of Karl's head where that single upstart hair grew. He awoke and looked up at her, bewildered.

Rose, stretching out of sleep, said, "You hear about May Stonehill? She ran down the corridor at the home naked one night to Andy Wallbank's room and tucked herself into his bed. The night nurse caught them at it and shooed May back to her room. That must have been a sight, eh?"

"Why didn't the nurse step back out the door?" said Augusta. "She should have left them to it. Neither of them are children." Although Andy spent most of his time thinking he was eighteen and working in a mine. Who would be worse off if May crawled down into that mine with him for a night? she wondered. Only the night nurse's stiff sensibility would be dented by it.

Augusta supposed the young never thought of the love-making that went on between old bodies, or if they did it was material for jokes. She still wanted to be found beautiful, desirable. No one ever outgrew that. Yet she knew how the boys on the train today had seen her, how they had laughed at her. They could not conceive of growing old—metamorphosing in this odd way—any more than Augusta could have at their age. They expected to grow older, to sprout manly muscles, but not to progress to gray brittleness, as she had. Could they have imagined that she had once been smooth-skinned, young, like them? A different animal altogether, and yet the same. Right there on the train she had glanced down at her lap, expecting to see those smooth young hands gripping her purse, and been surprised to find these old things instead. She didn't feel any different than she had at thirty, except for the aches and pains. She had expected that her desires would slacken after the possibility of a child was gone, but they hadn't. She almost wished they had. What cruel joker gave old women such heated desires at the very time in their lives when they were likely widowed, or when any menfolk they had were grown flaccid and tired? I'm not being fair to the old guys, she thought. What was that psalm? *Do not cast me off in the time of old age; do not forsake me when my strength fails.*

There were certainly some old men still willing and able. Or willing, anyway. There were a couple of men at the seniors' center always making the rounds of the women. One turned up for lunch every day dressed in a different outfit. One day it was a sailor's getup, complete with captain's hat, his potbelly hanging over his bell-bottom pants. Another day he was dressed as a pirate. Once it was a 1970s white suit with a shiny disco shirt. He sidled up to that noisy Faye Risby with his usual line of "Married? Got a lover? No? Well, now." Faye didn't waste any time with him. She said, "Who are trying to kid? You couldn't get it up if your life depended on it." She had a voice that carried; she caused quite a commotion in the lunch room. Mr. Dress-Up had a wife who wouldn't go anywhere with him. Augusta didn't wonder at it.

The few men who came to the dances were gallant; they did try, each of them, to dance with each woman. Lance Reed, tall and so skinny that his hipbones wore the fabric on his pants, came alone, as his wife, Maeve, was long past dancing. As Augusta could no longer dance, Karl was now a popular man. Faye Risby commandeered him with something very near ownership, and had most of the dances with him except the polkas. Rose got the polkas. Augusta sat at the table at the door taking toonies from everyone who came, and seeing that they signed in, and rattled on about bees to anyone who would listen. As much as the members would have liked them to be, these dances weren't the rollicking affairs of the forties. Music was provided by a tape machine or sometimes a balding, oily-scalped man who brought his keyboard and played requests, though he rarely played anything faster than a fox-trot.

Very few couples attended these events. A few single men came, but mostly it was women, and they sat in a long line against the windowed wall, watching the dance. Maybe, she thought, they should be sharing the few men who remained, as women did in warrior societies where the young men went off and got themselves killed. There the women clamored, demanded to share husbands, in bed, at the table, around the house and field. In the society of old

women they did share men. They took turns dancing with
other women's husbands, or borrowed them to fix the sink
or drive them to doctors' appointments. Or else they found
what they lacked in the company of the women themselves.

"Oh, there's the phone!" cried Augusta. "Grab it, Rose,
will you? I can never get up quick enough."

Rose peered down at the screen on the telephone. "It's
Ernest again."

"Good Lord, Ernest, give it up."

"Shall I answer?"

"No. No. I just wish Joy would phone, even to let us
know she hasn't heard anything yet."

"What would be the sense in that?" said Karl.

"It's all this waiting. I hate the waiting."

"About time you got a taste of your own medicine," said
Rose.

"That's a cruel thing to say, today of all days."

"I was only trying to lighten things up a little."

"No you weren't. You were trying to make me feel
guilty. I was the one waiting at the Parksville station today."

"What do you mean?" said Rose.

"It doesn't take two hours to drive from Courtenay to
Parksville."

"I hadn't had my breakfast. I'll be damned if I'm going
to drive that far on an empty stomach. I went out of my way
to pick up you and that Indian woman."

"Don't go blaming her again."

"I didn't. I'm just saying—"

"It wasn't her fault I got off. I had to use the washroom."

"They've got washrooms on those trains."

"I couldn't use that one."

"Why not?"

"I just couldn't." Augusta had in fact tried to use the train washroom. But the three boys had laughed as she walked past them down the aisle. She could guess what they were laughing at: the hole in her stocking, her puffed ankles, the dangling parrot earrings and the hot pink of her blouse. She ignored them and tried the handle on the bathroom. It was an odd, cantankerous affair that wouldn't at first turn and, when it finally did, the door didn't swing out as she expected, but in, toward the toilet. That made the room impossible to enter. The bathroom was tiny, and smelled hotly of cigarette smoke. The steel sink took up much of the space. If she slid in there, she wouldn't be able to turn to close the door. If she did somehow manage that, how would she get out again? How would she manage the cane, and the handle of the door, and her own balance? She couldn't bear the thought of having to cry for help from that coffin of a room, not with those three young goats guffawing at her.

She had closed the door to the bathroom and put on a face of disgust, as if she'd seen or smelled some awful thing that made her not want to use it. She switched her cane and purse to her left hand and made her way down the rumbling, shaking aisle to her seat. She sat and glanced at the young men as she placed her purse on her lap. "Is there another stop? Where I can use the bathroom?" she asked Esther. "I can't use that one."

"Parksville's coming right up. You all right to Parksville?"

Augusta nodded and sat back in the seat. Traveling—all that sitting—stopped her up terribly, and her doctor had suggested that prunes loosened people up like nothing else, so now prunes were a necessary companion on her trips.

She had once read, in some magazine in the doctor's office, that prunes were provided free of charge in Elizabethan brothels. Back then they were eaten with gusto to promote vigor; now they were foisted on the elderly to encourage bowel movements. A long way to fall, that.

As the train began to slow for the next stop, Esther sat forward and pointed out the window. "You see all those bushes? Blackberries. Big juicy blackberries. I'd like to pick some of those." Augusta nodded as the train lumbered to a stop. The conductor marched into the car and yelled, "Parksville!"

"Here we go," said Esther. "We'll get you to the washroom." Although the station bathroom at Parksville turned out to be not much easier to use than the train bathroom. There was no power in the building, and the windowless ladies' washroom was pitch-dark. Augusta couldn't bring herself to navigate around it. Instead she chose the men's washroom, as it had a window in it. She shut the door, put her purse in the sink, and hung her cane over the doorknob before lowering herself onto the toilet seat. She had only just settled herself when Esther knocked on the door. "Augusta, you okay in there? The train's going."

"I'm coming. I'm coming. Tell them to wait!"

"You've got to hurry."

"I'll just be a moment. Tell them!"

As she stood, her Depends pad slipped from her undergarment and slid into the toilet bowl. How was she going to get it out? There were no coat hangers in this place. The station was all but deserted. She hurriedly pulled her underwear up and adjusted her stockings and dress and tried to think what to do. If she flushed, wouldn't the pad block the toilet and wouldn't the toilet overflow? But she couldn't just leave it there, could she? Maybe she could get Esther's help. But that would be too humiliating. She rinsed her hands under the tap and patted them dry on her skirt, as there were no paper towels left, and then her hand made the decision for her. It reached out and flushed the toilet. The toilet bowl went brownish red for a moment, from the flush of rusty water, and then the water gurgled back to its normal level. Augusta sighed as she grabbed her cane and purse.

As she opened the bathroom door, the train horn sounded and sounded again. The train was leaving without her. She tried to make her old body move faster, but the pain in her hip slowed her. When she took that last step outside, she found herself looking at the back end of the train moving down the track. She stared after it, not quite believing that it had left without her. Esther was sitting on the bench, watching Augusta and eating an apple. "They didn't wait for me," said Augusta.

"No."

"Why didn't you tell the conductor to wait?"

"He wouldn't listen. He seemed to think I was making a joke or something."

"Weren't you going to Courtenay?"

"Yup."

"You missed the train for me?"

"I wasn't going to leave. I figured something was the matter."

"I'm so sorry." Augusta turned to the blackboard on the station wall that proclaimed the white numbers of the trains, but the spaces for departure times were blank.

"I guess if we're stuck here together I better introduce myself," said Esther. She held out her hand. "Esther Joseph."

Augusta glanced at the hand a moment before taking it. It was the hand of a gardener or farmer, callused and large, as big as a man's. She shook Esther's hand. "Augusta Olsen. Glad to meet you." Then she sat down and sighed. Had she been at home, she would have lain in her bed and had a good long nap, with the window open to let the air in. Then she would have awoken rested and had some tea and toast and jam.

"I guess we better get to a phone," said Esther. "Call a taxi or something."

"I'll call my friend Rose. She'll pick us up." They made their way down the road and across the highway to Buckerfield's, a farm and garden supplies store, where she used the phone. At first she told Rose to meet her at Buckerfield's. It would have been a nice enough place to wait. There was a greenhouse full of fall plants for sale: pansies, chrysanthemums, and potted dahlias that would go on flowering, in this climate, right into the coldest months of winter.

"No, tell her the train station," Esther said.

"What?" said Augusta.

"Blackberries."

"Who is that?" Rose said.

"Yes. Rose? I'll be at the Parksville train station. I'll wait there."

They must have made a sight, thought Augusta. Two old women waddling down that dirt road back to the train station, one nearly too fat to walk, one with a crippled hip, each of them carting their luggage on a day hot enough to make corn tips turn brown from thirst. The dust on the station road was so thick and fine that she felt like taking off her shoes and running in it. But that would have looked foolish, wouldn't it? A barefoot old woman hop-skipping through the dust because her hip wouldn't cooperate with her enough for a full run. It took them twenty minutes to cover the distance; it would have taken a young person five.

The Parksville station was painted a hideous green and its front windows were boarded over. On the station door there was a cardboard sign handwritten in black marker that said, "Sorry. No Hydro. Vandalism—cut power 96-07-23." Huge banks of broom bordered the gravel road leading to the station; they must have made for one glorious show of yellow come spring. Bunches of Queen Anne's lace thrived in the poor soil around the tracks. Here and there nests of California poppies bloomed in the gravel. Just under the plank bridge that led from the platform to the gravel road, salmonberry grew in thick exotic bushes. Esther's promised blackberries grew everywhere, but especially across the tracks, at the edge of bush. They were too big to be believed: as big as the end of Augusta's thumb. Such a deep purple they looked black. And sweet. They grew everywhere on the island, along the highways, train tracks, down the sides of gravel roads. People on the island had come to think of them as common weeds, and few braved the bramble to pick them. But Augusta and Esther picked them that morning, though they were scratched by bramble and bothered by wasps attracted to the juice of berries on their faces and hands. Augusta had a good old chat with Esther while eating blackberries off those bushes, about her visions and the men she loved, about Gabe's illness and how her daughter didn't need her anymore.

"I know about that," said Esther. "Nobody's got time for us old ladies. When we're young, the men chase after us and make us have babies. Then the babies want all our time.

But when the babies are grown up, nobody's got any use for us. But what the hell, eh? What the hell."

"I wish I still had my beekeeping business," said Augusta. "Something that was my own, you know?"

"My father kept bees."

"Really? That's wonderful. Did you?"

"No. They always fascinated me, though. I used to poke around with my father when he was working on them. He called them white man's flies."

Augusta laughed. Until that moment she'd felt a little uneasy with Esther, a little unsure. She had been afraid she would say something that might upset her, or that Esther might act in some strange way Augusta couldn't imagine. But if Esther's father had kept bees, well, she couldn't have lived so very differently than Augusta had.

When Rose finally turned up, both Augusta's and Esther's hands were purple from the blackberries; their lips were smeared purple as if they were a couple of kids trying out their mom's lipstick. They were both excited after their excursion, breathless and giggly as schoolgirls. Rose crossed the tracks and joined them at the bushes. "I guess I better stop eating and start collecting these berries," said Esther. She plucked several and put them into the huge basket she carried.

"I love that basket," said Augusta. "Karl bought a baby basket for Joy like it, years and years ago."

"Yeah, I used a basket like that for my first, too," said Esther. She popped several berries in her mouth and talked with her mouth full. "When I was carrying my son—before I knew I was pregnant—I dreamt about his coming. He was coming toward me from a long way off, not running to me or anything like that but moving fast toward me somehow, but without moving. You know how dreams are. When I woke up I knew that I was pregnant and that I'd have a son. In the dream I called him Philly, so that's what I ended up calling him. I was, what? Sixteen? Not even that, when I got pregnant."

"That's strange," said Rose. "That you dreamt you were pregnant."

Esther shrugged. "I know lots of women who dreamed about their babies before they knew," she said. "I figure my body knew before I did, and found some way to tell me. Like when you're asleep and you've got to go pee and you dream about outhouses or bathrooms; that's your body telling you, 'Wake up! You've got to go pee.' " She laughed. "That vision about your father drowning when you were having your baby, *that's* strange."

"You told her that?" said Rose.

"It just came up."

"I think it was the stress that gave you that vision," said Esther. "I don't mean the labor pains, necessarily, though that would be enough on its own. I bet it was the stress of knowing you were going to have a baby that wasn't your husband's. That was a terrible thing to have happen back then. Having my Philly out of wedlock was bad enough."

"You told her about Joe?"

Augusta shrugged.

Esther patted Augusta's arm. "But it turned out okay, didn't it? Things cooled down. You got a daughter out of the deal. And that Joe fellow got to see his daughter after all those years. Things have a way of turning out all right."

"Joe saw Joy?" said Rose. "When did he see Joy? You never told me that."

"At the auction sale. Just before we sold the farm. I'm sure I told you."

"No. I'd remember that."

"It was no big deal, really."

"Well, let's hear it."

"I don't want to bore Esther with that all over again. I'll tell you later."

"And now," said Esther, "when you give Joy that brooch, maybe you can tell *her* all about it. Settle unfinished business. Though it sounds like she knows most of it already."

"Are we talking about the amber brooch, here?" asked Rose. "You mean to tell me you're going to give that to Joy?"

"I'll tell you about it later."

Esther chuckled. "I still can't get over you giving those boys hell."

"What boys?" said Rose.

"I'll tell you about it—"

"—later. I know." Rose stuffed her mouth full of blackberries. Then she cried out, "Ouch! Damn it!"

"What? What happened?" said Augusta.

"One of your precious bees stung me."

"That wasn't a bee," said Esther. "That was a wasp. A yellow jacket."

"Exactly," said Augusta. "Yellow jackets are often mistaken for honeybees. You've got a good eye, Esther."

"I don't give a damn what it was. It stung me. Look!" Rose held out her finger.

"I don't know what I can do for you," said Augusta. "If we had sugar or baking soda, I'd make up a paste." She turned to Esther. "You'll have to come over and see my hive."

"I'm going home," said Rose. "Are you coming?"

"Yes, I guess we should. Karl will be wondering what's happened to us. You don't mind if Esther comes along, do you?"

"Will you excuse us, Esther?" said Rose. She pulled Augusta across the tracks and around the corner of the train station. "I don't want to take that woman anywhere."

"Why not? It's on our way."

"I just don't."

"She stayed with me. She missed the train for me. To make sure I was all right."

"She didn't have to, did she? She could have got the conductor to wait."

"She tried. He wouldn't listen."

"You don't have to take me," said Esther. She was leaning against the station building, just around the corner, listening in. "I'll get a taxi."

"To Courtenay?" said Augusta. "That'll cost a fortune. Don't be silly. Come with us."

What was Rose going to say, with the woman standing right there? They all piled into Rose's car, Rose in the front and Augusta and Esther in back, as Augusta couldn't pull her leg into the front and had to lie down in the back to work her way in. Once she was sitting upright Esther sat beside her, as the seatbelt in front wouldn't do up around her belly, but the one in the back would.

As they were driving along the ocean, they passed a group of people standing in a circle on the shore. They were Native, all of them. Several of them, three women and a man, were elderly. The rest were young people, dressed in jeans and sweatshirts. What were they up to, Augusta wondered. A ceremony of some kind? One of the old women gestured as if she was telling them something.

"What are those people doing?" Rose said.

"What?" said Esther.

"Those Indians, in the river. They were all standing in a circle."

"I don't know."

"I thought you might know—"

"Rose—" said Augusta. They peered at each other in the mirror. Augusta shook her head. Rose didn't say another word for the rest of the drive. When they dropped Esther off at the mall, where she said she wanted to be left, Rose didn't say good-bye or even look at her. Augusta felt she had to make up for Rose's rude behavior. She got out of the car, limped around to the other side, and gave Esther a hug and exchanged phone numbers. Once Esther was heading off to the mall, she had to get help from Rose to get back in.

Rose sat back down on the couch. Augusta grinned at her. "I told Esther how you wouldn't let go of your purse when that boy tried to steal it," she said.

"Yeah?" said Rose.

"She called you *skookum*."

"What the hell does that mean?"

"Really good. The best. Top of the line. She said you must be one *skookum* woman."

"Yeah? She called me that?"

Karl's chin had dropped to his chest. "Karl," said Augusta. "Karl!"

"Hmm? What?"

"Why don't you go into the bedroom to have your nap? So Rose and I don't have to listen to your snoring."

"Yep. Sure." He stood and limped a little as he made his way to the bedroom door.

Rose sat in Karl's chair beside Augusta. "Good, good, good," she said. "Now, let's have it."

"What?"

"The story. Tell me about Joe. Seeing Joe after all those years."

But the phone rang and Augusta made her way to it and grabbed the receiver. "Oh, for Christ's sake," said Rose.

"Hello?"

"Linda?"

"Ernest, you've got the wrong number again."

"What's that?"

"The number. You have the wrong number."

"Where's Linda?"

"She doesn't live here. Why don't you check your phone number. Okay?"

"Okay." He sounded dubious, as if she were trying to pull a fast one. "Are you sure Linda isn't there?"

"Nobody named Linda lives here. Or ever has."

"All right, then. If you see her, tell her I phoned."

"Good-bye, Ernest."

"Good-bye."

Augusta put down the receiver and sighed. She supposed he must be forgiven, as even the clearest minds among their old set forgot what they had done just yesterday, or found their slippers in the refrigerator, and all of them took forays backward in time now and again. When Augusta and Karl were about to leave the farm, Gabe came over to help them whip the place into shape to be sold. Augusta went inside the house to make coffee. As she busied herself in the kitchen she happened to glance out the window, and there, standing on a ladder propped against the stout arm of the tree, was Karl. His back was turned to her and he was putting up the rope of the swing for Joy. A good crop of carroty blond hair blazed from the top of his head in the early evening sun. She stood there for several moments, amazed. Somehow she'd tripped through a hole in time. Karl worked quickly, capably, looping the rope and knotting it in place with those huge hands—hands that were always warm, even on cold nights when hers had gone white as the blood retreated. On nights like that those big farmer hands had been there to enclose hers, to bring back the blood. Those hands. But then Karl climbed down the ladder and faced the house and wasn't Karl at all. He was Gabe. And when she looked down at her hands, they weren't the hands of a young mother, they were the hands of an old woman.

The phone rang again. "Damn it, Ernest," said Augusta. Without checking the call display, she picked up the phone. But Ernest wasn't there. The line was crackling and hollow, like the old phone lines out at the farm. "Hello?" she said.

"I'm okay." It was Gabe's voice. *Wasn't it?*

"Gabe?" she said. Rose put her hand on Augusta's shoulder. Then the line went dead. Augusta put the receiver down, feeling a chill run up her neck.

"That was Gabe?" said Rose.

"I'm not sure. You wouldn't think they'd let him use the phone, even if he was out of surgery, would you?"

Rose shrugged. "Maybe. They get them on their feet pretty quick these days. Check whose number it was." But the screen read "Unknown name, unknown number." Rose shuddered. "That's spooky," she said. "You think he's dead?"

Augusta grimaced at her. "No, I don't think he's dead. If anything, I think he was telling me he's alive and well."

"So you think it was one of your visions?"

"I don't know. You heard the phone ring too, didn't you?"

"Yes." They both stared down at the phone for a while.

"Well," said Rose, "enough interruptions. Tell me about Joe."

"What do you want to know?"

"How Joe got to see Joy. Did Joy see him? Did they meet?"

"No, no. He turned up at the auction held at the farm, before we sold the place. He saw the auction notice in the newspaper." They had hired an auction company to come on site to sell off almost everything but the buildings. Augusta had arranged for the church ladies to set up a concession stand, and that got the community out to the sale; no one wanted to miss the opportunity for a bit of socializing over coffee and pie, or for snooping around in their neighbors' stuff.

All the decades of Augusta and Karl's life were lined up outside the house and in the farmyard: decades of stoves, first wood, then electric; the copper boiler and wringer washers—both the hand-cranked one Helen had struggled with, and the gas-powered one the Reverend had brought Augusta; crocks and butter churns; coffeepots and canning jars; water kettles; teapots; coal-oil lamps and lanterns; syrup pails; egg crates; cream separators; the kitchen cupboard the Grafton boy had left in the house so many years before; the ancient radio Karl had packed up the mountains in the years when he still ranched with Olaf; the horse harnesses and doubletrees and tractors; discs and rakes; wooden-handled saws and gas-powered chain saws; wooden barrels and wheelbarrows; wire-stretcher and fencing tools; shovels and pitchforks; and the electric fish smoker Karl had never got around to using. There it was: all the decades of work and memories laid out in front of the community. She felt naked, exposed at having her things inspected, and weepy at seeing that so many years had gone by so quickly. The auctioneer rattled her whole life away. Not the apiary equipment, though. She gave all that to Gabe to get him started on his honey business. She couldn't have sold it if she'd tried.

The crowds were noisy and the auctioneer was noisier yet. Two people could carry on a conversation in the center of the crowd and feel pretty safe no one around them was going to hear a thing. Augusta saw Joe making his way toward her through the crowd but she didn't watch him coming. She glanced over at Martha Rivers and the other church ladies at the concession to see that they were all busy and not looking in her direction, and then she kept her eyes on the auctioneer, who was selling off the kitchen table she'd sat at for so many years with Karl, Joy, and the Reverend. When Joe reached her, he stood at her side, watching the auctioneer, as if he were interested in the sale and not in Augusta standing right there. She was aware of the heat from his arm brushing against hers, and she could smell the soap on him.

"That the kid?" he said, nodding at the house, where Joy stood in the doorway, guarding the house so no one would stray inside. Karl and Gabe were leaning against the house beside her, talking.

"Yes, that's Joy at the door."

"She's pretty."

"Do you think?"

"Looks like her mother."

"Good Lord, no."

"And that's the boy?"

"That's Karl, and Joy's husband, Gabe, talking to him."

"He's better looking than I thought."

"Karl?"

"Where you moving?"

"The island."

"Victoria?"

"Joy and Gabe are there."

"What's she doing now?"

"Receptionist. She went to college after she left home. She does bookkeeping on the side."

"And her husband?"

"This and that. Construction work mostly. I've just got him started in beekeeping."

"She ever ask again?"

"No."

"What's she like?"

"Stubborn. Restrained. Religious. Good with money."

"Just like her mother."

"Like Karl, more like it."

"Doesn't sound like she inherited much from me."

"Her eyes."

"Nose, maybe."

"The chin. Definitely the chin."

The auctioneer offered the gas-powered iron the Reverend had given her a few years before the power line reached them; he sold it with a box of assorted tins, as if it meant nothing at all, as if it hadn't saved her hours of labor because she didn't have to keep stopping to heat the thing on the fire while she was ironing clothes. Her favorite old Tetley tea caddy went with that box too, the one with the bees and sunflowers painted on it. Why had she put that with the stuff up for sale? What had she been thinking?

"I think of you quite a bit," said Joe. "Wondering how you're doing. I've got something for you. When I saw it in the display case a few years back, I knew it had to be for you, though I had no idea when I'd see you again, or *if* I'd see you. I figured if Sally found it I could say it was for her."

"Sally's your wife?"

"Yes. I guess I never talked much about her."

"No."

"As I recall, you did most of the talking."

Augusta laughed. "I was making up for lost time. Karl and I weren't much for talking. Still aren't, I guess."

"Well, here." Their hands met while they both watched the auctioneer. Augusta put the little box Joe gave her in her pocket.

"What is it?"

"You'll see when you open it." He looked around at the bits and pieces of Augusta's life displayed on the tables. "I'd like it if you could make sure that it's passed on to Joy when you're gone. Not that I bought it for her, you understand. I'd just hate to think it ended up in the hands of strangers."

"Sure. I understand."

"Is there someplace we could go for a few minutes?"

"In the house, I suppose. But Joy's there at the door."

"Let's chance it."

"You want to meet her? We can make something up."

He shook his head. "I don't think I have the nerve." Then he said, in a louder voice, "I was wondering if you wouldn't mind showing me the cupboards you've got."

Augusta led him through the crowd toward the house. When she reached Joy she said, "This man wants to see the buffet in the parlor."

"I thought you weren't going to sell that."

"We'll see."

Joy got a good look at Joe when he stopped briefly in front of her, but let him pass. To Augusta's relief neither Joy nor Karl nor Gabe followed her and Joe into the house. She led him to the back room, the dark parlor she never used for entertaining as it had no windows. There were a few photos here, family pictures scattered in frames around the room. "This was Joy when she was eight," she told him. "All dressed up to play an angel at a Christmas concert. And this is her when she was six weeks. This is her and Gabe on their wedding day."

It was at that point that she looked into his face for the first time. When she'd first seen him across the crowd he hadn't appeared much different than he had the day she'd met him at the Silver Grill to discuss Joy. But seeing him this close, she realized how terribly old he was. He must have been eighty-five, because he'd been a good twenty years older than Augusta. When she handed him Gabe and Joy's wedding photo his hands were shaky. He whistled through his teeth to hide a wheeze. He put down the photo and cupped Augusta's face with both hands and kissed her there, in the darkest room in a house surrounded by gossiping neighbors. It was a tender kiss, from a dear wobbly old face, that said: *We had something good going, didn't we? And I'm so sorry for this growing old business. If I could stop it, I would.*

"Mom, they're selling off the stoves now," called Joy. "You said you wanted to see what the stove from the honey house would sell for?"

"Coming."

Joe led the way outside and headed for the concession. Joy caught Augusta's arm as she came out the door. "Who was that old man?"

"I'm not sure. I think he said he was from Kamloops."

"He looks familiar. Have I met him?"

"I don't think so."

Joy examined her mother's face a moment too long, then leaned back into the doorway and let her go, but she watched Joe as he milled around the tables and machinery. Joe in his turn snuck glances at Joy and at Augusta. He left late in the afternoon—Augusta watched him get into his truck and drive off—and Joy never said another word about it.

A few weeks later, on the day they were in town closing down their power account and rerouting their mail to Victoria, Augusta bought a Kamloops paper to read at the café while Karl was picking up a few things at the hardware store. She turned the page and scanned the obituaries and suddenly all the sound in the café receded. Joe was dead. There was a picture of him and his death notice was skillfully and solemnly written, containing the date he had married, the ages of his children (a daughter nearly as old as Augusta!). There was no mention of a military career. He'd been a farmer during the war and at the time of their affair, then worked in a mill until it shut down. She'd once asked him about the army jacket he wore. "Tell me about the war. Tell me how you got those medals."

"There's nothing to talk about."

"Come on, tell me."

"I said no!"

So he hadn't been to war at all. That was the role he'd played for himself, and for her. Soldier. She realized now, reading the obituary over and over, how little she had known him.

Augusta tore the death notice from the newspaper, there in the busy café, barely able to see what she was doing for the sting in her eyes. He'd died in the early morning, of a heart attack. Wasn't that the way, she thought. Death came suddenly to men, in the morning. It was different for women; it wasn't quite the surprise. Women knew they risked death in giving life. They probed their bodies monthly, knowing cancers might consume their breasts, their life-giving places. Old women who fell and broke their hips knew they likely wouldn't recover; with their wings clipped they waited. Death chased women slowly, a rolling comical porcupine they could watch coming, and if they chose to they could learn to laugh at it, to grow comfortable with it. Men, though, men feared death because it hunted them silently, hit swiftly, and took them by surprise.

Augusta pulled the clipping out of her purse and showed it to Rose.

"So what was in the box," asked Rose.

"Hmm?"

"The present Joe gave you."

"The brooch, of course. The bee caught in amber." Augusta rummaged through her purse and held it up. The light from the kitchen window lit the amber so the bee made a striking silhouette within it. "I don't wear it, for Karl's sake, but I like to keep it with me."

Rose shook her head. "And now you want to give it away?"

Augusta shrugged. "It's not giving it away. It's passing it on."

The apartment door flew open, sending the cats hissing into corners, and Joy barged in with Karl trailing behind her. Augusta and Rose looked at each other. They hadn't heard Karl leave the bedroom or the apartment. Had he heard anything of their conversation? He patted Joy on the shoulder as he passed her, and carried a large grocery bag into the bedroom. Augusta slipped the brooch back in her purse and went to greet Joy. She was red-faced and sobbing. She leaned against the wall next to the door and slid down to the floor. "Joy?" said Augusta. "Joy, what is it? What's happened? Is it Gabe?"

Joy rolled her head back and forth against the wall. Her legs were straight out in front of her, and her hands drooped on either side of her like those of a rag doll. "Oh, my God," said Augusta. "It's Gabe, isn't it?" Joy went on rolling her head back and forth and Augusta wasn't sure if she was saying no or not. Augusta handed Joy a tissue and she blew her nose several times.

"I hit a deer," she said.

"What?"

"I was driving too fast, I guess. I don't know. It was suddenly *there*. There was an awful crunch. My grille is wasted."

"Oh, sweetie. Get up. Come on. Sit on the couch." Joy pushed herself up using the wall, then flopped on the couch. Augusta sat beside her. "Rose, put the kettle on, will you?" Karl closed the bedroom door quietly behind him and sat in his chair opposite Joy and Augusta.

"It was lying there by the road," said Joy, "all bloody, and its legs were jerking around."

"That's just the nerves," said Karl. "It wasn't feeling anything. That's the nerves going after it's dead."

"It was just like Gabe when he had the seizure. Just like that." She sobbed and leaned into Augusta. Augusta wrapped her arms around her and rocked her as she had so many years ago, when Joy had cried for the unhatched chicks that had died in the school fire. "I waited and waited at the hospital," said Joy. "Finally I went home. But I couldn't stand it. I phoned the hospital, then I phoned again, and the operation still wasn't over. Then I had to get out and *drive*, you know? So I left your number at the hospital and got in the car. I didn't think I'd come all the way here. But once I got in the car I couldn't stop driving. Then I hit the deer. Just outside of town. Oh, *God!*"

"So you haven't heard anything yet?"

"No. They didn't phone?"

"I don't think so. Someone phoned—"

"Oh, I can't stand this." She grabbed the phone and dialed the hospital, then walked to the kitchen, waving a hand for them to leave the room or not listen to her. Augusta and Rose glanced at each other and went out onto the balcony. Karl went to the bedroom. "You going to tell her about hearing Gabe on the phone?" said Rose.

"I don't know. If the operation isn't over yet it would scare her."

They stared down at the garden and beehive below until Joy hung up the phone and sat back on the couch. "Anything?" asked Augusta as she joined her in the living room.

"No. He's still in the operating room. The nurse said things are going okay."

Augusta sat next to her and put an arm around her. "That sounds hopeful, doesn't it?" Joy began to cry again and Augusta pulled her close and rocked her. "Shush, now," she said. "Gabe's going to be fine."

"How can you say that? He may not be able to walk, or even talk. He might *die*."

"He's okay."

"How do you know that?"

"I just know." She tapped her temple and glanced at Rose. "I'm psychic, remember?" Joy laughed, and cried, and laughed. Augusta went on rocking her. "Did you know there's a dance the bees do that's named after you?"

"Yeah. You used to tell me all the time, when I was a kid."

"It's the joy dance. It's called that because the bees do that dance when everything's going really well. They do it to celebrate the birth of a new queen, or when honey flow is excellent. They jitter around giving each other little hugs. Sooner or later we're going to get a phone call from the hospital and we're all going to do that joy dance." Augusta let go of Joy and motioned for Rose to hand her her purse. "I have a surprise for you, Joy," she said. "Something I've been meaning to give you."

Rose scowled at her, but handed her the purse. "I think I should be getting home," she said. "You phone me when you hear something?"

Augusta nodded and turned to watch Rose leave, then glanced at the bedroom door to see that it was closed. She could hear Karl rummaging in the bag he'd brought. She lowered her voice. "I want you to have this," she said, and held out the bee caught in amber.

"Oh, that's too much; you can't give me that."

"I never wear it. I saw how much you liked it."

"Are you sure?"

"There's a story behind it."

"I'm not sure I'm up to another bee story right now."

"No. Sometime when things are going better, you ask me about it."

Joy blew her nose. "I'm so sorry about sending you home like that."

Augusta shrugged. The phone rang and Joy rushed to pick it up. Augusta walked out to the balcony, as she knew Joy would hate being listened to. Karl left the bedroom and came out onto the balcony and put his arm around Augusta. He kissed her temple. He smelled fresh, of soap and shaving cream, and the skin on his cheeks was smooth. He'd shaved just before she'd arrived. He'd shaved for her.

Joy shrieked. "He's okay! He's okay!" She was jumping up and down when they joined her in the living room. "He's already awake and talking! The nurse said he's got full use of his hands and legs!"

"Thank God," said Augusta.

"Yes, exactly!" said Joy. "Thank the Lord! Hallelujah! I've got to get down there." She grabbed her coat and purse and then turned to Augusta. "Is it okay—do you mind if I drive down alone? If I spend tonight alone with him? You can come tomorrow."

"No, no. Go on. Go see your husband. I understand."

"All right. Bye."

"Bye."

Joy stopped again at the door and pinned the brooch to her blouse, and patted it. "Thanks for this. I'm glad I came. It helped."

"You mean you still need me?"

Joy came back into the room and hugged her. "Of course I need you. Where'd you get the idea I didn't?" Augusta knew it was a lie, or nearly a lie, but she was grateful for it nevertheless.

-ten-

Augusta took Karl's hand and together they walked onto
the balcony to wave across the garden as Joy got in the car
and drove off. Karl put his arm around Augusta. "She's a
brave girl," he said. "I don't think I could stand it if you got
sick like Gabe did. I wouldn't know what to do."

"Yes you would," said Augusta. She cupped his face in
the palm of her hand and kissed him. It was a sweet kiss. He
tasted of peppermint and the cookies he'd eaten that afternoon. He gave her shoulders a squeeze, kissed her forehead,
and walked through the living room back to the bedroom.
She heard him rustling around in there. Likely wrapping an
anniversary gift, she thought. She felt a great tenderness for
him wash over her. She wanted to run her fingers over the
papery skin on the back of his hand; to touch and be surprised yet again by the youthful flesh hidden away from sun
under shirt and pants. She wanted to stroke the hair in those
secret spots, hair that was no longer coarse and coiled but
had grown thin and smooth with age, a baby's hair in
grown-up places.

Would Joy and Gabe's marriage survive into old age?
she wondered. Would it even survive these next few years

as Gabe recovered? She knew her daughter well enough to know that Joy believed God had given her the miracle she'd been after, that He had healed Gabe. She doubted that Joy gave much credit to the surgeon. But of course the surgery was no miracle, and it would be a long time before Gabe was truly healed. One of the nurses at the hospital had given Joy and Augusta a book on head injuries, and what Augusta had read made it clear that Gabe would be a real handful until he recovered, and that he might never recover completely. He wouldn't be able to do much or concentrate, and it would be a long time before he realized what had happened to him, that he wasn't as capable as he had been before. He would have to be watched constantly, because he might endanger himself, and other people, if he tried things he could no longer do. It would be some time before he was able to work, or even drive. Augusta wasn't sure Joy was up to managing all that, or if she fully understood what she was up against. Did she think everything was going to go back to normal now, Augusta wondered, under God's divine hand?

She looked down at her beehive in Rose's garden. The bees were calmer; there were fewer bees dancing around the hive. Now, in late August, when there were fewer flowers and honey flow was coming to an end, her bees made do with the nectar and pollen of asters. But they longed for the sweeter nectars; they watched the dances of returning foragers more closely than they did at other times of the year, hoping for news of fields of sweet clover. When she had still been on the farm, she had had to be careful to keep the car windows shut, because the bees, then more than ever, were drawn to the smell of honey drifting from the warm jars and tin buckets she delivered to her customers. They would hover in clouds around the car, confused by the sweet smell, muddled by longing for something they couldn't find.

Augusta went back inside the apartment and stretched out on the couch. She felt pleasantly emptied, as if she were resting after some great effort. It was the relief of finally hearing about Gabe, she thought. She had wondered briefly if that dream of the pit full of flowers had been a premonition of Gabe's death, and not her own. Now she knew it was her own. But what did it matter? Her mother had been right, that day Augusta described the vision of Helen's death. She was no better off knowing about it beforehand. Augusta didn't know when she'd die or how. She didn't know any more than anyone ever did about their own death. She was perhaps worse off, she thought, for all her worrying. She wondered if any of it was even real. She wondered if the visions she saw—of Gabe, of her mother's coffin, of Karl's mother walking out into the snow, of Helen in the honey house—were products of her own powerful imagination, the back of her head offering warnings and solutions, in the way nighttime dreams sometimes solved problems. Had years of telling and retelling stories, a little differently each time, obscured her memory of what had actually happened? Had she really told Karl that Manny would drown a week before it happened? Yes, she thought so, and Karl said he remembered her telling him. But maybe what he remembered was the story she had told so many times, with all its additions and exclusions, all the fuzzy details that had found their way into that story from others. Sometimes she believed her own stories as truth; other times she believed them as fiction.

Karl slid back into the living room and turned on the television for the evening news. This disappointed her.

When she had heard him coming, she had thought he was bringing out her anniversary surprise. "Didn't you have plans—" she said.

"What?"

"Did you have plans for supper?"

"No. I hadn't thought about it." He *had* forgotten. Augusta got up and slammed around in the kitchen, taking out her disappointment on the cutlery and plates, and prepared Karl a pointedly modest supper—sardines, fried potatoes, bread, and tea—a small revenge because he had not thought to take her out for an anniversary supper. They ate in front of the television set. Because the day was hot and the fans were going, the volume on the TV was turned high so Karl could hear it. They didn't try to talk.

Her hands were stained purple from the blackberries she'd picked that morning. She wished she'd had some container to collect them in, as Esther had. She would have taken them home to bake a blackberry pie. No, she would have baked *two* pies, and taken one down to the old man's house and left it there on his doorstep, with a note: *Love your garden!* Or maybe she would have drummed up the courage and knocked on his door and given him the pie herself. Maybe she would go armed with a clutch of dahlia tubers, to exchange for some bittersweet, and start a friendship that way. Or maybe she would invite him to one of the many garden shows at the civic center or at one of the churches, and then work up to dinner or an evening out. But there was Karl to contend with, and all the gossiping women at the seniors' center. And besides that, the old man of the garden seemed as uninterested in companionship as that old man she'd worked for in Kamloops so many years ago. She hadn't been able to engage him in a game of crib, much less a bit of conversation; the old man of the garden showed all the signs of being much the same. Her feelings for him were conjured up; this was as much a fantasy as her first love for a demon-possessed boy.

After dinner Augusta chastised herself for her sulkiness. After all, she could have made dinner reservations herself. She decided to do something cheerful. She went into the kitchen to make popcorn with the popper Karl had given her one Christmas, a contraption she hadn't quite mastered. But her absence from the living room, or the sound of popping, brought Karl into the kitchen. He said, "Shouldn't you warm the machine first?" And, "You don't put butter inside the machine!" When, in frustration, she dumped the popcorn into the sink, he said, "It'll plug up the drain!" Augusta began to cry and Karl, because he had never known what to do with tears, went back to the television set.

Augusta slapped the kitchen counter, then stomped into the bedroom and slammed the door behind her. It was hot in there; the sun had cooked the south side of the apartment building. She drew the curtains and plunked herself on the bed. *Impossible, niggardly man,* she thought. How could she have spent so many years with him? She lay in the dark, sweltering room, fuming. He should have come to see what was wrong, to make amends.

A couple of months before, Augusta had dreamed that she was in an expensive carriage pulled by two black high-spirited stallions and driven by a man in tails and a top hat. This man wasn't Karl but he was her husband. She was young, dressed in high fashion for the Victorian era, in a black dress with ruffles around the neck, and she had a muff that she was proud of because it had real fur trim. She put her hands in the muff and showed it off to those passing by in carriages and motorcars. But no one would look; no one even glanced her way. It was as if she were invisible. All around them, in the night, a carnival was going on. She could hear the music and laughter of crowds, but as there were no lights she couldn't see anything but the many carriages and cars that passed close by.

Her husband, this Victorian gentleman, pulled the carriage to a stop in front of a large black building, stepped out, and strutted up the dark steps and disappeared. Where had he gone? she wondered. No light leaked through an open door. There were no windows. She waited.

A coach stopped nearby and a group of elegant young men stepped out, lighting cigarettes in silver holders. She tried to overhear their conversation but couldn't—the music of the carnival overwhelmed their voices. They were handsome men, just boys, really, so much younger than her husband. She waved to them, opened the carriage door, and lifted her long dress to expose a shapely young leg, but the boys didn't glance her way either.

A parade of horse skeletons pranced by in the dark, glowing phosphorus, and then the parade and the carnival music disappeared abruptly as her husband walked back down the steps. As he made his way to the driver's side he became Karl, dressed in the outfit he wore on the farm: white shirt and armbands, wool pants held up by suspenders, and a big, wide-brimmed hat. The fashionable carriage and horses rippled and dissolved into the old International they had become engaged in. As Karl turned the truck around, the elegant young men in the carriage finally saw Augusta. They nodded in recognition and faded away. She knew she couldn't tell Karl about any of what she had seen at the carnival—the gleaming skeleton horses, the longing she felt for the young men—how could she tell him? So they drove in silence up the familiar dusty hills of their early marriage.

Augusta went into the bathroom and washed her face with cold water; she soaked a facecloth with water and wiped the sweat from the back of her neck, from between her breasts, under her arms, behind her knees. She put on a fresh dress and went back into the coolness of the sitting room to watch television from her chair next to Karl's. Once there she tried to ignore him, to keep a stony silence, but her anger didn't last; it drained away. She forgave him his inadequacies, just as he had forgiven hers so many times in the past, because Karl, resourceful as all farmers were, found a way to say the things he wished he had said over the years, all the things he had been unable to say. It wasn't much: a simple gesture he had been planning for a day or two, a message contained in flowers. He handed Augusta a bouquet tied in ribbon that he had hidden beside his chair: a clutch of pearly everlastings with white woolly stems, and flowers that would last until the first snows of winter.

-About the Author-

GAIL ANDERSON-DARGATZ lives with her husband, Floyd, on
Vancouver Island, British Columbia. She is also the author of
the award-winning, best-selling novel *The Cure for Death by
Lightning*.